THE POSTHUMOUS MEMOIRS
OF BRAS CUBAS

MACHADO DE ASSIS

GET TO KNOW OUR BOOKS
BY ACCESSING HERE!

Copyright of this edition © IBC - Instituto Brasileiro De Cultura, 2024

All rights reserved and protected by law 9.610 of 2.19.1998.

President: Paulo Roberto Houch
MTB 0083982/SP

Editorial Coordination: Priscilla Sipans and Paola Houch
Art Coordination: Rubens Martim
Editorial Production: Eliana S. Nogueira
Translation: Francine Cervato
English Text Review: Francine Oliveira

Sales: Phone: (55 11) 3393-7723 (vendas@editoraonline.com.br)

Legal deposit has been made.

Printed by PlenaPrint.
1st Print 2025

International Data of Cataloging in Publication (CIP)
according to ISBD

A848p   Assis, Machado de

The Posthumous Memoirs of Brás / Machado de Assis. –
Barueri : Camelot Editora, 2025.
176 p. ; 15,1cm x 23cm.

ISBN: 978-65-6095-318-5

1. Brazilian literature. 2. Romance. I. Title.

2025-1808   CDD 869.89923
                             CDU 821.134.3(81)-31

Elaborated by Odilio Hilario Moreira Junior - CRB-8/9949

IBC — Instituto Brasileiro de Cultura LTDA
CNPJ 04.207.648/0001-94
Avenida Juruá, 762 — Alphaville Industrial
ZIP CODE: 06455-010 — Barueri/SP
www.editoraonline.com.br

TO THE WORM

THAT

FIRST GNAWED ON THE COLD

FLESH OF MY CORPSE

I DEDICATE

THESE POSTHUMOUS

MEMOIRS AS A

NOSTALGIC REMEMBRANCE

PROLOGUE OF THE FOURTH EDITION

The first edition of these *Posthumous Memoirs of Bras Cubas* was published in sections in the *Revista Brasileira*[1], in the 1880s. Later, compiled in book format, I corrected the text in several places. Now that I had to review it, this work comes to light again, which seems to have found some benevolence among the public.

Capistrano de Abreu, announcing the publication of the book, asked, "Are *The Posthumous Memoirs of Bras Cubas* a novel?" Macedo Soares, in a letter he wrote to me at that time, fondly recalled the *Travels in My Homeland* [by Almeida Garrett]. To the first, the late Bras Cubas already replied (as the reader saw and will see in his prologue below) "yes" and "no," saying that it was a novel for some and not for others. As for the second, this is how the deceased explained: "It is a diffuse work, in which I, Bras Cubas, adopted the free form of a Sterne or a Xavier de Maistre, I do not know if I added some grumpiness of pessimism to it." All these people traveled: Xavier de Maistre around his room, Garrett in his homeland, and Sterne in the homeland of others. It might be said of Bras Cubas that he traveled around life.

What makes my Bras Cubas a particular author is what he calls "grumpiness of pessimism." There is in the soul of this book, however cheerful it may seem, a bitter and harsh feeling, which is far from coming from its models. It is a goblet that may have a similar design, but it contains another wine. I do not say more so as not to criticize a deceased person who painted himself and others as he thought was best and most correct.

MACHADO DE ASSIS

---

1   A magazine published by ABL - Brazilian Academy of Letters (translator's note).

TO THE READER

That Stendhal confessed to having written one of his books for a hundred readers is something that brings on wonder and concern. What does not cause wonder and probably no concern is if this other book does not have Stendhal's one hundred readers, not fifty, not twenty, but, at most, ten. Ten? Maybe five. It is, in fact, a diffuse work, in which I, Bras Cubas, adopted the free form of a Sterne or a Xavier de Maistre, I do not know if I added some grumpiness of pessimism to it. It is possible. The work of a dead man. I wrote it with a playful pen and the ink of melancholy, and it is not difficult to foresee what can come out of this marriage. Furthermore, serious people will find in the book some appearances of pure novels, while frivolous people will not find their usual novel in it; here it is, deprived of the esteem of the serious and the love of the frivolous, which are the two main pillars of opinion.

But I still hope to gain a sympathetic opinion, and the first remedy is to avoid an explicit and long prologue. The best prologue is the one that contains the fewest things, or the one that says them in an obscure and truncated way. Consequently, I avoid recounting the extraordinary process I used to compose these memoirs, which I worked on here, in the other world. It would be curious, but minimally extensive, and, in fact, unnecessary for an understanding of this work. The work itself is everything: if it pleases you, dear reader, I will be well paid for the task; if I do not please you, I will pay you with a flick, and goodbye.

BRAS CUBAS

CHAPTER I
THE AUTHOR'S DEATH

For some time, I hesitated whether I should open these memoirs at the beginning or the end, that is, whether I should put my birth or my death in the first place. Supposing the common usage is for beginning with birth, two considerations led me to adopt a different method: the first is that I am not exactly a writer who is dead but a dead man who is a writer, for whom the grave was another cradle; the second is that the writing would be more gallant and newer. Moses, who also wrote about his death, did not place it in the introit, but in the ending — a radical difference between this book and the Pentateuch.

With that said, I expired at two o'clock in the afternoon of a Friday in the month of August 1869, on my beautiful farm in Catumbi. I was about sixty-four years old, strong, and prosperous. I was single, I had about three hundred *contos de réis*[2] and I was accompanied to the cemetery by eleven friends. Eleven friends! The truth is that there were no letters or announcements. Furthermore, it was raining — drizzling — a soft, sad, and constant rain, so constant and so sad that it led one of those last-minute faithful friends to intersperse this ingenious idea in the speech he gave at the edge of my grave: "You who knew him, gentlemen, you can say with me that nature seems to be crying over the irreparable loss of one of the most beautiful characters that has honored humanity. This dark air, these drops from heaven, those dark clouds that cover the blue like a funereal crepe, all of this is the raw and evil pain that gnaws at nature's deepest entrails; all of this is a sublime praise to our illustrious deceased." Good and faithful friend! No, I do not regret the twenty policies I left him. And this is how I reached the closure of my days; that was how I headed towards Hamlet's *undiscovered country*, without the anxieties or doubts of the young prince, but slowly and shambling, like someone leaving the show late. Late and bored. About nine or ten people saw me go, including three ladies: my

---

2   Brazilian currency at the time.

sister Sabina, married to Cotrim, — their daughter, a lily of the valley — and... be patient! In a moment, I will tell you who the third lady was. Be content to know that this anonymous woman, although not a relative, suffered more than the relatives. It is true, she suffered more. I am not saying that she wailed, I am not saying that she rolled on the ground in convulsions. Or that my death was a highly dramatic thing... a bachelor who expires at the age of sixty-four does not seem to gather all the elements of a tragedy in himself. And even if that was the case, what least suited this anonymous woman was to show such feelings. Standing by the head of the bed, with stupid eyes, her mouth half open, the sad lady could hardly believe my extinction.

— Dead! Dead! — she said to herself.

And her imagination, like the storks that an illustrious traveler saw taking flight from the Ilissus to the African shores, without the hindrance of ruins and time, — this lady's imagination also flew over the present wreckage to the shores of a youthful Africa... let it go; there we will go later; there we will go when I return to my early years. Now, I want to die peacefully, methodically, listening to the ladies sobbing, the men's low speeches, the rain that drums on the farm's vine leaves, and the strident sound of a razor that a grinder is sharpening outside, at the door of a saddler. I swear to you that this orchestra of death was much less sad than it might have seemed. From a certain point onwards, it became delightful. Life was churning in my chest, with the surging of a sea wave, my consciousness was disappearing, I was descending into physical and moral immobility, and my body was becoming a plant, mud, and nothing else.

I died of pneumonia, but if I tell you that it was less pneumonia than a grand and useful idea that caused my death, you may not believe me, and, nevertheless, it is true. I will briefly explain the case to you. Judge it for yourself.

CHAPTER II
THE POULTICE

In fact, one day in the morning, while I was walking around the farm, an idea started hanging from the trapeze I had in my brain. Once hanging there, it came in, waving its arms and legs, doing the most daring antics of a tightrope-walker one can believe. I let myself contemplate it. Suddenly, it took a great leap, extended its arms and legs, until it took the shape of a X: decipher me, or I will devour you.

This idea was nothing less than the invention of a sublime medicine, an antihypochondriac poultice, intended to alleviate our melancholic humanity. In the patent application that I drew up, I called the government's attention to this truly Christian result. However, I did not deny my friends the pecuniary advantages that should result from the distribution of a product with such far-reaching and profound effects. Now, however, that I am here on the other side of life, I can confess everything: what mainly influenced me was the pleasure of seeing printed in newspapers, on displays, in leaflets, on street corners, and finally on medicine boxes, these three words: *Bras Cubas Poultice*. Why deny it? I had a passion for the noise, the limelight, the fireworks. Maybe the modest ones argue this defect to me; I believe, however, that the skilled ones will recognize this talent. So, my idea had two faces, like a medal, one facing the public, the other facing me. On the one hand, philanthropy, and profit; on the other hand, a thirst for fame. Let's say: love of glory.

An uncle of mine, a canon with full prebend, used to say that the love of temporal glory was the perdition of souls, which should only covet eternal glory. To which another uncle, an officer from one of the former infantry regiments, retorted that the love of glory was the most truly human thing in man and, consequently, his most genuine trait.

The reader decides between the military man and the canon; I return to the poultice.

CHAPTER III
GENEALOGY

But, since I mentioned my two uncles, let me make a short genealogical outline here.

The founder of my family was a certain Damiao Cubas, who flourished in the first half of the 18th century. He was a cooper by trade, born in Rio de Janeiro, where he would have died in penury and obscurity if he had only worked as a cooperage. But he did not; he became a farmer. He planted, harvested, exchanged his product for good and honorable silver *patacas*[3] until he died, leaving a nice inheritance to his son, the undergraduate Luis Cubas. It was with this young man that the series of my grandfathers truly begins — the grandfathers that my family

---

3   In Brazil, these were ancient silver coins (translator's note).

always admitted to —, because Damiao Cubas was, after all, a cooper, and maybe a bad cooper, while Luis Cubas studied in Coimbra, excelled in that state, and was one of the personal friends of the viceroy Count da Cunha.

As this surname Cubas smelled excessively of cooperage, my father, Damiao's great-grandson, claimed that the said surname was given to a knight, a hero of the African campaigns, as a reward for a deed he performed: the capture of three hundred kegs from the Moors. My father was a man of imagination; he escaped from the cooperage on the wings of a pun. He had a good character, my father, a dignified and loyal man like few others. He had, it is true, a touch of laziness; but who is not a little lazy in this world? It is important to note that he did not resort to inventiveness until after an attempt at falsification; firstly, he had the family branch off from that famous namesake of mine, the captain-general, Bras Cubas, who founded the village of Sao Vicente, where he died in 1592, and for that reason, he gave me the name Bras. However, the captain-general's family refuted him, and it was then that he imagined the three hundred Moorish kegs.

Some members of my family are still alive, my niece Venancia, for example, the lily of the valley, which is the flower of the ladies of her time; her father, Cotrim, is still alive, a fellow who… But let's not anticipate the events; let's finish with our poultice once and for all.

CHAPTER IV
THE FIXED IDEA

My idea, after so many mistakes, had become a fixed one. God forbid you, dear reader, from a fixed idea; rather a speck, rather a mote in the eye. Look at Cavour; it was the fixed idea of the Italian unit that killed him. It is true that Bismarck did not die; but it is important to remember that nature is terribly fickle and history is an eternal harlot. For example, Suetonius gave us Claudius, who was a simpleton, — or "a pumpkinhead," as Seneca called him — and Titus, who deserved to be the delight of all Rome. A professor came along in modern times and found a way to demonstrate that of the two Caesars, the delight one, the true delight one, was Seneca's "pumpkinhead." And you, Madame Lucrezia, the flower of the Borgias, if a poet painted you as the Catholic Messalina, along came an incredulous Gregorovius who erased that quality from you, and, even if you did not become a lily, you did not become a swamp either. I will take my position between the poet and the sage.

So, long live to history, the fickle history that can be used for everything; and, returning to the fixed idea, I will say that it is what makes men strong and crazy; the mobile, vague, or iridescent idea is what produces a Claudius — according to the formula of Suetonius.

My idea was fixed, fixed like... I cannot think of anything that is quite fixed in this world: maybe the moon, maybe the Egyptian pyramids, maybe the dead Germanic diet. Let the reader see the comparison that best suits him, let him see it and don't be upset, just because we did not reach the narrative part of these memoirs yet. We will get there. I believe he prefers anecdotes to reflection, like other readers, his confreres, and I think he is right. So, let's get on with it. However, it is important to say that this book is written with patience, with the patience of a man now freed of the brevity of the century, a supinely philosophical work, and an unequal philosophy, now austere, then playful, something that neither builds nor destroys, neither inflames nor cools, and yet it is more than a pastime and less than an apostolate.

Let's go; straighten your nose, and let's go back to the poultice. Let's leave history with the whims of an elegant lady. None of us fought the battle of Salamina, none of us wrote the Augsburg Confession; for my part, if I ever remember Cromwell, it is only because of the idea that His Highness, with the same hand that locked parliament, would have imposed the Bras Cubas poultice on the English people. Do not laugh at this common victory of pharmacy and puritanism. Who does not know that beneath every great, public, ostentatious flag, there are often several other modestly private flags, which are unfurled and waving in the shadow of the first, and not infrequently outlive it? Barely comparing, it is like the rabble huddled in the shadow of a feudal castle; when the latter fell, the rabble huddled remained. The truth is that they became big and castellans... No, the comparison is useless.

CHAPTER V
IN WHICH A LADY'S EAR APPEARS

But when, while I was busy preparing and refining my invention, I was caught in a strong draft; I fell ill right after, and did not take care of myself; I had the poultice on my brain; I brought with me the fixed idea of the crazy and the strong. I could see myself, in the distance, rising up from the ground of the crowd, and rising back to heaven, like an immortal eagle, and it is not in the face of such an exalted spectacle that a man can feel the pain that stings him. The next day I was worse; I finally treated myself, but in an incomplete way, without method, care, or persistence; such was the origin of the illness that brought me to eternity. You already know that I died on a Friday, an unlucky day, and I believe I have proven that it was my invention that killed me. There are less lucid and no less triumphant demonstrations.

— You are wrong — replied the animal — we are going to the origins of centuries.

It was not impossible, however, for me to have climbed to the heights of a century, and appear on public pages, among macrobes. I was healthy and robust. Suppose that, instead of laying the foundations of a pharmaceutical invention, I was trying to bring together the elements of a political institution, or a religious reform. The current of air came, which surpasses human calculation in efficiency, and there went everything. This is how the fate of men goes.

With this reflection, I said goodbye to the woman, I will not say the most discreet, but certainly the most beautiful among her contemporaries, the anonymous one from the first chapter, the one, whose imagination was similar to the storks on the Ilissus... She was then 54 years old, she was a ruin, an imposing ruin. Let the reader imagine that she and I loved each other many years before, and that one day, already ill, I see her appearing at the door of my bedroom...

CHAPTER VI
CHIMÈNE, QUI L'EÛT DIT? RODRIGUE, QUI L'EÛT CRU?

I see her appearing at the door of my bedroom, pale, moved, dressed in black, and remaining there for a minute, not in the mood to enter, or be detained by the presence of a man who was with me. From the bed, where I was lying, I contemplated her during that time, forgetting to say anything to her or make any gesture. We had not seen each other for two years, and now I saw her not as she was, but as she had been, as we both were, because a mysterious Hezekiah had turned the sun back to youthful days. The sun turned back, I shook off all my miseries, and this handful of dust, which death was going to scatter into the eternity of nothingness, was more powerful than time, which is the minister of death. No water from Juventas could match the simple nostalgia there.

Believe me, the least bad thing is to remember; no one should trust in present happiness; there is a drop of Cain's drool in it. With the passing of time and the end of spasm, then yes, then maybe it is really possible to enjoy it, because between one and the other of these two illusions, the one that you enjoy without hurting is the better.

The evocation did not last long; reality soon took over; the present expelled the past. Maybe I will explain to the reader, in some corner of this book, my theory of human editions. What is important to know for now is that Virgilia — her name was Virgilia — entered the room with a firm step, with the seriousness that her clothes and years gave her, and came to my bed. The stranger got up and left. He was a guy who visited me every day to talk about the exchange rate, colonization, and the need to develop railways; nothing more interesting for a dying man. He left; Virgilia remained standing; for a while, we looked at each other without saying a word. Who would say something? Of two great lovers, of two unbridled passions, there was nothing left there, twenty years later; there were just two withered hearts, devastated by life and satiated with it, I do not know if in the same dose, but finally satiated. Virgilia now had the beauty of old age, an austere and maternal look; she was less thin than when I last saw her, at a Saint John's festival in Tijuca; and as she was someone who had a great resistance, only now were a few silver threads beginning to mingle with her dark hair.

— Are you visiting dying men? — I asked her. — Come on, dying men! — Virgilia answered with a sigh. And after shaking my hands: — I am seeing if I can put the strays out on the street.

It did not have the tearful caress of another time, but her voice was friendly and sweet. She sat down. I was alone at home, a simple sick person; we could talk to each other without danger. Virgilia gave me long news from the world outside, narrating it with grace, with a certain touch of bad language that was the salt of the talk; I, about to leave the world, felt a satanic pleasure in making fun of it, in persuading myself that I was leaving nothing behind.

— What kind of ideas are those?! — Virgilia interrupted me, somewhat angry.
— Look, I am not coming back. Dying! We all have to die; it is enough just being alive.

And looking at the clock:

— Jesus! It is three o'clock. I've got to go.

— So soon?

— Yes. I will come tomorrow or the day after.

— I do not know if it is good, — I replied — the patient is a bachelor and the house has no women in it...

— What about your sister?

—She is going to come here and spend a few days, but she cannot get here until Saturday. — Virgilia reflected for a moment, raised her shoulders and said seriously:

— I am old! Nobody pays any attention to me anymore. But, to eliminate doubts, I will come with Nono.

Nono was a bachelor, the only child from her marriage, who, at the age of five, had been an unconscious accomplice in our love affairs. They came together, two days later, and I must confess that, when I saw them there, in my room, I was taken by a feeling of shyness that did not even allow me to immediately respond to the guy's kind words. Virgilia sensed this and told her son:

— Nono, do not pay any attention to that sly guy over there; he does not want to talk to make people believe he is dying.

Her son smiled, I believe I also smiled, and everything ended up as a big joke. Virgilia was serene and smiling, she had the appearance of an immaculate life. No suspicious look, no gesture that could betray anything; equality of word and spirit, control over oneself, which seemed and perhaps was rare. As we casually talked about some illegitimate, half-secret, half-known love affairs, I saw her speak with disdain and a little bit of indignation about the woman involved, who was in fact her friend. Her son felt satisfied, hearing that dignified and strong word, and I asked myself what the hawks would say about us, if Buffon had been born a hawk...

It was the start of my delirium.

CHAPTER VII
DELIRIUM

As far as I know, no one has yet reported their own delirium; I do it, and science will thank me. If the reader is not keen on the contemplation of these mental phenomena, you can skip the chapter and go straight to the narration. But if you have the slightest bit of curiosity, I always tell you that it is interesting to know what went on in my head for twenty or thirty minutes…

Firstly, I took the figure of a Chinese barber, big-bodied, right-handed, shaving a Mandarin, who paid me for the work with pinches and sweets: the whims of a Mandarin.

Soon after, I felt transformed into the *Summa Theologica*, by St. Thomas, printed in one volume, and bound in Moroccan, with silver clasps and illustrations; this idea gave my body the most complete immobility; and even now I remember that, with my hands being the clasps of the book, and crossing them over my stomach, someone uncrossed them (certainly Virgilia), because the attitude gave her the image of a deceased.

Lately, restored to human form, I saw a hippopotamus come and carry me away. I let myself go, silent, I do not know if it was out of fear or trust; but, after a short while, the career became so dizzying that I dared to question it, and, in some way, I told it that the journey seemed to me to have no destination.

— You are wrong — the animal replied — we are going to the origins of the centuries.

I insinuated that it must be very far away; but the hippopotamus did not understand me or did not hear me, unless it was pretending one of those things; and, asking it, since it could talk, if it was a descendant of Achilles' horse or Balaam's ass, it answered me with a gesture peculiar to these two quadrupeds: it flapped its ears. For my part, I closed my eyes and let myself go on the adventure. I must confess now, however, that I felt some sort of tickle of curiosity, to know where the origin of the centuries was, if it was as mysterious as the origin of the Nile, and, most of all, if it was worth something more or less than the consummation of the same centuries: reflections of a sick brain. Since I was going along with my eyes closed, I could not see the path; I just remember that the feeling of cold increased with the journey, and that there came a time when it seemed to me that I was entering the region of eternal ice. Indeed, I opened my eyes and saw that my animal was galloping on a snow-white plain, with an occasional snow mountain, snow vegetation, and several large snow animals. All snow; the snowy sun was freezing us. I tried to speak, but I could only grunt this anxious question:

— Where are we?
— We just passed Eden.
— Good. Let's stop at Abraham's tent.
— But we are traveling backwards! — my mount retorted, mockingly.

— I was vexed and stunned. The journey started seeming boring and extravagant to me, the cold was uncomfortable, the ride was violent, and the result was impalpable. And then - the cogitations of a sick man - given that we reached the indicated destination, it was not impossible that the centuries, annoyed with having their origins devastated, would crush me between their nails, which must have been as secular as they were. While I thought so, we were devouring the path, and the plain ground flew beneath our feet, until the animal stopped, and I was able to look more calmly around me. Just look; I saw nothing, other than the immense whiteness of the snow, which this time invaded the sky itself, until then blue. Maybe, at intervals, one or another plant appeared to me, huge, brutish, waving its broad leaves in the wind. The silence of that region was like that of the tomb: it was said that the life of things had become stupid before man. Did it fall out of the air? Did it detach itself from the earth? I do not know; I know that a huge shape, the figure of a woman, appeared to me then, looking at me with eyes as bright as the sun. Everything about this figure had the vastness of wild forms, and everything escaped the understanding of the human eye, because the outlines were lost in the environment, and what seemed thick was often diaphanous. Stunned, I said nothing, I did not even let out a scream; but, after some time, which was brief, I asked who she was and what her name was: curiosity of delirium.

— Call me Nature or Pandora. I am your mother and your enemy.

When I heard that last word, I stepped back a little, overcome by fear. The figure let out a laugh, which produced the effect of a typhoon around us; the plants twisted, and a long groan broke the muteness of external things.

— Do not be scared, — she said — my enmity does not kill; it is confirmed most of all by life. You are alive: that is the only torment I want.

— Alive? — I asked, digging my nails into my hands, as if to make sure of my existence.

— Yes, worm, you are alive. Do not be afraid to lose that rag that is your pride; you are still going to taste, for a few hours, the bread of pain and the wine of misery. You are alive: even now that you are going crazy, you are alive; and if your conscience gets an instant of wisdom, you will say that you want to live.

Saying this, the vision reached out her arm, grabbed me by the hair, and lifted me into the air, as if I was a feather. Only then could I see her face up close, which was huge. Nothing more serene; no violent contortion, no expressions of hatred or ferocity; the single, general, complete feature was that of selfish impassibility, that of eternal deafness, that of immobile will. Anger, if she had any, remained closed in her heart. At the same time, in that face of glacial expression, there was an air of youth, a mixture of strength and freshness, before which I felt like the weakest and most decrepit of beings.

— Did you understand me? — she said, after some time of mutual contemplation.

— No — I answered — I do not even want to understand you; you are absurd, you are a fable. I am dreaming, certainly, or, if it is true that I went crazy, you are nothing more than an alienated conception, that is, a vain thing that an absent eason cannot control or touch. You, Nature? The Nature I know is only a mother and not an enemy; she does not make life a torment, nor, like you, carries a face as indifferent as the tomb. And why Pandora?

— Because I carry in my bag the good and the evil, and the greatest thing of all, hope, the consolation of men. Are you trembling?

— Yes; your gaze fascinates me.

— I believe it; I am not just life; I am also death, and you are about to give me back what I loaned you. You, great lascivious, the voluptuousness of nothingness awaits you.

When this word, "nothingness," echoed, like a thunder, in that huge valley, it seemed to me that it was the last sound that reached my ears; I seemed to feel my own sudden decomposition. Then I faced her with pleading eyes and asked for a few more years.

— Poor minute! — she exclaimed. — Why do you want a few more moments of life? To devour and be devoured later? Are you not tired of the spectacle and the fighting? You know in depth everything that I presented to you that is less awkward or less distressing: the dawn of the day, the melancholy of the afternoon, the stillness of the night, the aspects of the earth, sleep, in short, the greatest benefit of my hands. What more do you want, you sublime idiot?

— Just to live, I do not ask you for anything else. Who put this love of life in my heart, if not you? And, if I love life, why should you strike yourself, killing me?

— Because I no longer need you. Time does not care about the minute that passes, but about the minute that comes. The minute that comes is strong, powerful, it is supposed to bring eternity within itself, and it brings death, and it perishes like the other, but time subsists. Selfishness, conversation. The jaguar kills the calf because the jaguar's reasoning is that it must live, and if the calf is tender, so much the better: this is the universal statute. Come up and take a look.

Saying this, she carried me up to the top of a mountain. I cast my eyes down to one of the slopes, and contemplated, for a long time, in the distance, through a fog, a unique thing. Imagine, reader, a reduction of centuries, and a parade of all of them, all the races, all the passions, the tumult of empires, the war of appetites and hatreds, the reciprocal destruction of beings and things. Such was the spectacle, a harsh and curious spectacle. The history of man and the earth thus had an intensity that neither imagination nor science could give it, because science is slower and imagination is vaguer, while what I saw there was the living condensation of all times. To describe it, it would be necessary to make a lightning stand still. The centuries passed by in a whirlwind, and, nevertheless, because the eyes of delirium are different, I saw everything that passed before me – torments and delights, from that thing that is called glory to that thing that is called misery, and I saw love multiplying misery, and I saw misery intensifying weakness. Then came the greed that devours, the anger that inflames, the envy that drools, and the hoe and the pen, damp with sweat, and ambition, hunger, vanity, melancholy, wealth, love, and all of them shaking man like a rattle, until they destroy him, like a rag. They were the different forms of an evil, that sometimes bit the gut, sometimes bit the thought, and walked eternally in its harlequin clothes, around the human species. The pain sometimes gave way, but it gave way to indifference, which was a dreamless sleep, or to pleasure, which was a bastard pain. So man, scourge and rebel, ran before the fatality of things, behind a nebulous and elusive figure, made of patches, a patch of the impalpable, another of the improbable, another of the invisible, all sewn together with a precarious stitch by the needle of imagination; and that figure, — nothing less than the chimera of happiness, — either runs away from him perpetually, or lets itself be caught by the diaper, and the man would hold it to his chest, and then she laughed, like a mockery, and disappeared, like an illusion.

When contemplating so much calamity, I could not hold back a cry of anguish, which Nature or Pandora heard without protesting or laughing; and I do not know by what cerebral disorder law, I was the one who started laughing, — an out-of-control and idiotic laugh.

— You are right, — I said — this is amusing and worth something; maybe monotonous, but it is worth it. When Job cursed the day he was conceived, it was because he wanted to see the spectacle from above. Come on, Pandora, open up your womb and digest me. It is amusing, but digest me.

Her answer was to strongly compel me to look down, and to see the centuries that continued to pass, fast and turbulent, the generations that overlapped the generations, some sad, like the Hebrews of captivity, others happy, like the profligates of Commodus, and all of them punctual at the grave. I wanted to run away, but a mysterious force held back my feet; then I said to myself: — Well, the centuries keep passing, my century will come, and it will also pass, until the last one, which will give me the decipherment of eternity. And I fixed my eyes, and continued to see the ages, which were coming and going, now calm and resolute, even happy — I do not know. Maybe happy. Each century brought its share of shadow and light, of apathy and combat, truth and error, and its cortege of systems, of new ideas, and new illusions; in each of them, the greenery of springtime was bursting for, and then turned yellow, to be rejuvenated later on. So in that way life had the regularity of a calendar, history, and civilization were made, and man, naked and unarmed, armed and dressed himself, built the tugurium and the palace, the crude village and Thebes of a Hundred Doors; created science, which scrutinizes, and art that captivates; made himself an orator, mechanic, philosopher, covered the face of the globe, descended to the womb of the earth, ascended to the sphere of the clouds, thus collaborating in the mysterious work, with which he entertained the necessity of life and the melancholy of helplessness. My gaze, bored and distracted, finally saw the present century arrive and, behind it, the future ones. That one came along agile, dexterous, vibrant, self-confident, a little diffuse, bold, knowledgeable, but in the end, it was as miserable as the first ones, and so it passed, and that was how the others passed, with the same speed and equal monotony. I doubled my attention; I sharpened my sight; I was finally going to see the last one — the last one! But then the speed of the march was such that it escaped all understanding; at its foot, the lightning would be a century. Maybe that is why the objects started changing; some grew, others shrank, others were lost in the environment; a fog covered everything, except the hippopotamus that had brought me there, and which in fact started getting smaller, smaller, smaller, until it was the size of a cat. It was actually a cat. I looked at it well; it was my cat, Sultan, who was playing at the door of the room with a ball of paper...

CHAPTER VIII
REASON VERSUS FOLLY

The reader now understood that it was Reason that returned to the house, and invited Folly to leave, proclaiming, with perfect right, the words of Tartuffe:

La Maison est à moi, c'est à vous d'en sortir.

But it is Folly's old passion to create love for other people's houses, so that, just being the owner of one, it is difficult for her to be evicted. It is a quirk; there is no getting rid of her; She was hardened to shame a long time ago. Now, if we take note of the huge number of houses she occupies – some permanently, others during the calm seasons, we will conclude that this friendly pilgrim is the terror of the householders. In our case, there was almost a disturbance at the door of my brain, because the intruder did not want to hand over the house, and the owner did not give up on her intention to take what was hers. After all, Folly was content with a little corner in the attic.

— No, ma'am — Reason replied. — I am tired of giving you attics, sick and tired. What you want is to move smoothly from the attic to the dining room, then to the living room and everywhere else.

— All right, just let me stay a little longer, I am on the trail of a mystery...

— What mystery?

— Two of them — Folly corrected. — That of life and that of death; I ask you for just ten minutes.

Reason started laughing.

— You will always be the same... Always the same... Always the same...

And so saying, Reason grabbed Folly by the wrists and dragged her outside. Then she went in and closed the door. Folly still moaned some pleas, grunted some curses, but she soon gave up, stuck out her tongue as a jeer, and went on her way...

CHAPTER IX
TRANSITION

And now see with what dexterity, with what art I make the greatest transition in this book. See: my delirium started in the presence of Virgilia; Virgilia was the great sin of my youth; there is no youth without childhood; childhood presumes birth; and here is how we come, effortlessly, to that day of October 20, 1805, on which I was born. Did you see it? No apparent joints, nothing that diverts the reader's attention: nothing. So, the book goes on like this, with all of the advantages of the method. In fact, it was time. Because this business of method, being, as it is, an indispensable thing, it is still better to have it without a tie or suspenders, but a little cool and loose, like someone who does not care about the neighboring border or the inspector of the block. It is like eloquence, where there is a genuine and vibrant one, with natural and enchanting art, and another that is stiff, starched, and stale. Let's go to October 20th.

CHAPTER X
ON THAT DAY

On that day, the Cubas family tree sprouted a graceful flower. I was born; Pascoela, a distinguished midwife, who boasted of having opened the door to the world to an entire generation of nobles, welcomed me into her arms. It is not impossible that my father heard such a statement; I believe, however, that paternal feeling is what induced him to gratify her with two half-doubloons. Washed and bandaged, I was immediately the hero of our house. Each one predicted for me what suited them best. My uncle Joao, the former infantry officer, thought I had a certain Bonaparte look in my eyes, something that my father could not hear without nausea; my uncle Ildefonso, then a simple priest, sensed a canon in me.

— A canon is what he will be, and I say no more so that it will not look like pride; but I would not be surprised if God destined him for a bishopric... That is right, a bishopric; it is not an impossible thing. What do you say, Brother Bento?

My father told everyone that I would be whatever God wanted; and he lifted me into the air, as if he intended to show me to the city and the world. He was asking everybody if I looked like him, if I was intelligent, handsome...

I say these things haphazardly, as I heard them narrated years later; I ignore most of the details of that famous day. I know that the neighborhood came or was sent to greet the newborn, and that, during the first weeks, there were many visits to our house. There was no chair that did not work; there were a lot of jackets and a lot of coats. If I do not mention the treats, the kisses, the admiration, the blessings, it is because, if I did, I would not finish the chapter, and it needs to be finished.

Note: I cannot say anything about my baptism, because nothing was mentioned to me about it, except that it was one of the most gallant celebrations of the following year, 1806; I was baptized in the church of S. Domingos, on a Tuesday in March, a clear, luminous, and pure day, with Colonel Rodrigues de Matos and his wife as godparents. They were both descendants of old northern families and truly honored the blood that ran through their veins, once shed in the war against the Netherlands. I think their names were some of the first things I learned; and I certainly said them with great grace, or revealed some precocious talent, because there was no stranger in front of whom I was not forced to recite them.

— Young man, tell these gentlemen what your godfather's name is.

— My godfather? He is the Honorable Colonel Paulo Vaz Lobo Cesar de Andrade e Sousa Rodrigues de Matos; my godmother is the Honorable Mrs. Maria Luisa de Macedo Resende e Sousa Rodrigues de Matos.

— Your boy is very smart — the listeners exclaimed.

— Very smart — my father agreed; and his eyes drooled with pride, and he spread his hand over my head, looked at me for a long time, lovingly, bursting with pride.

Note: I started walking, I do not know exactly when, but ahead of time. Maybe in order to speed up nature, they forced me to grab chairs early, picked me up by my diaper, gave me wooden carts. — By yourself, by yourself, little master, by yourself, by yourself, — said the nursemaid to me. And I, attracted by the tin rattle that my mother shook in front of me, went forward, fell here, fell there; and I walked, probably poorly, but I walked, and I kept walking.

CHAPTER XI
THE BOY IS THE FATHER OF THE MAN

I grew up; and in this, the family did not intervene; I grew up naturally, like magnolias and cats do. Maybe cats are less sly, and certainly magnolias are less restless than I was in my childhood. A poet said that the boy is the father of the man. If this is true, let's look at some of the markings of the boy.

Since I was five years old, I deserved the nickname "devil boy;" and I really was just that; I was one of the most malevolent children of my time, evasive, indiscreet, mischievous, and willful. For example, one day I broke a slave's head, because she had refused me a spoonful of the coconut candy she was making, and, not happy with the evil deed, I threw a handful of ashes into the bowl, and, not satisfied with that mischief, I went to tell my mother that the slave had ruined the candy "out of a prank," and I was only six years old. Prudencio, a houseboy, was my everyday horse; he would put his hands and knees on the ground, take a cord in his mouth as a bridle, and I climbed on his back; with a stick in my hand, I whipped him, making a thousand turns from one side to the other, and he obeyed – sometimes moaning – but he obeyed without saying a word, or, at most, an — ouch, little master! — to which I retorted: — Shut up, beast! — Hiding visitors' hats, pinning paper tails on serious people, pulling the ponytails of their hair, pinching the arms of matrons, and many other deeds of this kind, were signs of an indocile nature, but I must believe that they were also expressions of a robust spirit, because my father held me in great admiration; and if he sometimes scolded me, in the presence of people, he did it as a simple formality: in private he gave me kisses.

Do not conclude from this that I spent the rest of my life breaking other people's heads or hiding their hats; but opinionated, selfish, and somewhat contemptuous of men, that was me; if I did not spend my time hiding their hats, I did once pull the ponytails of their hair.

Furthermore, I became fond of contemplating human injustice, I was inclined to mitigate it, to explain it, to classify it into parts, to understand it, not according to a rigid standard, but according to the circumstances and places. My mother indoctrinated me in her own way, made me memorize some precepts and prayers; but I felt that, more than prayers, my nerves and blood governed me, and the good rule lost its living spirit and became a vain formula. In the morning, before porridge, and at night, before bed, I asked God to forgive me, just as I forgave my debtors; but between morning and night I did great evil, and my father, after the commotion was over, pat me on the cheek and exclaimed, laughing: — Oh, you little devil! You little devil!

Yes, my father adored me. My mother was a weak woman, with little brain and a lot of heart, quite credulous, sincerely pious — homely, despite being beautiful, and modest, despite being wealthy; afraid of thunder and her husband. Her husband was her god on Earth. From the collaboration of these two creatures, my education was born, which, if there was anything good, was generally vicious, incomplete, and, in parts, negative. My uncle, the canon, sometimes made some repairs to his brother, telling him that he was giving me more freedom than education, and more affection than correction; but my father answered that he applied a system to my education that was entirely superior to the usual system; and in this way, without confusing his brother, he deceived himself. Along with education, there was also the outside example, the domestic environment. We saw the parents; let's see the uncles. One of them, Joao, was a man with a loose tongue, a gallant life, and picaresque conversation. From the age of eleven on, I was admitted to his anecdotes, real or not, all contaminated with obscenity or filth. He did not respect my adolescence, just as he did not respect his brother's cassock; with the difference that the latter ran away as soon as he embarked on a scandalous subject. I did not; I let myself be, not understanding anything at first, then understanding it, and finally finding him funny. After a certain time, I was the one looking for him; and he liked me a lot, he gave me candy, he took me for walks. At home, when he was there for a few days, I often found him, at the back of the farm, in the laundry, talking to the slaves who were washing clothes; then it was a parade of jokes, sayings, questions, and a burst of laughter that nobody could hear, because the laundry was too far away from the house. The black women, with clothes around their stomachs, their dresses hiked up a little, some inside the tank, others outside, leaning over the article of clothing, beating them, soaping them, twisting them, listening, and retorting to Uncle Joao's jokes, and commenting on them from time to time, saying:

— God forbid!... This Master Joao is the devil!

My uncle, the canon, was quite different. This one had austerity and purity; such qualities, however, did not enhance a superior spirit, they only compensated for a mediocre spirit. He was not a man to aim at the substantial part of the church; he saw the external side, the hierarchy, the pre-eminences, the surplices, the genuflections. He was closer to the sacristy than to the altar. A gap in the ritual excited him more than an infraction of the commandments. Now, so many years away, I am not sure whether or not he could easily understand a passage from Tertullian, or expound, without hesitation, the history of the symbol of Nicea; but no one, at the sung parties, knew better the number and type of courtesies that were owed to the officiant. Being canon was his only ambition in life; and he said from his heart that it was the greatest dignity to which he could aspire. Pious, severe in his habits, precise in his observance of the rules, limp, shy, subordinate, he possessed some virtues, in which he was exemplary, but he absolutely lacked the strength to instill them, to impose them on others.

I am not saying anything about my maternal aunt, Mrs. Emerenciana, and in fact she was the person who had the most authority over me; this one differed greatly from the others; but she lived in our company for a short time, about two years. Other relatives and some close friends are not worth mentioning; we did not have a common life, but intermittent, with great spans of separation. What matters is the general expression of the domestic environment, and this is indicated there — vulgarity of characters, love of flashy appearances, of noise, laxity of will, dominance of whim, and so on. Out of that land and that manure, this flower was born.

CHAPTER XII
AN EPISODE FROM 1814

But I do not want to go ahead without summarily telling a gallant episode from 1814. I was nine years old.

Napoleon, when I was born, was already in all the splendor of his glory and power; he was emperor, and had entirely conquered the admiration of men. My father, who, on the strength of having persuaded others of our nobility, had ended up persuading himself, kept on feeding a completely mental hatred of him. This was the reason for fierce disputes in our house, because my uncle Joao, I do not know if it was due to class spirit and professional sympathy, forgave in the despot what he admired in the General. My priest uncle was inflexible in his opposition to the Corsican, and my other relatives were divided. That was the basis of the controversy and the raids.

When the news of Napoleon's first fall arrived in Rio de Janeiro, there was naturally a great shock in our house, but no chaos or revolt. The defeated, witnesses of public rejoicing, judged silence to be more decorous; some went further and clapped their hands. The population, cordially happy, did not haggle on demonstrations of affection for the royal family; there were torches, salutes, *Te-Deum*, parades, and acclamations. I appeared on those days with a new rapier, which my godfather gave me on Saint Anthony's Day; and, frankly, I was more interested in the rapier than in the fall of Bonaparte. I never forgot about this phenomenon. I never stopped thinking to myself that our rapier is always greater than Napoleon's sword. And note that I heard a lot of speeches when I was alive, I read a lot of noisy pages of great ideas and greatest words, but I do not know why, in the background of the applause that drew from my mouth, sometimes that voice of experience echoed:

— Go away, all you care about is your rapier.

My family was not content with having an anonymous share in the public rejoicing. They considered it opportune and indispensable to celebrate the emperor's dismissal with a dinner, and such a dinner that the noise of the acclamations reached the ears of His Highness, or at least, of his ministers. No sooner said than done. All the old silverware, inherited from my grandfather Luis Cubas, was taken down;

the tablecloths from Flanders were unpacked, the large vases from India; a pig was killed; jams and marmalade were ordered from the nuns of Ajuda; everything was washed and polished: the rooms, stairs, candlesticks, sconces, the vast glass items, all the things of classic luxury. Given the hour, a select society was gathered together: the district judge, three or four military officers, some businessmen and scholars, several government officials, some with their wives and daughters, others without them, but all with a common desire to stuff a turkey with Bonaparte's memory. It was not a dinner, but a *Te- Deum*; that was more or less what one of the scholars present, Dr. Vilaca, said. He was a famous glosser who added the tidbit of muses to the dishes of the house. It reminds me as if it was yesterday, it reminds me of seeing him standing up, with his long ponytail, silk coat, an emerald on his finger, asking my priest uncle to repeat the motto, staring at a lady's forehead, then coughing, raising his right hand, all clenched, except for the index finger, which had pointed towards the ceiling; and, thus stated and composed, return the glossed maxim. He did not make one gloss, but three; then he swore to his gods that it would never end. He asked for a maxim, they gave him one, he quickly glossed it, and then asked for another, and another, to the point that one of the ladies present could not keep her admiration silent.

— You say that — Vilaca modestly retorted — because you never heard Bocage, like I heard, at the end of the century, in Lisbon. That was something! How easy! And what verses! We had fights lasting one and two hours, in Nicola's bar, shouting, amidst applause and cheers. Bocage had a tremendous talent! That is what Her Grace the Duchess of Cadaval told me a few days ago...

And these last three words, expressed with great emphasis, produced a thrill of admiration and astonishment throughout the entire assembly. Because this man, so cordial, so simple, in addition to competing with poets, was close to duchesses! Bocage and Cadaval! Being in contact with such a man, the ladies felt super fine; the men looked at him with respect, some with envy, often with incredulity. He, however, was on his way, accumulating adjective upon adjective, adverb upon adverb, listing everything that rhymed with *tyrant* and *usurper*. It was dessert time. No one was thinking about eating anymore. During the intervals of the glosses, there was a happy buzz, a chatter of satisfied stomachs; their eyes, sluggish and moist, or lively and warm, lounged or leaped from one end to the other of the table, loaded with candies and fruits — sliced pineapple here, the carved melon there, the crystal jam jars displaying the thinly shredded coconut candy, yellow like a yolk — or the molasses, thick and dark, not far from the cheese. From time to time a jovial, broad, unbuttoned laugh — a family laugh — came to break the political gravity of the banquet. In the midst of the great and common interest, the small and private ones were also moving about. The girls talked about the songs they would sing to the accompaniment of the harpsichord, and about the minuet and the English solo; there was no shortage of matrons who promised to dance an octave, only to show how much fun she had enjoyed in her good childhood days. A guy, next to me, was giving recent news to another about new slaves who were coming, according to letters he had received from Luanda, a letter in which his nephew told him that he had already traded around forty heads, and another letter in which... He had them in his pocket, but he could not read them on that occasion. What he guaranteed is that from this one shipment, we can count on some hundred and twenty slaves at least.

— Shh... shh... shh... — Vilaca was saying, clapping his hands. The noise quickly stopped, like a pause of an orchestra, and all eyes turned to the glosser, who was far away, with his hands behind his ears so as not to miss a word. Most of them, even before the gloss, had already given a chuckle of approval, mild and sincere.

As for me, there I was, lonely and out of it, making eyes at a certain dessert that was my passion. At the end of each gloss, I was very happy, hoping it was the last, but it was not, and the dessert remained intact. Nobody remembered giving the first word. My father, at the head of the table, savored the joy of the guests with long sips, he had eyes only for the happy faces, the dishes, the flowers. He was delighted with the familiarity between the most distant spirits, the influence of a good dinner. I could see that because I dragged my eyes from the jam to him and from him to the jam, as if begging him to serve me some. But it was in vain. He did not see anything; he was seeing himself. And the glosses went on one after the other like sheets of water, forcing me to withdraw my desires and requests. I was patient as much as I could; but I could not be for long. I asked loudly for the candy; finally, I shouted, roared, and stamped my feet. My father, who would be able to give me the sun if I asked him to, called a slave to serve me the candy; but it was too late. Aunt Emerenciana pulled me out of my chair and handed me over to a slave girl, despite my screams and shoves.

The glosser's crime was only that: he delayed the dessert and caused my exclusion. So much was enough for me to consider revenge, whatever it was, but huge and exemplary, something that somehow would make him ridiculous. Since Dr. Vilaca was a serious man, mannerly and calm, forty-seven years old, married, and a father. I was not content with a paper tail; it had to be worse. I started scrutinizing him for the rest of the afternoon, following him around the farm, where everyone went for a walk. I saw him talking to Ms. Eusebia, sister of Sergeant Major Domingos, a robust maiden, who, if she was not pretty, was not ugly either.

— I am very angry with you, sir — she was telling him.

— Why?

— Because... I do not know why... Because it is my fate... Sometimes I believe it is better to die...

They had entered a small bush; it was twilight. I followed them. There was a spark of wine and sensuality in Vilaca's eyes.

— Let go of me — she said.

— Nobody can see us. Dying, my angel? What kind of idea is that? You know that I would die too... What am I saying?... I die every day, of passion, of longing...

Ms. Eusebia put the handkerchief to her eyes. The glosser searched his memory for some literary fragment, and found this one, which I later discovered was from an opera by Antonio Jose da Silva, the Jew:

— Do not cry, my dear; do not wish for the day to break with two dawns.

He said that and pulled her toward him; she resisted a little, but let herself go. Their faces came together, and I heard, very lightly, a kiss, the most fearful of kisses.

— Dr. Vilaca gave Ms. Eusebia a kiss! — I shouted running through the farm. Those words of mine were an explosion; stupefaction immobilized everyone.

Eyes looked out all over. Smiles were exchanged, furtive whispers. Mothers dragged their daughters, with the pretext of the dew. My father pulled my ears, surreptitiously, but really annoyed by my indiscretion; but, the next day, at lunch, remembering the case, he tweaked my nose, laughing: — Oh, you little devil! You little devil!

CHAPTER XIII
A LEAP

Let's put our feet together now and leap over school, the irksome school where I learned to read, write, count, whack noggins, get mine whacked, and make mischief, sometimes up on the hills, sometimes on the beaches, wherever it was convenient for a loaf.

They were bitter times. There were the scoldings, the punishments, the arduous long lessons, and little else, very little and very slight. The only really bad part was the whacking of the palms with a ruler, and even then... Oh, ruler, terror of my childhood, you who were the *compelle intrare* with which an old teacher, bony and bald, instilled in my brain the alphabet, prosody, syntax, and everything else he knew, blessed ruler, so cursed by modern people, if only I could have remained under your yoke with my beardless soul, my ignorance, and my rapier, that rapier from 1814, so superior to Napoleon's sword! What was it that my old primary teacher wanted, after all? Memorization and behavior in the classroom. Nothing more, nothing less than what life, the final class, wants, with the difference that if you put fear into me, you never put anger. I can still see you now, coming into the room with your white leather slippers, cape, handkerchief in hand, bald head on display, clean-shaven chin. I see you sit down, snort, grunt, take an initial pinch of snuff, and then call us to order for the lesson. And you did that for twenty-three years, quiet, obscure, punctual, stuck in a little house on Louse Street, not bothering the world with your mediocrity, until one day you took the great dive into the shadows and nobody wept for you except an old black man—no one, not even I, who owe you the rudiments of writing.

The teacher's name was Ludgero. Let me write his full name on this page: Ludgero Barata — a disastrous name whose second part means cockroach and that gave the boys an eternal basis for crude jokes. One of us, Quincas Borba, was cruel to the poor man at that time. Two or three times a week, he would put a dead roach into his pants pocket — wide trousers tied with a cord — or in the desk drawer, or by his inkwell. If he found it during school hours, he would leap up, pass his flaming eyes over us, call us by our last names: we were parasites, ignoramuses, brats, scoundrels... Some trembled, others snorted. Quincas Borba, however, allowed himself to remain quiet, his eyes staring into space.

A delight, Quincas Borba. Never in my childhood, never in my whole life, I found a funnier, more inventive, more mischievous boy. He was a delight not only in school but all over the city. His mother, a widow of certain means, worshiped her son and brought him to school pampered, well-dressed, all decked out, with a striking houseboy following, a houseboy who would let's play hooky, go hunt for birds' nests or lizards on *Livramento* and *Conceiçao* hills, or simply roam the streets on the loose like two idle loafers. And as emperor! It was a pleasure to see Quincas Borba playing the emperor during the festival of the Holy Spirit. In our children's games, he always chose the role of king, minister, general, or someone supreme, whoever he might be. The rascal had poise and gravity, a certain magnificence in his stance, in his walk. Who would have said that... Let's hold back our pen, let's not get ahead of events. Let's take a leap to 1822, the date of our political independence and of my first personal captivity.

CHAPTER XIV
THE FIRST KISS

I was seventeen. My upper lip was beginning to sprout as I strove to grow a mustache. My eyes, lively and resolute, were my really masculine features. Since I showed a certain haughtiness, it was hard to tell whether I was a child with the arrogance of a man or a man with the look of a boy. In short, I was a handsome young fellow, handsome and bold, who was entering life in boots and spurs, a whip in his hand and blood in his veins, mounted on a nervous, robust, swift steed, like the steeds in ancient ballads, for whom romanticism went looking in medieval castles, only to run into him on the streets of our century. The worst is that the romantics wore the fellow out so much that it became necessary to lay him aside, where realism came to find him, eaten by leprosy and worms, and, out of compassion, they bore him off for their books.

Yes, I was that handsome, graceful, well-to-do young fellow, and it is easy to imagine how more than one lady lowered her pensive brow before me or lifted her covetous eyes up to me. Of them all, however, the one who captivated me immediately was a... a... I do not know if I should say it. This book is chaste, at least in its intention. In its intention, it is ever so chaste. But out with it, either you say everything or nothing. The one who captivated me was a Spanish woman, Marcela, "beautiful Marcela," as the boys of those times called her. And the boys were right. She was the daughter of a gardener from Asturias. She told me so herself during a day of sincerity, because the accepted version was that she was the daughter of a lawyer from Madrid, a victim of the French invasion, wounded, jailed, and shot when she was only twelve years old. *Cosas de España.* Whatever her father was, however, a lawyer or gardener, the truth is that Marcela did not have any rustic innocence and hardly understood the morality of the law. She was a good girl, cheerful, without scruples, a little hampered by the austerity of the times, which would not allow her to haul her flightiness and her gossip games through the streets, fond of luxury, impatient, a friend of money and young men. That year, she was madly in love with a certain Xavier, a wealthy and tubercular fellow— a pearl.

I saw her for the first time on *Rossio Grande*, the night of the luminaries, celebrating the Declaration of Independence, a springtime festival, the dawn of the public soul. We were a couple of youths, the people and me. We were coming out of childhood with all the ecstasy of youth. I saw her get out of a sedan chair, graceful and eye-catching, with a slim, swaying body, elegant, something I never found in chaste women. — Follow me — she said to her page. And I followed her, as much a page as the other, as if the order had been given to me. I let myself go, in love, vibrant, full of the first inklings of a dawn. Along the way, they called out to her: Beautiful Marcela! I remembered that I heard that name from my uncle Joao and I stood there, I must confess, I stood there stupefied.

Three days later, my uncle asked in secret if I wanted to have dinner with some "girls" in *Cajueiros*. We went. It was Marcela's house. Xavier, along with all his tubercles, presided over the nocturnal feast, at which I ate little or nothing because I only had eyes for the lady of the house. The Spanish woman was so elegant! There were more than half a dozen women — all in the amorous profession — and pretty, lively, but the Spanish... The enthusiasm, a few swallows of wine, an imperious temperament, hotheaded — all of that led me to do a singular thing. On leaving, at the street door, I told my uncle to wait a moment and I went back up the steps.

— Did you forget something? — Marcela asked, standing on the landing.

— My handkerchief.

She went to open the way back to the room for me. I grasped her hands, pulled her toward me, and gave her a kiss. I do not know whether she said anything, cried out, or called anyone. I do not know anything. I know that I went back down the steps as swiftly as a typhoon and as unsteadily as a drunkard.

CHAPTER XV
MARCELA

It took me thirty days to get from *Rossio Grande* to Marcela's heart, no longer riding the steed of blind desire but the ass of patience, crafty and stubborn at the same time, for there are really two ways of enticing a woman's will: the violent way like Europa's bull and the insinuative way like Leda's swan or Danae's shower of gold — three inventions of Father Zeus, which, being out of fashion, have been replaced by the horse and the ass.

I will not mention the plots I wove or the bribes or the alternation of confidence and fear or the wasted waiting or any other of those preliminary things. I can tell you that the ass was the equal of the steed — an ass like Sancho's, a philosopher, really, who bore me to her house at the end of the period mentioned above. I got off, patted it on the haunch, and sent it off to forage.

Oh, first agitation of my youth, how sweet you were to me! That was what the effect of the first sunlight must have been like in biblical creation. Just imagine the effect of the first sun beating down on the face of a world in bloom. Because it was the same thing, dear reader, and if you have ever counted eighteen years, you must certainly remember that it was exactly like that.

Our passion, or union, or whatever name it went by, because I do not hold much to names, had two phases: the consular phase and the imperial phase. During the first, which was short, Xavier and I ruled without him ever thinking he was sharing the government of Rome with me. But when credulity could no longer resist evidence, Xavier lowered his standards, and I gathered all power into my hands. It was the Caesarean phase. It was my universe, but, alas, it was not free. I had to gather money together, multiply it, invent it. First, I exploited my father's largesse. He gave me anything I asked for without scolding, without delay, without coldness. He told everybody that I was young, and that he had been young once himself. But the abuse reached such extremes that he put restrictions on his liberality, then more, then still more. Then I went to my mother and induced her to turn something my way, which she did in secret. It was not much. Then I laid hands on a final resource: I started drawing my father's inheritance, signing notes that I would redeem one day at usurious rates.

— In fact, — Marcela told me when I brought her something in silk, some piece of jewelry — in fact, you are trying to start a fight with me... Because this is something... Such an expensive gift...

And if it was a jewel — she said that as she examined it between her fingers, looking for the best light, trying it on, laughing, and kissing me with an impetuous and sincere obstinacy, but protesting, though happiness was pouring out of her eyes and I felt happy seeing her like that. She liked our ancient gold doubloons very much, and I brought her as many as I could get hold of; Marcela put them all together in a little iron box whose key was kept where no one ever knew. She hid it because she was afraid of the slaves. The house in which she lived in Cajueiros belonged to her. The carved rosewood furniture was solid and good as were all the other items, mirrors, pitchers, a silver plate — a beautiful plate from India that an appeals judge had given her. You devilish plate, you always got on my nerves. I told its owner herself many times. I did not hide from her the annoyance that these and other spoils from her loves of other times brought on in me. She listened to me and laughed, with an innocent look — innocence and something else that I did not understand too well at the time, but now, recalling the case, I think it was a mixed laugh, as if it was coming from a creature born to a witch of Shakespeare's by a seraph of Klopstock's. I do not know if I am explaining myself. So, it happened one day when I was unable to give her a certain necklace she saw at a jeweler's; she retorted that it was all a game, that our love did not need such a vulgar stimulant.

— I will never forgive you if you get that awful idea of me — she concluded, threatening me with her finger.

And then, quick like a bird, she opened her hands, grasped my face in them, pulled me to her, and put on a funny expression, the mummery of a child. Afterward, reclining on the settee, she continued talking about it with simplicity and frankness. She never wanted people to buy her affection. She sold the appearance of it many times, but the reality she saved for a few. Duarte, for example, Second Lieutenant Duarte, whom she really loved two years before. Only after a struggle was he able to give her something of value, as had happened with me. She would only willingly accept keepsakes with a low price tag, like the gold cross he gave her once as a gift.

— This cross…

She said that putting her hand into her breast and taking out a delicate gold cross attached to a blue ribbon and tied around her neck.

— But that cross — I observed — didn't you tell me it was your father who…

Marcela shook her head with a look of pity:

— Couldn't you tell it was a lie, that I told you that in order not to upset you? Come here, *chiquito*, do not be so mistrustful with me… I was in love with someone else. What difference does it make? It is all over. Someday, when we break up…

— Do not say that! — I shouted.

— Everything comes to an end! Someday…

She could not go on. A sob was strangling her voice. She held out her hands, took mine, snuggled me against her breast, and whispered softly in my ear: — Never, never, my love! — I thanked her, teary-eyed. The next day I brought her the necklace she had refused to get.

— For you to remember me when we break up — I said.

Marcela at first maintained an indignant silence. Then she made a grand gesture: she made it as if to throw the necklace into the street. I held back her arm, kept begging her not to do such an awful thing to me, to keep the jewel. She smiled and kept it.

In the meantime, she was rewarding me abundantly for my sacrifices. She would ferret out my most hidden thoughts. There was no desire of mine that she would not hasten to fulfill with all her heart, without any effort, by some kind of law of awareness of the needs of the heart. The desires were never reasonable, but pure whims, some childish wish to see her dress in a certain way, with such and such accessories, this dress and not that one, to go for a walk or something like that, and she would accede to everything, smiling and chattering.

— You are a regular expert — she told me.

And she went to put on the dress, the lace, and the earrings with bewitching obedience.

CHAPTER XVI
AN IMMORAL REFLECTION

An immoral reflection occurs to me, one which at the same time is a correction of style. I think I said in chapter XIV that Marcela was dying with love for Xavier. She was not dying, she was living. Living is not the same as dying. That is attested to by all the jewelers in this world, people held in great esteem for their grammar. My good jewelers, what would become of love were it not for your trinkets and your credit? A third or a fifth at least of the universal trade in hearts. This is the immoral reflection I was trying to make, which is really more obscure than immoral because what I am trying to say is not easily understood. What I am trying to say is that the most beautiful head in the world will be no less beautiful if ringed by a diadem of fine stones, neither less beautiful nor less loved. Marcela, for example, who was quite pretty, Marcela loved me...

CHAPTER XVII
OF THE TRAPEZE AND OTHER THINGS

... Marcela loved me for fifteen months and eleven *contos de réis*, no more, no less. My father, as soon as he got wind of the eleven *contos de réis*, he was really taken by surprise. He thought the case was reaching beyond the bounds of a juvenile whim.

— This time, — he said — you are going to Europe. You are going to study at a university, probably in Coimbra. I want you to be a serious man, not a loafer and a thief. — And since I showed an expression of surprise: — Thief, yes sir. A son who does this to me is nothing but...

He took from his pocket my I.O.U.s that he had already redeemed and waved them in my face. — Do you see these, you rascal? Is this how a young man is supposed to protect his family name? Do you think my grandfathers and I earned our money in gambling houses or drifting about in the streets? You playboy! This time, either you take care of yourself or you will be left with nothing.

He was furious, but with a tempered and short fury. I listened to him in silence and did not oppose the trip in any way, as I had done at other times. I was pondering the idea of taking Marcela with me. I went to see her. I explained the crisis and made my proposal. Marcela listened to me with her eyes in the air, without responding immediately. As I insisted, she told me that she would stay, that she could not go to Europe.

— Why not?

— I cannot — she said with a sorrowful look — I cannot breathe that air while I think of my poor father, killed by Napoleon.

— Which one, the gardener or the lawyer?

Marcela furrowed her brow, hummed a *seguidilla*, then complained about the heat and sent for a glass of pineapple wine. A slave girl brought it on a silver tray, which was part of my eleven *contos de réis*. Marcela politely offered me the refreshment. My answer was to strike the glass and the tray. The liquid spilled into her lap, and the black girl cried out. I roared at her to get out. When we were alone, I poured out all the despair in my heart. I told her that she was a monster, that she never loved me, that she let me drop to the bottom without even the excuse of sincerity. I called her all sorts of ugly names, making wild gestures. Marcela kept herself seated, tapping her teeth with her nails, cold as a piece of ivory. I had an urge to strangle her, humiliate her at least, make her crawl at my feet. Maybe I would have, but my actions took the opposite turn: it was I who threw myself at her feet, contrite and supplicant. I kissed them, I remembered those months of our happiness alone together, I repeated our pet names from past times to her, sitting on the floor with my head between her knees, squeezing her hands, gasping, delirious, I begged her, tearfully, not to abandon me... Marcela sat looking at me for a few seconds, both of us silent, until she pushed me away softly and with an annoyed air:

— Stop annoying me — she said.

She stood up, shook her dress, still wet, and went to her bedroom. — No! — I shouted — You are not going in there... I do not want you to... — I went to reach out my hands to her. It was too late; she entered and locked the door.

I ran out, crazy. I spent two fatal hours wandering through the most distant and deserted neighborhoods, where it would have been hard to find me. I went along, gnawing on my despair with a kind of morbid gluttony. I brought back the days, the hours, the instants of delirium, and now I was gratified in believing that they were eternal, that all of this was a nightmare. Deceiving myself now, I tried to push them away like a useless burden. Then I decided to embark immediately in order to cut my life into two halves, and I pleased myself with the idea that Marcela, learning of my departure, would be tormented by longing and remorse. Since she had been madly in love with me, she would have to feel something, some kind of remembrance, like that of Lieutenant Duarte... At that point, the fangs of jealousy buried themselves in my heart. All nature roared that I had to take Marcela with me.

— By force... By force... — I kept saying, hitting the air with my fist.

Finally, I got an idea that would save things... Oh! trapeze of my sins, trapeze of abstruse notions! The saving idea worked out on it like the one about the poultice (chapter II). It was nothing less than bewitching her, bewitching her greatly, dazzling her, pulling her along. It reminded me to ask her by more concrete means than through entreaty. I did not measure the consequences: I had recourse to one last loan. I went to the Street of Goldsmiths, bought the finest piece of jewelry in the city, three large diamonds inlaid on an ivory comb. I ran to Marcela's house.

Marcela was lying in a hammock with a soft and weary expression, one leg hanging down, showing her little foot clad in a silk stocking, her hair loose and flowing, her look quiet and dreamy.

— Come with me — I said. — I will get the money... We got lots of money, you can have anything you want... Look, take it.

And I showed her the comb with the diamonds. Marcela gave a slight start, raised halfway, and, leaning on an elbow, looked at the comb for a few short seconds. Then she withdrew her eyes, got control of herself. I thrust my hands into her hair, drew it together, quickly wove it into braids, improvised a hairdo that was not very neat, and topped it off with the comb and the diamonds. I drew back, went closer again, adjusted the braids, lowered the comb on one side, tried to find some kind of symmetry in that disorder, all with the careful touch and care of a mother.

— There — I said.

— Crazy! — it was her first response.

The second was to pull me to her and reward my sacrifice with a kiss, the most ardent ever. Then she took off the comb, admired the material and the craftsmanship for a long time, looking at me every so often and nodding her head with a scolding look:

— What am I going to do with you! — she said.

— Are you coming with me?

Marcela thought for a moment. I did not like the expression with which her eyes passed from me to the wall and from the wall to the jewel. But that bad impression vanished completely when she answered resolutely:

— I will go. When do you embark?

— Two or three days from now.

— I will go.

I thanked her on my knees. I found my Marcela of my early days and I told her that. She smiled and went to put the jewel away while I went down the stairs.

CHAPTER XVIII
A VISION IN THE HALL

At the bottom of the stairs, at the rear of the dark hall, I stopped for a few seconds to catch my breath, to touch myself, to call forth scattered ideas, to see myself in the midst of ever so many deep and contrary feelings once more. I thought I was happy. The diamonds, true, were corrupting my happiness a bit, but no less true was the fact that a pretty lady was quite capable of loving the Greeks and their gifts. And, after all, I trusted my good Marcela. She may have defects, but she loved me...

— An angel! — I muttered, looking at the hall ceiling.

And there, like mockery, I saw Marcela's gaze, the gaze that a short time before had given me a shade of mistrust, gleaming over a nose that was Bakbarah's nose and mine at the same time. Poor lover from *The Arabian Nights*! I could see you right there, running along the gallery after the vizier's wife, she beckoning to you with possession, and you are running, running, up to the long tree-lined drive from where you came out onto the street where all the harness-makers jeered at you and thrashed you. Then it seemed to me that Marcela's hallway was the drive and the street was in Baghdad. As a matter of fact, looking toward the door, I saw three harness-makers on the sidewalk, one in a cassock, another in livery, another in civilian clothes. As all three entered the hallway, they took me by the arms, put me into a carriage, my father on the right, my canon uncle on the left, the one in livery on the driver's seat, and from there they took me to the house of a police official, from where I was transported to a ship that was to leave for Lisbon. You can imagine my resistance, but all resistance was useless.

Three days later, I left the harbor behind, downcast and silent. I was not even weeping. I had a fixed idea... Damned fixed idea! The one on that occasion was to dive into the ocean, repeating Marcela's name.

CHAPTER XIX
ON BOARD

We were eleven passengers: a crazy man accompanied by his wife, two youths going on an excursion, four businessmen, and two servants. My father entrusted me to all of them, starting with the ship's captain, who had much of his own to look after as well because, on top of everything else, he was carrying his wife, who was in the last stages of tuberculosis.

I do not know whether the captain suspected anything of my lugubrious project or whether my father had put him on alert, but I do know that he never took his eyes off me, called to me everywhere. When he could not be with me, he brought me to his wife. The woman was almost always on a low couch, coughing a lot, and promising to show me the sights in Lisbon. She was not thin, she was transparent. It was impossible to know why she did not die from one moment to the next. The captain pretended not to believe in her approaching death, perhaps to deceive himself. I did not know or think about anything. What did the fate of a tubercular woman in the middle of the ocean matter to me? The world for me was Marcela.

One night, after a week had passed, I thought it was a propitious time to die. I went cautiously up on deck, but I found the captain standing beside the rail with his eyes fixed on the horizon.

— Expecting a storm? — I asked.

— No — he replied, shivering. — No, I was only admiring the splendor of the night. Take a look. It is heavenly!

The style did not fit the person, rather crude and a stranger to recherche expressions. I stared at him. He seemed to be savoring my surprise. After a few seconds, he took my hand and pointed to the moon, asking me why I was not writing an ode to the night. I replied that I was not a poet. The captain snorted something, took two steps, put his hand in his pocket, took out a piece of crumpled paper, and then, by the light of a lantern, he read a Horatian ode on the freedom of maritime life. It was his poetry.

— What do you think?

I cannot remember what I told him, but I remember that he took my hand with a great deal of strength and a great deal of thanks. Right after that, he recited two sonnets for me. He was going to recite another when they came to get him for his wife. — I will be right there — he said, and recited the third sonnet for me, slowly, with love.

I was left alone, but the captain's muse had swept away all evil thoughts from my spirit. I preferred going to sleep, which is an interim way of dying. The following day, we awakened in the midst of a storm that put fear into everyone except the madman. He started leaping about, saying that his daughter was sending for him in a brougham. The death of a daughter had been the cause of his madness. No, I will never forget the hideous figure of the poor man in the midst of the tumult of the people and the howls of the hurricane, humming and dancing, his eyes bulging from his pale face, his hair bristly and long. Sometimes he stopped, lifted up his bony hands, made crosses with his fingers, then a checkerboard, then some rings, and he laughed a lot, desperately. His wife could no longer take care of him; given over to the terror of death, she was praying to all the saints in heaven for herself. Finally, the storm abated. I must confess that it was an excellent diversion from the storm in my heart. I, who thought about going to meet death, did not dare look it in the eye when it came to meet me.

The captain asked me if I was afraid, if I felt threatened, if I had not found the spectacle sublime. All of that with the interest of a friend. Naturally, the conversation turned to life at sea. The captain asked me if I liked piscatorial idylls. I answered ingenuously that I did not know what they were.

— You will see — he replied.

And he recited a little poem for me, then, another — an eclogue — and finally five sonnets, with which he capped literary confidence for that day. The following day, before reciting anything, the captain explained to me that only because of the gravest reasons he had embraced the maritime profession, because his grandmother had wanted him to be a priest, and, indeed, he had some schooling in Latin. He did not get to be a priest, but he never stopped being a poet, which was his natural vocation. In order to prove it, he immediately recited for me, in person, a hundred lines. I noticed one phenomenon: the gestures he used were such that they made me laugh once. But the captain, as he recited, looked so deep inside himself that he did not see or hear anything.

The days passed, and the waves, and the poetry, and, with them, the life of his wife was also passing. She was not for long. One day, right after lunch, the captain told me that the sick woman might not last for the week.

— So soon! — I exclaimed.

— She had a very bad night.

I went to see her. She was almost moribund, really, but she still talked about resting in Lisbon a few days before going to Coimbra with me, because it was her proposal to take me to the university. I left her, disconsolate, and went to find her husband, who was looking at the waves as they came to die against the hull of the ship, and I tried to console him. He thanked me, told me the tale of their love, praised his wife's fidelity and dedication, remembered the verses he wrote for her, recited them to me. At that point, they came from her to get him. We both ran. It was a crisis. That day and the following one were cruel. The third was the day of her death. I fled from the sight; it was repugnant to me. A half hour later, I found the captain sitting on a pile of hawsers, his head in his hands. I said some things to comfort him.

— She died like a saint – he answered. And so those words would not be taken as a sign of weakness. He immediately stood up, shook his head, and peered at the horizon with a long, deep expression. — Let's go, — he continued — let's consign her to the grave that is never opened again.

Indeed, a few hours later, her corpse was cast into the sea with the customary ceremony. Sadness had shriveled all the faces. That of the widower had the look of a hillock struck by a great bolt of lightning. Deep silence. The wave opened its womb, received the remains, closed — a slight ripple — and the ship went on. I let myself linger at the stern for a few minutes, with my eyes on that uncertain spot in the sea where one of us had been left behind... I went off to find the captain, and distract him.

— Thank you — he told me, understanding my intent. — You must believe that I will never forget her good care. God is the one who will pay her for it. Poor Leocadia! Think of us in heaven.

He wiped an inconvenient tear with his sleeve. I tried to find a way out in poetry, which was his passion. I spoke to him about the verses he read to me and offered to get them published. The captain's eyes lighted up a little. — They might take them, — he said — but I do not know... They are rather weak verses.

I swore to him that they were not. I asked him to put them together and give them to me before we landed.

— Poor Leocadia! — he muttered, without answering my request. — A corpse... The sea... The sky... The ship...

The next day he came to read me a newly composed elegy in which the circumstances of the death and burial of his wife were memorialized. He read it to me with a truly emotional voice and his hand trembled. At the end, he asked if the poem was worthy of the treasure he had lost.

— Yes — I answered.

— It may not have style, — he pondered after an instant — but no one can deny me feeling, unless that very feeling is harmful to the perfection...

— I do not think so. I think it is a perfect poem.

— Yes, I think that... The poem of a sailor.

— Of a sailor poet.

He shrugged his shoulders, looked at the piece of paper, and recited the composition again, but this time without trembling, stressing the literary intent, giving emphasis to the imagery and melody of the lines. In the end, he confessed to me that it was his most accomplished piece of work. I said that it was. He shook my hand and predicted a great future for me.

CHAPTER XX
I AM GRADUATED

A great future! With that word pounding in my ears, I turned my eyes back to the distance, to the mysterious and uncertain horizon. One idea drove out another, ambition was displacing Marcela. Great future? Maybe a naturalist, a literary man, an archeologist, a banker, a politician, or even a bishop, — let it be a bishop — as long as it meant responsibility, preeminence, a fine reputation, a superior position. Ambition, since it was an eagle, had broken the shell of its egg on that occasion and removed the cover from that tawny, penetrating eye. Farewell, love! Farewell, Marcela! Days of delirium, priceless jewels, ungoverned life, farewell! Here I come for toil and glory. I leave you with the short pants of childhood.

And that was how I disembarked in Lisbon and continued on to Coimbra. The university was waiting for me with its difficult subjects. I studied them in a very mediocre way, but even so, I did not lose my law degree. They gave it to me with all the solemnity of the occasion, following years of custom, a beautiful ceremony that filled me with pride and nostalgia — mostly nostalgia. In Coimbra, I earned a great reputation as a carouser. I was a profligate, superficial, riotous, and petulant student, given to larks, following romanticism in practice and liberalism in theory, living with pure faith in dark eyes and written constitutions. On the day that the university certified me, on parchment, knowledge that was far from rooted in my brain, I must confess that I thought myself hoodwinked in some way, even though I was proud. Let me explain: the diploma was a certificate of emancipation. It gave me freedom, but it also gave me responsibility. I put it away, I left the banks of the Mondego, and I came away rather disconsolate but already feeling a drive, a curiosity, a desire to elbow others aside, to influence, to enjoy, to live — to prolong the university for my whole life forward...

CHAPTER XXI
THE MULETEER

Going on, then, the donkey I was riding balked. I whipped it and it gave two bucks, then three more, and finally another one that shook me out of the saddle so disastrously that my left foot got stuck in the stirrup. I tried to hold on to the beast's belly, but by then, spooked, it took off down the road. I am not telling it right: it tried to take off and took a couple of bounds, but a muleteer who happened to be there ran up in time to grab the reins and hold it, not without some effort and danger. With the animal under control, he untangled me from the stirrup and stood me on my feet.

— You were lucky to escape, sir — the muleteer said.

And he was right. If the donkey had run away, I really would have got bruised, and I am not sure if death would not have been the outcome of the disaster. My head split open, congestion, some kind of internal injury, all my budding knowledge leaving me. The muleteer may have saved my life. I was sure of it. I felt it in the blood that was pounding through my heart. Good muleteer! While I was taking care of myself, he was carefully adjusting the donkey's harness with great skill and zeal. I decided to give him three gold coins from the five I was carrying with me.

Not because it was the price of my life — that was inestimable —but because it was just recompense for the dedication with which he saved me. All settled, I would give him the three coins.
— All ready — he said, handing me the reins to my mount.
— Not quite yet — I answered. — Let me wait a bit. I am still not myself...
— Come on, sir!
— Well, isn't it a fact that I was almost killed?
— If the donkey had run off, maybe so, but with the help of the Lord, you can see that nothing happened, sir.

I went to the saddlebags, took out an old waistcoat in the pocket of which I was carrying the five gold coins, but during that interval, I got to thinking that maybe the gratuity was excessive, that two coins might be sufficient. Maybe one. As a matter of fact, one coin was enough to make him quiver with joy. I examined his clothing. He was a poor devil who had never seen a gold coin, one coin, therefore. I took it out, saw it glitter in the sunlight. The muleteer did not see it because I had my back turned, but he may have suspected something. He started talking to the donkey in a meaningful way. He was giving it advice, telling it to watch out, that the "good doctor" might punish it. A paternal monologue. Good Lord! I even heard the smack of a kiss. It was the muleteer kissing it on the forehead.
— Hurray! — I exclaimed.
— Begging your pardon, sir, but the devilish creature was looking at us with such charm...

I laughed, hesitated, put a silver *cruzado*[4] in his hand, mounted the donkey, and went off at a slow trot, a little bothered, I should really say a little uncertain of the effect of the piece of silver. But a few yards away I looked back and the muleteer was bowing deeply to me as an obvious sign of contentment. I noted that it must have been just that. I paid him well; maybe I had paid him too much. I put my fingers into the pocket of the waistcoat I was wearing and I felt some copper coins. They were the pennies I should have given the muleteer instead of the silver *cruzado*. Because, after all, he did not have any recompense or reward in mind. He had followed a natural impulse, his temperament, the habits of his trade. Furthermore, the circumstance of his being right there, not ahead and not behind, but precisely at the point of the disaster, seemed to be the simple instrument of Providence. And, in one way or another, the merit of the act was positively nonexistent. I became

---

4   A type of silver coin (translator's note)

disconsolate with that reflection. I called myself a prodigal. I added the *cruzado* to my past dissipation. I felt… (why not come right out with it?), I felt remorse.

CHAPTER XXII
RETURN TO RIO

Blasted donkey, you made me lose the thread of my reflections! Right now, I am not going to say what I went through from there to Lisbon or what I did in Lisbon, on the Peninsula, or in other places in Europe, the old Europe that seemed to be rejuvenating at that time. No, I am not going to say that I was present at the dawn of Romanticism, that I, too, went off to write poetry to that effect in the bosom of Italy. I am not going to say a thing. I would have to write a travel diary and not memoirs like these, where only the substance of life will enter.

After some years of wandering, I heeded my father's entreaties: "Come home," he said in his last letter, "if you do not come quickly, you will find your mother dead!" That last word was a blow to me. I loved my mother very much. I still had the last blessing she gave me on board the ship before my eyes. — My poor child, I will never see you again! — the unfortunate lady had sobbed, clutching me to her breast. And those words echo in my ears now like a fulfilled prophecy.

Let it be noted that I was in Venice, still redolent with the verses of Lord Byron. There I was, sunk deep in dreams, reliving the past, thinking that I was in the Most Serene Republic. It is true. It occurred to me once to ask the innkeeper if the doge would take his walk that day. — What doge, *signore mio*? I came back to my senses, but I did not confess the illusion. I told him that my question was a kind of South American charade. He acted as if he understood and added that he liked South American charades a lot. He was an innkeeper. Well, I left all that, innkeeper, doge, Bridge of Sighs, gondolas, poetry of the Lord, ladies of the Rialto, I left it all and took off like a shot in the direction of Rio de Janeiro.

I came… But no, let's not lengthen this chapter. Sometimes I forget myself when I am writing, and the pen just goes along eating up paper to my great harm, because I am an author. Long chapters are better suited for logy readers, and we are not an *in-folio* public, but an *in-12* one, with not much text, wide margins, elegant type, gold trim, and ornamental designs… Designs above all… No, let's not lengthen the chapter.

CHAPTER XXIII
SAD, BUT SHORT

I came. I will not deny that when I caught sight of my native city, I had a new sensation. It was not the effect of my political homeland, it was that of the place of my childhood, the street, the tower, the fountain on the corner, the woman in a shawl, the black street sweeper, the things and scenes of childhood engraved in my memory. Nothing less than a rebirth. The spirit, like a bird, did not take into consideration the flow of years, it fluttered toward the original spring and went to drink its cool, pure waters, still not mingled with the torrent of life. If you take careful note, you will see a commonplace there. Another commonplace, sadly common, was the family's consternation. My father embraced me in tears.

— Your mother is not going to live — he told me. Indeed, it was not the rheumatism that was killing her anymore, it was a stomach cancer. The poor thing was suffering cruelly because cancer is indifferent to a person's virtues. My sister Sabina, married by then to Cotrim, was on the point of dropping from fatigue. Poor girl! She got only three hours of sleep a night, no more. Even Uncle Joao was downcast and sad. Ms. Eusebia and some other ladies were there, too, no less sad and no less dedicated.

— My son!

The pain held back its pincers for a moment. A smile lit the face of the sick woman, over whom death was beating its eternal wings. It was less a face than a skull. Its beauty had passed like a bright day. The bones, which never grow thin, were left. I could hardly recognize her. It had been eight or nine years since we had seen each other. Kneeling by the foot of the bed with her hands in mine, I remained mute and still, not daring to speak because every word would have been a sob, and we were afraid to tell her of the end. Vain fear! She knew that she was close to the end. She told me so. We found out the next morning.

Her agony was long, long and cruel, with a meticulous, cold, repetitious cruelty that filled me with pain and bewilderment. It was the first time I had seen someone die. I only knew death by hearsay. At most, I had seen it, petrified already, in the face of some corpse I accompanied to the cemetery, or I carried the idea of it wrapped up in the rhetorical amplifications of professors of ancient matters — the treacherous death of Caesar, the austere death of Socrates, the proud death of Cato. But that duel between to be and not to be, death in action, painful, contracted, convulsive, without any political or philosophical apparatus, the death of a loved one, that was the first time I had faced it. I did not weep. I remember that I did not weep during the whole spectacle. My eyes were dull, my throat tight, my awareness open-mouthed. Why? A creature so docile, so tender, so saintly, who never caused a tear of displeasure to fall, a loving mother, and an immaculate wife, why did she have to die like that, handled, bitten by the teeth of a pitiless illness? I must confess that it all seemed obscure to me, incongruous, insane...

A sad chapter. Let's pass on to a happier one...

CHAPTER XXIV
SHORT, BUT HAPPY

I was prostrate. And this in spite of the fact that I was a faithful compendium of triviality and presumption at that time. The problems of life and death had never weighed on my brain. Never, until that day, had I peered into the abyss of the inexplicable. I lacked the essential thing, which is a stimulus, the vertigo...

To tell you the truth, I mirrored the opinions of a hairdresser I met in Modena, who was distinguished by having absolutely none. He was the flower of hairdressers. No matter how long the operation on the coiffure took, he never got angry. He interspersed the combing with lots of maxims and jests, full of a certain malice, a zest... He had no other philosophy. Nor did I. I am not saying that the university had not taught me some philosophical truths. But I only memorized the formulas, the vocabulary, the skeleton. I treated them as I had Latin: I put three lines from Virgil in my pocket, two from Horace, and a dozen moral and political locutions for the needs of conversation. I treated them the way I treated history and jurisprudence. I picked up the phraseology of all things, the shell, the decoration...

Maybe I am startling the reader with the frankness with which I am exposing and emphasizing my mediocrity. Be aware that frankness is the prime virtue of a dead man. In life, the gaze of public opinion, the contrast of interests, the struggle of greed all force people to keep quiet about their dirty linen, to disguise the rips and stitches, not to extend to the world the revelations they make to their conscience. And the best part of the obligation comes when, by deceiving others, a man deceives himself, because in such a case he saves himself vexation, which is a painful feeling, and hypocrisy, which is a vile vice. But in death, what a difference! What a release! What freedom! Oh, how people can shake off their coverings, leave their spangles in the gutter, unbutton themselves, unpaint themselves, undecorate themselves, confess flatly what they were and what they have stopped being! Because, in short, there are no neighbors or friends or enemies or acquaintances or strangers anymore. There is no longer an audience. The gaze of public opinion, that sharp and judgmental gaze, loses its virtue the moment we tread the territory of death. I am not saying that it does not reach here and examine and judge us, but we do not care about the examination or the judgment. My dear living gentlemen and ladies, there is nothing as incommensurable as the disdain of the deceased.

CHAPTER XXV
IN TIJUCA

Drat! My pen got away from me there and slipped into the emphatic. Let's be simple, as simple as the life I led in Tijuca during the first weeks after my mother's death.

On the seventh day, when the funeral mass was over, I gathered together a shotgun, some books, clothing, cigarettes, a houseboy — Prudencio of chapter XI — and went off to establish myself in an old house we owned. My father made an effort to make me change my mind, but I could not and did not want to obey him. Sabina wanted me to go live with her for a while — two weeks at least. My brother-in-law was on the point of carrying me off forcibly. He was a good man, that Cotrim. He had gone from profligacy to circumspection. Now he was a food merchant, toiling from morning till night with perseverance. In the evening, sitting by the window and twirling his sideburns was all he had on his mind. He loved his wife and the son they had at that time, who died a few years later. People said he was avaricious.

I had given up everything. I was in a state of shock. I think it was around that time that hypochondria started blooming in me, that yellow, solitary, morbid flower with an intoxicating and subtle odor. "It is so good to be sad and say nothing!" When those words of Shakespeare's caught my attention, I must confess that I felt an echo in myself, a delightful echo. I remember that I was sitting under a tamarind tree with the poet's book in my hands, and my spirit was even more downcast than that of the character — or crestfallen, as we say of sad hens. I clutched my taciturn grief to my chest with a singular sensation, something that could be called the sensuality of boredom. The sensuality of boredom: memorize that expression, reader, keep it, examine it, and if you cannot understand it, you may conclude that you are ignorant of one of the most subtle sensations of this world and that time. Sometimes I would go hunting, at other times sleep, and at others read — I read a lot — other times, well, I did nothing. I let myself ramble from idea to idea, from imagination to imagination, like a vagrant or hungry butterfly. The hours dripped away, one by one, the sun set, the shadows of night veiled the mountain and the city. No one came to visit me. I had expressly asked to be left alone. One day, two days, three days, a whole week spent like that without saying a word was enough for me to shake off Tijuca and rejoin the bustle. Indeed, at the end of a week, I had more than enough of loneliness. My grief had abated. My spirit was no longer satisfied with only a shotgun and books or with the view of the woods and the sky. Youth was reacting, it was necessary to live. I packed away the problem of life and death, the poet's hypochondriacs, the shirts, the meditations, the neckties in a trunk, and I was about to close it when the black boy Prudencio told me that the day before, a person of my acquaintance had moved into a purple house a couple of hundred steps away from ours.

— Who?
— Do you remember Ms. Eusebia, Little Master?
— I remember... Is it her?
— She and her daughter. They came yesterday morning.

The episode from 1814 came to me immediately and I felt annoyed.

But I called my attention to the fact that: events proved me right. Actually, it had been impossible to prevent the intimate relations between Dr. Vilaca and the sergeant-major's sister. Even before I traveled, there was already a mysterious wagging of tongues about the birth of a girl. My uncle Joao wrote me later that Dr. Vilaca, when he died, had left a good legacy to Ms. Eusebia, something that caused a lot of talk in the neighborhood. Uncle Joao himself, greedy when it came to scandal, did not talk about anything else in the letter — several pages long.

Events had proved me right. Even though they had, however, 1814 was a long way back, and with it Vilaca's mischief and the kiss in the shrubbery. Finally, no close relationship existed between me and her. I made that reflection for myself and finished closing the trunk.

— Will you not visit Ms. Eusebia, Little Master? — Prudencio asked me. — She was the one who dressed the body of my late lady.

I remembered that I had seen her among other ladies on the occasion of the death and the burial. I did not know, however, that she had lent my mother that final kindness. The houseboy's reflection was reasonable. I owed her a visit. I decided to do it at once and then leave.

CHAPTER XXVI
THE AUTHOR HESITATES

Suddenly, I heard a voice: — Hello, my boy, this is no life for you! — It was my father, who arrived with two proposals in his pocket.

I sat down on the trunk and welcomed him without any fuss. He stood looking at me for a few moments and then extended his hand in an emotional gesture:

— My son, accept the will of God.

— I already accepted it — that was my answer, and I kissed his hand.

He hadn't had lunch. We lunched together. Neither of us mentioned the sad reason for my withdrawal. Only once we talked about it, in passing, when my father brought the conversation around to the Regency; it was then that he mentioned the letter of condolence that one of the Regents had sent him. He had the letter with him, already rather wrinkled, maybe from having been read to so many other people. I think he said it was one of the Regents. He read it to me twice.

— I already went to thank him for that mark of consideration, - my father said — and I think you should go, too...

— Me?

— You. He is an important man. He takes the place of the Emperor these days. Besides, I brought an idea with me, a plan, or... Yes, I will tell you everything. I brought two plans: a position as deputy and a marriage.

My father said that slowly, pausing, and not in the same tone of voice, but giving the words a form and placement with an end to digging them deeper into my spirit. The proposals, however, went so much against my latest feelings that I really did not get to understand them. My father did not falter, and he repeated them, stressing the position and the bride.

— Do you accept?

— I do not understand politics — I said after an instant. — As for the bride... Let me live like the bear I am.

— But bears get married — he replied.

— Then bring me a she-bear. How about the Ursa Major?

My father laughed, and after laughing, he went back to speaking seriously. A political career was essential for me, he said, for twenty or more reasons, which he put forth with singular volubility, illustrating them with examples of people we knew. As for the bride, all I had to do was see her. If I saw her, I would immediately go and ask her father for her hand, immediately, without waiting a single day. In that way, first, he tried fascination, then persuasion, then intimation. I gave no answer, sharpening the tip of a toothpick or making little balls of bread crumbs, smiling or reflecting. And, to say it outright, neither docile nor rebellious concerning the proposals. I felt confused. One part of me said yes, that a beautiful wife and a political position were possessions worthy of appreciation. Another said no, and my mother's death appeared to me as an example of the fragility of things, of affections, of family...

— I am not leaving here without a final answer — my father said. — Fi-nal an-swer! — he repeated, drumming out the syllables with his finger.

He drank the last sip of his coffee, relaxed, started talking about everything, the senate, the chamber, the Regency, the restoration, Evaristo, a carriage he intended to buy, our house in *Matacavalos*... I remained at a corner of the table, writing crazily on a piece of paper with the stub of a pencil. I was tracing a word, a phrase, a line of poetry, a nose, a triangle, and I kept repeating them over and over, without any order, at random, like this:

arma virumque cano

A

Arma virumque cano

arma virumque cano

arma virumque

arma virumque cano

virumque

All of it was mechanical, and nonetheless, there was a certain logic, a certain deduction. For example, it was the *virumque* that made me get to the name of the poet himself, because of the first syllable. I was going to write *virumque* — and Virgil came out, then I continued:

    Vir   Virgil
        Virgil   Virgil

                Virgil

                                Virgil

My father, a little put off by that indifference, stood up, came over to me, cast his eyes onto the paper...
— Virgil! — he exclaimed. — That's it, my boy. Your bride's name is Virgilia.

CHAPTER XXVII
VIRGILIA?

Virgilia? But, then, was it the same lady who, some years later...? The very same. It was precisely the lady who was to be present during my last days in 1869 and who before, long before, had played a great part in my most intimate sensations. At that time, she was only fifteen or sixteen years old. She was possibly the most daring creature of our race and, certainly, the most willful. I am not saying that she was already first in beauty, ahead of the other girls of the time, because this is not a novel, where the author gilds reality and closes his eyes to freckles and pimples. But I will not say that any freckle or pimple blemished her face either, no. She was pretty, fresh, she came from the hands of nature, full of that sorcery, uncertain and eternal, that an individual passes to another individual for the secret ends of creation. That was Virgilia, and she was fair, very fair, ostentatious, ignorant, childish, full of mysterious urges, a lot of indolence, and some devoutness —devoutness or maybe fear. I think fear.

There, in a few lines the reader has a physical and moral portrait of the person who was to influence my life later on. She was all that at sixteen. You who read me, if you are still alive when these pages come to life — you who read me, beloved Virgilia, have you noticed the difference between the language of today and the one

I first used when I saw you? Believe me, it was just as sincere then as it is now. Death did not make me sour, or unfair.

— But — you are probably saying — how can you discern the truth of those times like that, and express it after so many years?

Ah! So indiscreet! Ah! So ignorant! But it is precisely that which has made us lords of the earth; it is that power of restoring the past to touch the instability of our impressions and the vanity of our affections. Let Pascal say that man is a thinking reed. No. He is a thinking erratum; that's what he is. Every season of life is an edition that corrects the one before and which will also be corrected until the definitive edition, which the publisher gives to the worms for free.

CHAPTER XXVIII
PROVIDED THAT...

— Virgilia? — I interrupted.

— Yes, sir. That's the name of the bride. An angel, my silly, an angel without wings. Picture a girl like that, this tall, a lively scamp, and a pair of eyes... Dutra's daughter...

— What Dutra is that?

— Counselor Dutra. You do not know him, lots of political influence. All right, do you accept it? — I did not answer right away. I stared at my shoe tops for a few seconds. Then I declared that I was willing to think about both things over, the candidacy and the marriage, provided that...

— Provided that what?

— Provided that I am not forced to accept both things. I think that I can be a married man and a public man separately...

— All public men have to be married — my father interrupted, sententiously. — But do what you will. It is all right with me. I am sure that seeing will be believing! Besides, bride and parliament are the same thing... That is, not... You will find out later... Go ahead. I accept the delay, provided that...

— Provided that what?... — I interrupted, imitating his voice.

— Oh, you rascal! Provided that you do not let yourself sit there useless, obscure, and sad. I did not put out money, care, or effort not to see you shine the way you should and as suits you and all of us. Our name has to continue; continue it and make it shine even more. Look, I am sixty, but if it was necessary to start life over, I would not hesitate a single minute. Fear obscurity, Bras, flee from the negligible. Men are worth something in different ways, and the surest one of all is being worthy in the opinion of other men. Do not squander the advantages of your position, your means...

And the magician went ahead waving a rattle in front of me as they used to do when I was little in order to make me walk more quickly, and the flower of hypochondria retreated into its bud to leave another flower less yellow and not at all morbid — the love of fame, the Bras Cubas poultice.

CHAPTER XXIX
THE VISIT

My father had won. I was prepared to accept diploma and marriage, Virgilia and the Chamber of Deputies. — The two Virgilias — he said with a show of political tenderness. I accepted them. My father gave me two strong hugs. It was his own blood that he was finally recognizing.

— Are you coming back down with me?

— I will go down tomorrow. First, I am going to visit Ms. Eusebia...

My father wrinkled his nose but did not say anything. He said goodbye and went back down. The afternoon of that same day, I went to visit Ms. Eusebia. I found her scolding a black gardener, but she left everything to come and talk to me, with a fuss and such sincere pleasure that I immediately lost my shyness. I think she even put her pair of robust arms around me. She had me sit down by her feet on the porch in the midst of many exclamations of contentment:

— Just look at you, little Bras! A man! Who would have said years ago... A great big man! And handsome, I have to say! You do not remember me too well, do you?...

I said that I did, that it was impossible to forget such a familiar friend of our house. Ms. Eusebia started talking about my mother with great longing, with so much longing that it immediately got to me and I grew sad. She realized it in my eyes and changed the topic. She asked me to tell her about my travels, my studies, my love affairs... Yes, my love affairs, too. She confessed to me that she was an old gadabout. At that point, I remembered the episode of 1814; her, Vilaca, the shrubbery, the kiss, my shout. And as I was recalling it, I heard the creak of a door, a rustle of skirts, and this word:

— Mom... Mom...

CHAPTER XXX
THE FLOWER FROM THE SHRUBBERY

The voice and the skirt belonged to a young brunette who stopped in the doorway for a few seconds after seeing a stranger.

A short, constrained silence followed. Ms. Eusebia broke it with resolution and frankness:

— Come here, Eugenia, — she said — say hello to Dr. Bras Cubas, Mr. Cubas' son. He is back from Europe.

And turning to me:

— My daughter, Eugenia.

Eugenia, the flower from the shrubbery, barely responded to the courteous bow I gave her. She looked at me, surprised and shy, and slowly, slowly came forward to her mother's chair. Her mother fixed one of the braids of her hair, whose end had become undone. — Oh, you scamp! — she said. — You cannot imagine, doctor, what it is like... — And she kissed her with such great tenderness that it moved me a bit. It reminded me of my mother and — I will say it right out — I had an itch to be a father.

— Scamp? — I said. — But is she not beyond that age now? That's what it looks.

— How old would you say she is?
— Seventeen.
— One less.
— Sixteen. Well, then, she is a young lady.

Eugenia could not hide the satisfaction she felt with those words of mine, but she immediately got hold of herself and was the same as before — stiff, cold, mute. As a matter of fact, she looked even more womanly than she was. She could have been a child playing at being a young lady but, quiet, impassive like that, she had the composure of a married woman. That circumstance may have diminished her virginal grace a bit. We quickly became familiar. Her mother sang her praises, and I listened to them willingly, and she was smiling, her eyes sparkling as if inside her brain, a little butterfly with golden wings and diamond eyes were flying...

I say inside because what was fluttering outside was a black butterfly that had come to the porch all of a sudden and started flapping its wings around Ms. Eusebia.

Ms. Eusebia cried out, stood up, swore with some disconnected words: — Away with you!... Get away, you devilish thing!... Holy Mother of God!...

— Do not be afraid — I said, and, taking out my handkerchief, I shooed the butterfly away. Ms. Eusebia sat down again, puffing, a little embarrassed. Her daughter, pale with fear, maybe concealed that impression with great willpower. I shook hands with them and left, laughing to myself at the two women's superstition, a philosophical, disinterested, superior laugh. In the afternoon, I saw Ms. Eusebia's daughter pass by on horseback, followed by a houseboy. She waved to me with her whip. I must confess that I flattered myself with the idea that, a few steps ahead, she would look back, but she did not turn her head.

CHAPTER XXXI
THE BLACK BUTTERFLY

The next day as I was getting ready to go back down, a butterfly entered my bedroom, a butterfly as black as the other one and much larger. I remembered the episode of the day before and laughed. I immediately started thinking about Ms. Eusebia's daughter, the fright she had, and the dignity that she managed to maintain in spite of it all. The butterfly, after fluttering everything about me, landed on my forehead. I shook it off. It went on to land on the counterpane, and because I chased it off again, it left there and settled on an old portrait of my father. It was as black as night. The soft movement with which it started moving its wings after landing had a certain mocking way about it that bothered me a lot. I turned my back, left the room, but when I returned a few minutes later and found it in the same place, I felt a nervous shock. I laid hands my on a towel, struck it, and it fell.

It did not fall down dead. It was still twisting its body and moving its antennae. I regretted what I had done, took it in the palm of my hand, and went over to put it down on the windowsill. It was too late. The poor thing expired after a few seconds. I was a little upset, bothered.

— Why the hell wasn't it blue? — I said to myself.

And that reflection — one of the deepest that has been made since butterflies were invented — consoled me for the evil deed and reconciled me with myself. I let myself contemplate the corpse with a certain sympathy, I must confess. I imagined that it had come out of the woods, having had breakfast, and that it was happy. The morning was beautiful. It came out of there, modest and black, having fun butterflying under the broad summit of a blue sky, which is always blue for all wings. It came through my window and found me. I suppose it had never seen a man before. It did not know, therefore, what a man was. It executed infinite turns around my body and saw that I moved, that I had eyes, arms, legs, a divine look, colossal stature. Then it said to itself, "This is probably the inventor of butterflies." The idea subjugated it, terrified it, but fear, which is also suggestive, hinted to it that the best way to please its creator was to kiss him on the forehead, and it kissed me on the forehead. When I drove it away, it went to land on the counterpane. There it saw my father's picture, and it is quite possible that it discovered a half-truth there, namely, that this was the father of the inventor of butterflies, and it flew over to beg his mercy.

Then the blow of a towel put an end to the adventure. The blue immensity was of no use to it, nor was the joy of the flowers, nor the splendor of the green leaves against a face towel, two palms of raw linen. See how fine it is to be superior to butterflies! Because, it is proper to say, had it been blue, or orange, its life would not have been any more secure. It was quite possible that I would have run it through with a pin for the pleasure of my eyes. It was not. That last idea gave me back my consolation. I put my middle finger against my thumb, gave it a flick, and the corpse fell into the garden. It was time. The provident ants were already arriving... No, I go back to the first idea: I think it would have been better if it had been born blue.

CHAPTER XXXII
LAME FROM BIRTH

I went on from there to finish my preparations for the trip. I am not going to delay it anymore. I am going down immediately. I am going down even if some circumspect reader holds me back to ask if the last chapter is only a disagreeable incident or whether I have been made a fool of... Then, I did not count on Ms. Eusebia. I was all ready when she came into the house. She was coming to invite me to postpone my descent and come have dinner with her that day. I tried to refuse, but she insisted so much, so very much, ever so much, that I could not help but accepting it. Besides, I owed her that compensation. I went.

Eugenia did not put on her adornments for me that day. I think they had been for me — unless she went around like that a lot of times. Not even the gold earrings she had worn the day before were hanging from her ears now, two delicately shaped ears on the head of a nymph. A simple white dress without any decorations, having a mother-of-pearl button at the neck instead of a brooch and another button at the wrists, closing the sleeves, and no shadow of a bracelet.

That was how she was in body, and no less in spirit. Clear ideas, simple manners, a certain natural grace, the air of a lady, and, I do not know, maybe something else. Yes, a mouth exactly like her mother's, which recalled the episode in 1814 for me, and then I had an urge to gloss the same verse for the daughter...

— Now let me show you the property — and it was then that I noticed something. Eugenia was limping slightly, so slightly that I asked her if she had hurt her foot. Her mother fell silent. The daughter answered without hesitation:

— No, sir, I am lame from birth.

I cursed myself into every hell there was. I called myself clumsy, rude. Really, the simple possibility of her being lame was enough not to ask anything. Then I remember the first time I saw her — the day before —the girl had approached her mother's chair slowly and, on that same day, I had already found her at the dinner table. It might have been to hide the defect. But what was her reason for confessing it now? I looked at her and noted that she was sad.

I tried to get rid of the remains of my blunder — it was not difficult, because the mother was, as she had confessed, an old carouser, and she quickly started a conversation with me. We looked over the whole property, trees, flowers, duck pond, laundry tank, an infinity of things that she kept showing me and commenting on while I, surreptitiously, scrutinized Eugenia's eyes...

I give my word that Eugenia's look was not lame, but straight, perfectly healthy. It came from a pair of dark and quiet eyes. I think that they were lowered two or three times, a little cloudy, but only two or three times. In general, they looked at me with frankness, without timidity or false modesty.

CHAPTER XXXIII
BLESSED ARE THOSE WHO DO NOT DESCEND

The worst of it was that she was lame. Such lucid eyes, such a fresh mouth, such ladylike composure — and lame! That contrast could lead one to believe that nature is sometimes a great mocker. Why pretty if lame? Why lame if pretty?

That was the question I kept asking myself on my way back home at night without hitting upon the solution to the enigma. The best thing to do when an enigma is unsolved is to toss it out the window. That was what I did. I laid my hand on another towel and drove off that other black butterfly fluttering in my brain. I felt relieved and went to bed. But dreams, which are a loophole in the spirit, let the bug back in, and I spent the whole night delving into the mystery without explaining it.

It was raining that morning, and I postponed my descent. But the next day, the morning was clear and blue, and despite that, I let myself stay, the same on the third day, the fourth, right to the end of the week. Beautiful, cool, inviting mornings. Down below, the family, the bride, parliament were calling me, and I was unable to attend to anything, bewitched at the feet of my Crippled Venus. Bewitched is just a way of enhancing style. There was no bewitchment but, rather, pleasure, a certain physical and moral satisfaction. I loved her, true. At the feet of that so artless creature, a spurious, lame daughter, the product of love and disdain, at her feet I felt good, and she, I think, felt even better at my feet. And all that in Tijuca. A simple eclogue. Ms. Eusebia kept watch over us, but not so very much. She tempered necessity with expedience. The daughter, in that first explosion of nature, gave me her soul in bloom.

— Are you going back down tomorrow? — she asked me on Saturday.
— I am planning to.
— Do not go.

I did not go back down and I added a verse to the Gospel: "Blessed are those who do not descend, for theirs is the first kiss of young girls." Indeed, Eugenia's first kiss came on a Sunday — the first ever, which no other male had taken from her, and it was not stolen or snatched, but innocently offered, the way an honest debtor pays a debt. Poor Eugenia! If you only knew what ideas were drifting out of my mind on that occasion! You, quivering with excitement, your arms on my shoulders, contemplating your welcome spouse in me, and I, my eyes on 1814, on the shrubbery, on Vilaca, and suspecting that you could not lie to your blood, to your origins...

Ms. Eusebia entered unexpectedly, but not so suddenly as to catch us at each other's feet. I went to the window. Eugenia sat down to adjust one of her braids. Such delightful pretense! Such infinitely delicate skills! Such profound Tartuffeanism! And all of it was natural, alive, unstudied, as natural as appetite, as natural as sleep. So much the better! Ms. Eusebia did not suspect anything.

CHAPTER XXXIV
FOR A SENSITIVE SOUL

There, among the five or six people reading me, is some sensitive soul who must surely be a bit upset with the previous chapter and who started trembling over Eugenia's fate and, maybe... Yes, maybe deep down inside, the reader is calling me a cynic. I, a cynic, sensitive soul? By Diana's thigh, that insult deserves to be washed away in blood, if blood can wash anything away in this world. No, sensitive soul, I am not a cynic, I was a man. My brain was a stage on which plays of all kinds were presented: sacred dramas, austere, scrupulous, elegant: comedies, wild farces, short skits, buffoonery, pandemonium, sensitive soul, a hodgepodge of things and people in which you could see everything, from the rose of Smyrna to the rue in your own backyard, from Cleopatra's magnificent bed to the corner of the beach where the beggar shivers in his sleep. Crossing it are thoughts of varied types and shapes. There was not only the atmosphere of water and hummingbirds there; there was also that of snails and toads. Take back the expression, then, sensitive soul, control your nerves, clean your glasses — because this is sometimes due to glasses — and let's be done with this flower from the shrubbery.

CHAPTER XXXV
THE ROAD TO DAMASCUS

It so happened that a week later, as if I was on the road to Damascus, I heard a mysterious voice that whispered the words of the Scripture (Acts, 9:6) to me: "Arise, and go into the city." That voice was coming from me, and it had a double origin: the pity that rendered me helpless before the innocence of the little one, and the terror of really falling in love with her and marrying her. A lame woman! As for that being the reason for my descent, there is no doubt that she thought so and she told me. It was on the porch, on a Monday afternoon, when I told her I would be going back down the next morning. — Goodbye — she sighed, holding out her hand with simplicity. — You are doing the right thing. — And since I did not say anything, she went on: — You are doing the right thing in running away from the ridiculous idea of marrying me. — I was going to tell her no. She withdrew slowly, swallowing her tears. I caught up with her after a few steps and swore to her by all the saints in heaven that I was forced to go back down, but that I had not stopped loving her very much. All cold hyperbole, which she listened to without saying anything.

— Do you believe me? — I finally asked.
— No, and I say you are doing the right thing.

I tried to hold her back, but the look she gave me was no longer a plea, but a command. I went down from Tijuca the next morning, a little embittered but also a little satisfied. I went along saying to myself that it was right to obey my father, that it was fitting to take up a political career... That the constitution... That my bride... That my horse...

CHAPTER XXXVI
ON BOOTS

My father, who was not expecting me, embraced me, full of tenderness and appreciation.

— Is it true, then? — he said. — Can I finally...?

I left him with that reticence and went to take off my boots, which were tight. Once relieved, I took a deep breath and stretched out while my feet and all that extended up from them went into relative bliss. Then I pondered the fact that tight boots are one of the best bits of good fortune on earth, because by making one's feet hurt, they give occasion to the pleasure of taking them off. Punish your feet, wretch, then unpunish them, and there you have cheap happiness, at the mercy of shoemakers and worthy of Epicurus. While that idea was working out on my famous trapeze, I cast my eyes up toward Tijuca and saw the little cripple disappearing over the horizon of the past, and I felt that my heart would not be long in taking off its boots either. And they were taken off by lechery. Four or five days later, I was savoring that quick, ineffable, and irrepressible moment of pleasure that follows a sharp pain, a concern, an indisposition... From that, I inferred that life is the most ingenious of phenomena because hunger only becomes sharp with the aim of bringing on the occasion for eating, and that life only invented calluses because they perfect earthly happiness. In all truth, I can tell you that all of human wisdom is not worth a pair of short boots.

You, my Eugenia, never took them off. You went along the road of life, limping from your leg and from love, sad as a pauper's burial, lonely, silent, laborious, until you, too, came to this other shore... What I do not know is whether your existence was quite necessary for the century. Who knows? Maybe one less walk-on would make the human tragedy a failure.

CHAPTER XXXVII
FINALLY!

Finally! Here is Virgilia. Before going to Councilor Dutra's house, I asked my father if there was any commitment to marriage.

No commitment. Some time back, while I was talking to him about you, I confessed my desire to see you as a deputy. And I talked in such a way that he promised to do something, and I think he will. As for the bride — that is the name I give to a lovely creature who is a jewel, a flower, a star, something rare... She is his daughter. I imagined that if you married her, you would get to be a deputy quicker.

— Is that all?
— That is all.

From there, we went to Dutra's house. The man was a delight, smiling, jovial, patriotic, a bit irritated by public ills, but not despairing about curing them quickly. He thought my candidacy was legitimate. It was best, however, to wait a few months. And then he introduced me to his wife — an estimable lady — and his daughter, who in no way belied my father's panegyric. I swear to you, in no way. Reread chapter XXVII. I, who had an idea regarding the little one, stared at her in a certain way. She, who I am not sure had one or not, did not stare at me any differently. And that first look was purely and simply conjugal. At the end of a month, we were close.

CHAPTER XXXVIII
THE FOURTH EDITION

— Come and have dinner with us tomorrow — Dutra told me one night. I accepted the invitation. The next day, I told the carriage to wait for me on the Largo Sao Francisco de Paula, and I went to take a stroll. Do you still remember my theory of human editions? Well, you should know then, that at that time, I was in my fourth edition, reviewed and corrected, but still contaminated with careless errors and incorrect usage. A defect that, on the other hand, was compensated for by the type, which was elegant, and the binding, which was deluxe. After my stroll, as I went along the Street of Goldsmiths, I looked at my watch, and the crystal fell to the sidewalk. I went into the first shop at hand. It was a cubicle, a little more — dusty and dark. In the back, behind the counter, a woman was sitting and her yellow, pockmarked face was not visible at first sight. But as soon as it was, it became a curious spectacle. She could not have been ugly, on the contrary, it was obvious that she had been pretty, quite pretty. But the illness and a precocious old age had destroyed the flower of her beauty. The smallpox had been terrible. The marks, large and plentiful, formed bumps and notches up and down her face, and they gave the feeling of thick sandpaper, enormously thick. The eyes were the best part of the figure, and yet they had a singular and repugnant expression that changed, however, as soon as I started talking. As for her hair, it was gray and almost as dusty as the doorway to the shop. A diamond gleamed on one of the fingers of her left hand. Can you believe it, you, future generations? That woman was Marcela.

 I did not recognize her right away. It was difficult. She, however, recognized me as soon as I talked to her. Her eyes sparkled and changed their usual expression for another, half sweet and half sad. I caught a movement by her, as if to hide or flee. It was the instinct of vanity, which only lasted for an instant. Marcela settled down and smiled.

 — Do you want to buy something? — she asked, holding out her hand to me.

 I did not answer. Marcela understood the cause of my silence (it was not difficult) and only hesitated, I think, in deciding which was stronger, the fright of the present or the memory of the past. She brought me a chair, and with the counter between us, she talked to me at length about herself, the life she had led, the tears I had caused her to shed, the longing, the disasters, finally the smallpox that had scarred her face, and time, which the illness had helped in bringing on her early decline. The truth is that she had a decrepit soul. She had sold everything, almost everything. A man who had loved her in past times and died in her arms had left her that jewelry store, but to make misfortune complete, there were not many customers coming to the shop now — maybe because of the odd situation that it was run by a woman. She immediately asked me to tell her about my life. I did not spend much time telling it. It was neither long nor interesting.

 — Did you get married? — Marcela asked after my narration.

 — Not yet — I replied dryly.

Marcela cast her eyes out to the street with the weakness of someone reflecting or remembering. I let myself go into the past then and, in the midst of memories and nostalgia, asked myself what could have been the reason for me to have done so much nonsense. This one certainly was not Marcela of 1822, but was the beauty of times gone by worth a third of my sacrifices? That was what I was seeking to find out by interrogating Marcela's face. The face told me no. At the same time, the eyes were telling me that back then, the same as today, the flame of greed burned in them. My eyes had not been able to see it in her. They were the eyes of the first edition.

— So, why did you come in here? Did you see me from the street? — she asked, coming out of that kind of torpor.

— No, I thought I was coming into a watchmaker's shop. I wanted to buy a crystal for this watch. I will go somewhere else. You will have to excuse me; I am in a hurry.

Marcela smiled sadly. The truth is that I felt distressed and annoyed at the same time, and I was anxious to get myself out of that place. Marcela, however, called a black boy, gave him the watch, and, despite my objections, sent him to a shop in the neighborhood to buy the crystal. There was no way out. I sat down again. Then she said that she wanted the protection of people she knew in times gone by. She thought that sooner or later it would be natural for me to get married and swore to me that she would get me fine jewelry at a cheap price. She did not say cheap, but she used a delicate and transparent metaphor. I started suspecting that she had not suffered any disaster (except for the illness), that she had her money safely put away, and that she was bargaining with the sole aim of satisfying her passion for profit, which was the worm that gnawed at her existence. That was exactly what I was told later.

CHAPTER XXXIX
THE NEIGHBOR

While I was reflecting on that to myself, a short fellow, hatless and leading a girl of four years old by the hand, entered the shop.

— How are you this morning? — Marcela asked him.

— So, so. Come here, Maricota.

The fellow picked up the child by the arms and passed her over the counter.

— Go ahead — he said. — Ask Mrs. Marcela how she spent the night. She was anxious to come here, but her mother was not able to dress her... So, Maricota? Ask her for a blessing... Watch out for the punishment! That is the way... You cannot imagine what she is like at home. She talks about you all the time, and here she acts like a dummy. Just yesterday... Shall I tell her, Maricota?

— No, do not tell her, Papa.

— Was it something naughty, then? — Marcela asked, patting the girl's face.

— I will tell you. Her mother taught her to say Our Father and Hail Mary every night to Our Lady, but yesterday the little one asked me in a very timid voice... Can you imagine what?... If it was all right to offer them to Saint Marcela.

— Poor thing! — Marcela said, kissing her.

— It is a love affair, a passion, you cannot imagine... Her mother says she is bewitched...

The fellow told many other things, all very pleasant, until he left, taking the girl, but not before casting a curious or suspicious glance in my direction. I asked Marcela who he was.

— He is a watchmaker in the neighborhood, a good person. His wife, too. And the daughter is a charm, don't you think? She seems to like me a lot... They are good people.

As she was saying those words, there seemed to be a quiver of joy in Marcela's voice. And on her face, something that spread a wave of happiness across it...

CHAPTER XL
IN THE CARRIAGE

At that point, the black boy came in carrying the watch with a new crystal. It was about time. It was already beginning to bother me to be there. I gave the boy a small silver coin, told Marcela that I would come back on another occasion, and went out with long strides. To tell the truth, I must confess that my heart was pounding a little. But it was a kind of death knell. My spirit was bound by opposing impressions. Remember that the day had dawned happily for me. My father had repeated in advance for me at breakfast the first speech I would make in the Chamber of Deputies. We were laughing a lot, and the sun was also brilliant, as on the most beautiful days in the world, in the same way that Virgilia should laugh when I tell her about our breakfast fantasies. All is going well when I lose the crystal of my watch, go into the first shop at hand, and, behold, the past rises up before me, lacerates and kisses me, interrogates me with a face scarred by nostalgia and smallpox...

I left it behind and hurriedly got into the carriage, which was waiting for me on the Largo Sao Francisco de Paula, and I ordered the coachman to drive fast. The coachman whipped up the animals, and the carriage started shaking me up. The springs groaned, the wheels cut rapidly through the mud that the recent rain had left, and yet it all seemed stock-still to me. Isn't there a kind of lukewarm wind that sometimes blows, not strong or harsh, but a little sultry, which does not blow the hat off your head or swirl women's skirts up, and yet is or seems to be worse than the one that does both those things because it lowers, weakens, kind of dissolves the spirit? Well, I had that wind with me, and I was certain that it was blowing on me because I found myself in a kind of gorge between the past and the present, I was longing to come out onto the plain of the future. The worst of it was that the carriage was not moving.

— Joao! — I shouted to the coachman. — Is this carriage moving or not?
— Oh, Little Master! We are already parked by the Councilor's door.

CHAPTER XLI
THE HALLUCINATION

He was right. I hurried in. I found Virgilia anxious, in a bad mood, frowning. Her mother, who was deaf, was with her in the living room. After the greetings, the girl told me dryly:
— We expected you sooner.

I defended myself as best I could. I mentioned a balky horse, a friend who had held me up. All of a sudden, my voice died on my lips, I was paralyzed with wonder. Virgilia... Could that girl be Virgilia? I took a good look at her, and the feeling was so painful, that I took a step back and turned my eyes away. I looked at her again. The smallpox had eaten her face. Her skin, so delicate and pink and pure before, just a day ago, looked yellow to me now, stigmatized by the same lash that had devastated the Spanish woman's face. Her eyes, which used to be lively, were dull, her lips were sad, and she had a weary air about her. I took a good look, took her hand, and softly drew her toward me. I had not been deceived; they were pockmarks. I think I took on an expression of repulsion.

Virgilia drew away from me and went to sit down on the sofa. I spent some time looking at my own feet. Should I leave or stay? I rejected the first suggestion, which was quite absurd, and walked over to Virgilia, who was sitting there without saying a word. I looked in vain for some vestiges of the illness on her face. There were none. It was the usual delicate and white skin.

— Have you never seen me before? — Virgilia asked, noticing that I was staring at her with insistence.

— Never so pretty.

I sat down while Virgilia, silent, clicked her fingernails. There was a pause of a few seconds. I talked to her about things that had nothing to do with the incident. She did not say anything in response, and she did not look at me. Except for the clicking of her nails, she was a statue of silence. Only once did she put her eyes on me, but far above me, raising the left corner of her mouth, knitting her brows to the point of bringing them together. That whole combination of things gave her face an intermediate expression, somewhere between comic and tragic.

There was a certain affection in that disdain. It was a kind of contrived expression. She was suffering inside, and quite a bit — it was either real suffering or just annoyance. And because the pain that is covered up hurts all the more, quite probably Virgilia was suffering twice over what she really should have been suffering. I think that is called metaphysics.

CHAPTER XLII
WHAT ARISTOTLE LEFT OUT

Another thing that seems metaphysical to me is this: put a ball into motion, for example. It rolls, touches another ball, transmits the impulse, and there you have the second ball rolling like the first.

Let us suppose that the first ball is called... Marcela — and it is only a supposition. The second Bras Cubas — the third Virgilia. Put the case that Marcela, receiving a flick from the past, rolls until she touches Bras Cubas — who, reacting to the impelling force, starts rolling, too, until he runs up against Virgilia, who had nothing to do with the first ball. And there you have it now, by the simple transmission of a force, two social extremes come into contact, and something is established that we can call... The solidarity of human aversion. How is it that Aristotle left that chapter out?

CHAPTER XLIII
A MARCHIONESS, BECAUSE I WILL BE A MARQUIS

Virgilia was positively a mischief-maker, an angelic mischief-maker, but one all the same...

Then Lobo Neves appeared, a man who was no slimmer than I, nor more elegant, nor better read, nor more pleasant, and yet it was he who snatched Virgilia and the candidacy away from me in a matter of a few weeks and with truly Caesarian drive. There was no anger preceding it, no family dispute at all. Dutra came to tell me one day that I should wait for another opportunity because Lobo Neves' candidacy was backed by people of great influence. I gave up. This was the start of my defeat. A week later, Virgilia asked Lobo Neves, smiling, when he was going to be a minister.

— As far as I am concerned, right now; according to others, a year from now. Virgilia replied:

— Promise me that you will make me a baroness someday?

— A marchioness, because I will be a marquis.

From that moment on, I was lost. Virgilia compared the eagle to the peacock and chose the eagle, leaving the peacock with his surprise, his spite, and the three or four kisses she had given him. Maybe five kisses. But even if there had been ten, they would not have meant anything. A man's lip is not like the leg of Atilla's horse, which sterilized the ground it trod on. Quite the opposite.

CHAPTER XLIV
A CUBAS!

My father was astounded at the outcome, and I would like to think that there was nothing else that caused his death. So many were the castles that he had built, ever so many the dreams, that he could not bear to see them demolished without suffering a great shock to his organism. At first, he refused to believe it. A Cubas! A twig of the illustrious tree of the Cubas! And he said that with such conviction that I, aware by then of our cooperation, forgot the fickle lady for a moment to think only about that phenomenon, not strange, but curious: imagination raised up to certitude.

— A Cubas! — he repeated to me the next morning at breakfast.

It was not a joyful breakfast. I myself was dropping from lack of sleep. I had stayed awake for a good part of the night. Because of love? Impossible. One cannot love the same woman twice, and I, who would love that one some time later, was not held at that time by any other bond than a passing fantasy, a certain obedience to my own fatuousness. And that was enough to explain my wakefulness. It was spite, a sharp little spite with the prick of a pin, which disappeared with cigars, pounding fists, scattered reading, until dawn broke, the most quiet of dawns.

But I was young, I had the cure in myself. It was my father who could not bear the blow so easily. When I think about it, it might be that he did not die precisely because of the disaster, but the disaster surely complicated his final ailments. He died four months later — disheartened, sad, and with an intense and continuous concern, something like remorse, a fatal disenchantment that went along with his rheumatism and coughing. He had a half hour of joy all the same. It was when one of the ministers came to call. I saw that he had — I remember it well — I saw that he had the pleased smile of other days and a concentration of light in his eyes that was, so to speak, the last flash of an expiring soul. But the sadness returned immediately, the sadness or dying without seeing me in some high position as befitted me.

He died a few days after the minister's visit one morning in May, between his two children, Sabina and me, along with uncle Ildefonso and my brother-in-law. He died despite the physicians' science or our love or our care, which was great, or anything else. He had to die, and he died.

— A Cubas!

CHAPTER XLV
NOTES

Sobs, tears, the house all prepared, black velvet over the doorways, a man who came to dress the corpse, another who took measurements for the coffin, bier, candleholders, invitations, guests slowly entering, stepping softly, shaking hands with the family, some sad, all serious and silent, priest and sacristan, prayers, the sprinkling of holy water, nailing shut the coffin, six people lifting it and carrying it down the steps in spite of the cries, sobs, the new tears on the part of the family, and going up to the hearse, placing it on top and tying it down, the hearse rolling along, and the carriages, one by one... What looks like a simple inventory here are notes I have taken for a sad and banal chapter that I will not write.

CHAPTER XLVI
THE INHERITANCE

Let the reader take a look at us now, a week after my father's death — my sister sitting on a sofa — Cotrim a little in front of her, leaning against a sideboard, his arms folded and nibbling on his mustache — I, walking back and forth staring at the floor. Deep mourning. Deep silence.

— But, after all, — Cotrim was saying — this house cannot be worth much more than thirty *contos de réis*. Let's say thirty-five...

— It is worth fifty — I figured. Sabina knows it costed fifty-eight...

— It could cost sixty — Cotrim replied — but it does not mean that it was worth it, much less that it is worth it today. You know that houses have gone down in price over the years. Look, if this one is worth the fifty *contos de réis*, how much do you think the one you want for yourself, the country house, is worth?

— Let's not talk about that. It is an old house.

— Old! — Sabina exclaimed, lifting her hands to the ceiling.

— Do you think it is new? I bet you do.

— Come on, brother, let's stop this — Sabina said, getting up from the sofa. — We can arrange everything in a friendly way, smoothly. For example, Cotrim will not take the slaves, only the coachman and Paulo...

— Not the coachman — I hastened to add — I am getting the carriage and I am not going to buy another driver.

— Well, I will stick with Paulo and Prudencio.

— Prudencio is free.

— Free?

— It has been two years.

— Free? How could our father have managed things here without telling anyone? That is great! What about the silver?... I do not imagine he freed the silver, did he?

We had talked about the silver, the old silverware from the time of D. Jose I, the most important part of the inheritance, for its workmanship, for its antiquity, for the origins of its ownership. My father said that the Count of Cunha, when he was Viceroy of Brazil, had given it to my great-grandfather, Luis Cubas, as a gift.

— About the silver — Cotrim went on — I would not care about it, if it were not for your sister's wish to keep it. And I think she is right. Sabina is a married woman, and she needs a fine setting, a presentable one. You are a bachelor, you do not entertain, you do not...

— But I can get married.

— What for? — Sabina interrupted.

That question was so sublime that, for a few moments, it made me forget all about my interests. I smiled, took Sabina's hand, patted her palm lightly, all with such a delicate appearance that Cotrim interpreted the gesture as one of acquiescence, and he thanked me.

— What is that? — I retorted — I did not give up anything and I am not going to.

— Are you not going to? I nodded.

— Never mind, Cotrim — my sister said to her husband. — Let's see if he wants the clothes on our bodies, too. That is all that is missing.

— Nothing more is missing. You want the carriage, you want the coachman, you want the silver, you want everything. Look, it would be quicker if you took us to court and proved with witnesses that Sabina is not your sister, that I am not your brother-in-law, and that God is not God. Do that, and you will not lose anything, not even a little teaspoon. Come on, my friend, try something else!

He was as annoyed as me, so that I thought of suggesting a means for conciliation: dividing up the silver. He laughed and asked me who would get the teapot and who would get the sugar bowl. And, after that question, he declared that we would have an opportunity to liquidate our demands in court at least. In the meantime, Sabina had gone to the window that looked out onto the grounds — and after a moment, she turned and proposed giving up Paulo and the other black on the condition that she get the silverware. I was going to say that I did not want that, but Cotrim came forward and said the same thing.

— Never! I do not take alms — he said.

We had a sad dinner. My uncle, the canon, appeared after dinner and witnessed yet another small altercation.

— My children, — he said — remember that my brother left a very large loaf of bread to be divided up for everyone.

But Cotrim said:

— I know, I know. But the question does not concern the bread, it concerns the butter. I cannot swallow dry bread.

The division was finally made, but peace was not. And I can tell you that, even so, it was very difficult for me to break with Sabina. We had been such good friends! Childhood games, childhood furies, the laughter and sadness of adult life, so many times we had divided that loaf of joy and misery like brother and sister, like the good brother and sister we were. But we were broken up. Just like Marcela's beauty, which had vanished with the smallpox.

CHAPTER XLVII
THE RECLUSE

Marcela, Sabina, Virgilia... Here I am putting together all the contrasts as if those names and people were only stages of my inner affections. Be sorry for bad habits, put on a stylish necktie, a less-stained waistcoat, and then, yes, come with me, enter this house, stretch out on this hammock that cradled me for the better part of two years, from the inventory of my father's estate until 1842. Come. If you smell some dressing-table perfume, do not think I had it sprinkled for my pleasure. It is the vestige of N, or Z, or U— because all those capital letters cradle their elegant abjection there. But if, in addition to the perfume, you want something else, keep that wish to yourself, because I do not keep portraits or letters or diaries. The excitement itself has vanished and left me with the initials.

I lived half like a recluse, attending, after long intervals, some ball or theater or a lecture, but I spent most of the time by myself. I was living, letting myself float on the ebb and tide of events and days, sometimes lively, sometimes apathetic, somewhere between ambitious and disheartened. I was writing politics and making literature. I sent articles and poems to newspapers, and I managed to attain a certain reputation as a polemicist and poet. When I thought of Lobo Neves, who was already a deputy, and Virgilia, a future marchioness, I asked myself whether I would not have been a better deputy and a better marquis than Lobo Neves — I, who was worth more, much more than he — and I said that looking at the tip of my nose...

CHAPTER XLVIII
A COUSIN OF VIRGILIA

— Do you know who arrived yesterday from Sao Paulo? — Luis Dutra asked me one night. Luís Dutra was a cousin of Virgilia, who was also an intimate of the muses. His poetry was more pleasing and was worth more than mine, but he had a need for the approval of some in order to confirm the applause of others. Since he was bashful, he never asked anyone, but he enjoyed hearing some words of appreciation. Then he created new strength and plunged into the work like an adolescent.

Poor Luis Dutra! As soon as he published something, he ran to my house and started hovering around me on the lookout for an opinion, a word, a gesture that would approve his recent production, and I told him about a thousand different things — the latest ball in Catete, salon discussions, carriages, horses — about everything except his poetry or prose. He answered me, with animation at first, then more sluggishly, turning the gist of the conversation toward his matter. He opened a book, ask me if I had done any new work, and I answered yes or no and turned the direction away, and there he was behind me, until he completely balked and went away, sad. My intent was to make him doubt himself, dishearten him, eliminate him. And all of that looking at the tip of my nose...

CHAPTER XLIX
THE TIP OF MY NOSE

Nose, conscience without remorse, you were very helpful to me in life... Have you ever meditated sometimes on the purpose of the nose, dear reader? Dr. Pangloss' explanation is that the nose was created for the use of eyeglasses — and I must confess that such an explanation, up until a certain time, seemed to be the definitive one for me. But it happened one day while ruminating on those and other obscure philosophical points that I hit upon the only true and definitive explanation. All I needed, really, was to follow the habits of a fakir. As the reader knows, a fakir spends long hours looking at the tip of his nose, with his only aim being to see the celestial light. When he fixes his eyes on the tip of his nose, he loses his sense of outside things, becomes enraptured with the invisible, learns the intangible, becomes detached from the world, dissolves, is etherealized. That sublimation of the being by the tip of the nose is the loftiest phenomenon of the spirit, and the faculty for obtaining it does not belong to the fakir alone. It is universal. Every man has the need and the power to contemplate his own nose with an aim to see the celestial light, and such contemplation, whose effect is subordination to just one nose, constitutes the equilibrium of societies. If noses only contemplated each other, mankind would not have lasted two centuries, it would have died out with the earliest tribes.

I can hear an objection on the part of the reader here: — How can it be like that, — he asks — if no one has ever seen men contemplating their own noses?

Obtuse reader, that proves you never got inside the brain of a hatter. A hatter passes by a hat shop, the shop of a rival who opened it two years before. It had two doors then, now it has four. It promises to have six or eight. The rival's customers are going in through the doors. The rival's hats are displayed on the windows. The hatter compares that shop with his, which is older and has only two doors, and those hats with his, which are less sought after even though priced the same. He is naturally mortified, but he keeps on walking, concentrating, with his eyes lowered or straight ahead, pondering the reasons for the other man's prosperity and his own backwardness, while he, as a hatter, is a much better hatter than the other hatter... At that moment, his eyes are fixed on the tip of his nose.

The conclusion, therefore, is that there are two capital forces: love, which multiplies the species, and the nose, which subordinates it to the individual. Procreation, balance.

CHAPTER L
VIRGILIA MARRIED

— The one who arrived from Sao Paulo was my cousin Virgilia, married to Lobo Neves — Luis Dutra went on.

— Oh!

— And today I knew something for the first time, you rogue...

— What was that??

— That you wanted to marry her.

— My father's idea. Who told you that?

— She did it herself. I talked about you a lot to her, and then she told me everything.

The next day, on Ouvidor Street, in the doorway of Plancher the printer, I saw a splendid woman appear in the distance. It was her. I only recognized her when she was a few steps away, she was so different, nature and art had given her their final touch. We greeted each other. She went on her way, joined her husband in the carriage that was waiting for them a little further on. I was astonished.

A week later, I met her at a ball. I think we had to exchange two or three words. But at another ball, about a month later, at the house of a lady, whose salons were the jewel of the first reign and were no less that of the second, the meeting was broader and longer because we chatted and waltzed. The waltz is a delightful thing. We waltzed. I will not deny that, as I pressed that flexible and magnificent body to my body, I had a singular sensation, the sensation of a man who was robbed.

— It is very hot — she said when we finished. — Shall we go to the balcony?
— No, you might catch a cold. Let's go to the other room.

In the other room was Lobo Neves, who paid me many compliments for my political writings, adding that he could not say anything about the literary ones because he did not understand them, but the political ones were excellent, well-thought-out, and well written. I replied with an equal show of courtesy, and we separated, pleased with each other.

About three weeks later, I received an invitation from him for an intimate gathering. I went. Virgilia greeted me with these gracious words: — You are going to waltz with me tonight.

The truth was that I had the reputation of being an eminent waltzer. Do not be surprised by the fact that she preferred me. We waltzed once and once again. If a book brought on Francesca's downfall, here it was the waltz that brought on ours. I think I grasped her hand that night with great strength, and she left it there, as if forgetful, and I embraced her, and with all eyes on us and on the others who were also embracing and turning... Delirium.

CHAPTER LI
SHE IS MINE!

— She is mine! — I said to myself as soon as I passed her on to another gentleman. And I must confess that for the rest of the evening, the idea was becoming embedded in my spirit, not with the force of a hammer, but with that of a drill, which is more insinuative.

— She is mine! — I said when I arrived at the door of my house.

But there, as if fate or chance or whatever it was remembered to feed my passionate flight of fancy, a round, yellow thing was gleaming at me on the ground. I bent over. It was a gold coin, a half doubloon.

— Mine! — I repeated and, laughing, put it in my pocket.

That night I did not think about the coin anymore, but on the following day, remembering the incident, I felt a certain revulsion in my conscience and a voice that asked me why the hell a coin that I did not inherit or earn, but only found in the street should be mine. Obviously, it was not mine; it belonged to somebody else, the one who had lost it, rich or poor, and maybe he was poor. A worker who did not have anything to feed his wife and children with. But even if he was rich, my duty remained the same. It was proper to return the coin, and the best method, the only method, was to do it through an advertisement or through the police. I sent a letter to the chief of police enclosing what I had found and begging him, by the means at his disposal, to return it to the hands of its true owner.

I sent the letter and ate a peaceful lunch; I might even say a jubilant one. My conscience had waltzed so much the night before that it had lost its breath, but giving back the half-doubloon was a window that opened to the other side of morality. A wave of pure air came in, and the lady breathed deeply. Ventilate your conscience! That is all I can tell you. Nevertheless, if for no other reason, my act was a nice one because it expressed the proper scruples, the feelings of a delicate soul. That was what my inner lady was telling me, in a way that was austere and tender at the same time. That was what she was telling me as I leaned on the sill of the open window.

— You did well, Cubas; you behaved perfectly. This air is not only pure but also balmy; it is the breath of the eternal gardens. Do you want to see what you did, Cubas? And the good lady took out a mirror and opened it, before my eyes. I saw, I clearly saw the half-doubloon of the night before, round, shiny, multiplying all by itself — becoming ten — then thirty — then five hundred — expressing in that way the benefits I would be given in, life and in death by the simple act of restitution. And I was pouring out my whole being into the contemplation of that act, I was seeing myself in it again, I found myself good — great, maybe. A simple coin, huh? See what it means to have waltzed just a little bit more.

So, I, Bras Cubas, discovered a sublime law, the law of the equivalencies of windows, and I established the fact that the method of compensating for a closed window is to open another, so that morality can continuously aerate one's conscience. Maybe you do not understand what is entailed in that. Maybe you want something more concrete, a package, for example, a mysterious package. Well, here is the mysterious package.

CHAPTER LII
THE MYSTERIOUS PACKAGE

The matter is that, a few days later, on my way to *Botafogo*, I tripped on a package lying on the beach. That is not quite exact. It was more of a kick than a trip. Seeing a package, not large, but clean and neatly tied together with strong twine, something that looked like something, I thought about giving it a kick, just for the experience, and I kicked it, and the package resisted. I cast my eyes around. The beach was deserted. Some children were playing far away — beyond them, a fisherman was drying his nets — no one could see my act. I bent over, picked up the package, and went on my way.

I went on my way, but not without some hesitation. It might have been a trick being played by some boys, I got the idea of taking what I found back to the beach, but I felt it and rejected the idea. A little further on, I changed course and headed home.

— Let's take a look — I said as I entered my office.

And I hesitated for a moment, out of shame, I think. The suspicion of a trick struck me again. It was certain that there was no outside witness there. But I had a boy inside myself who would whisper, wink, grunt, kick, jeer, cackle, do devilish things if he saw me open the package and find a dozen old handkerchiefs or two dozen rotting guavas inside. It was too late. My curiosity was sharpened, as the reader's must be. I unwrapped the package, and I saw... I found... I counted... and recounted nothing less than five *contos de réis*. Nothing less. Five *contos de réis* in good banknotes and coins, all clean and in neat order, a rare find. I wrapped them up again. At dinner, it seemed to me that one of the black boys was talking to the other with his eyes. Had they spied on me? I asked them discreetly and concluded that they had not. After dinner, I went back to my office, examined the money, and laughed at my maternal worries regarding the five *contos de réis* — I, who was wealthy.

In order not to think about it anymore, I went to Lobo Neves' house that night. He had insisted that I not miss his wife's receptions. There, I met the chief of police. I was introduced to him. He immediately remembered the letter and the half-doubloon I had sent him a few days before. He revealed the matter. Virgilia seemed to be savoring my act, and every one of those present came up with some analogous anecdote, to which I listened with the impatience of a hysterical woman.

The next night and during that whole week, I gave as little thought as I could to the five *contos de réis* and, I must confess, I left them ever so peacefully in my desk drawer. I liked talking about everything except money, and especially money that I found. It was not a crime to find money, however, it was a happy thing, good luck, maybe even a stroke of Providence. It could not be anything else. Five *contos de réis* are not lost the way you lose a pouch of tobacco. Five *contos de réis* are carried with thirty thousand feelings, you keep feeling them, you do not take your eyes off them, or your hands, or your thoughts, and for them to be lost foolishly like that, on a beach, it has to be... Finding them cannot be a crime. Neither a crime nor dishonor, nor anything that might sully a man's character. They were something discovered, a lucky strike, like the grand prize, like a winning bet on the horses, like the stakes in an honest gambling game, and I might even say that my good luck was deserved, because I did not feel bad or unworthy of the rewards of Providence.

— These five *contos de réis*, — I said to myself three weeks later — must be used for some good deed, maybe as the dowry of some poor girl, or something like that... I will see...

That same day, I took them to the Bank of Brazil. There I was received with many gracious references to the matter of the half-doubloon, the news of which was already spreading among people of my acquaintance. I replied with annoyance that the matter was not worth the great splurge. Then they praised my modesty — and since I got angry, they answered me that it was simply great.

CHAPTER LIII

● ● ● ● ● ● ●

Virgilia was the one who no longer remembered the half-doubloon. Her whole being been concentrated on me, on my eyes, on my life, on my thoughts — that was what she said and it was true.

There are some plants that are born and grow quickly. Others are late and stunted. Our love was like the former one. It burst forth with such drive and so much sap that, in a short while, it was the broadest, leafiest, and most luxuriant creation in the forest. I cannot tell you for certain the number of days that this growth took. I remember that on a certain night the flower, or the kiss, if you want to call it that, started budding, a kiss that she gave me trembling — poor thing — trembling with fear, because it was by the gate of the yard. That single kiss united us — just as the moment was brief, so was the love ardent, the prologue to a life of delights, terrors, remorse, pleasures that ended in pain, afflictions that opened up into joy — a patient and systematic hypocrisy, the only check rein on an unchecked passion — a life of agitation, rage, despair, and jealousy, which, one hour paid for fully and more than enough, but another hour came and swallowed it all, up along with everything else, leaving on the surface agitation and all the remains, and the remains of the remains, which are aversion and satiety. Such was the book with that prologue.

CHAPTER LIV
THE GRANDFATHER CLOCK

I left there, savoring the kiss. I could not sleep. I lay down on my bed, of course, but it meant nothing. I heard the hours of the night. Usually, when I could not sleep, the chiming of the grandfather clock used to upset me very much. The mournful tick-tock, slow and dry, seemed to say with every note that I was having one instant less of life. Then I pictured an old devil sitting between two sacks, one of life and one of death, taking out the coins of life and giving them to death, counting them like this:

— Another less...
— Another less...
— Another less...
— Another less...

The strangest thing is that, if the clock stopped, I wound it up so it did not stop ticking, and I could count all of my lost instants. There are inventions that are transformed or come to an end; institutions themselves die. A clock is both definitive and perpetual. The last man, as he says farewell to the cold and used-up sun, will have a watch in his pocket in order to know the exact time of his death.

On that night, I did not suffer that sad feeling of boredom, but a different and delightful one. Fantasies swarmed inside of me, coming one on top of another like the devout women who crush forward in order to get a look at the singing angel in processions. I did not hear the instants lost, but the minutes gained. From a certain time forward, I did not hear anything at all because my thought, wily and frisky, leaped out the window and flapped its wings toward Virgilia's house. There, it found Virgilia's thought on a windowsill. They greeted each other, remained chatting. We were tossing in bed, maybe cold, in need of rest, and those two idlers there were repeating the old dialogue of Adam and Eve.

CHAPTER LV
THE OLD DIALOGUE OF ADAM AND EVE

BRAS CUBAS

. . . ?

VIRGILIA

. . . .

BRAS CUBAS

. . . .

VIRGILIA

. . . . . !

BRAS CUBAS

. . . . . .

VIRGILIA

. . . .
. . . . ? . . . .
. . . .

BRAS CUBAS

. . . .

VIRGILIA

. . . .

BRAS CUBAS

. . . .

. . . .
. . . . ! . . . .
. . ! . . . .
. . . . !

VIRGILIA

. . . . ?

BRAS CUBAS

. . . . . !

VIRGILIA

. . . . . !

CHAPTER LVI
THE OPPORTUNE MOMENT

But, dash it all! Who can explain the reason for this difference to me? At one time we kept company, discussed marriage, broke up, and separated, coldly, painlessly, because there was no passion. I only carried away a little spite and nothing else. The years pass, I see her again, we take three or four turns in a waltz, and here we are, madly in love with each other. Virgilia's beauty, it is true, had reached a high degree of perfection, but we were substantially the same and I, for my part, had not become more handsome or more dashing. Who will explain the reason for that difference to me? The reason could not have been anything else, but the opportune moment, because if on that first occasion, neither of us was too green for love, both of us were for *our* love, a fundamental distinction. No love is possible without the opportunity of the subjects. I found that explanation myself two years after the kiss, one day when Virgilia was complaining to me about a guy who kept flirting with her tenaciously.

— How importunate! — she said, putting on an angry face.

I shuddered, stared at her, saw that the indignation was sincere. Then, it occurred to me that maybe I had brought on that same frown at some point, and I immediately understood the degree of my evolution. I had gone from importunate to opportune.

CHAPTER LVII
FATE

Yes, sir, we were in love. Now that all the social laws forbade it, now was when we truly loved each other.

We found ourselves yoked together like the two souls the poet encountered in Purgatory.

Di pari, come buoi, che vanno a giogo;

and I am wrong in comparing us to oxen, because we were a different species of animal, less sluggish, more roguish, and lascivious. There we were, going along without knowing where to go or on what secret roads, a problem that frightened me for a few weeks, but whose outcome I turned over to fate. Poor Fate! Where can you be walking now, great supervisor of human affairs? Maybe you are growing a new skin, a different face, different ways, a different name, and it is even possible that... I forget where I was... Ah, yes, on secret roads. I said to myself that now it would be whatever God willed. It was our fate to fall in love. If it had not been, how could we explain the waltz and all the rest? Virgilia was thinking the same thing. One day, after confessing to me that she had posthumous moments of remorse, since I had told her that, if she felt remorse, it was because she did not love me, Virgilia clasped me in her magnificent arms, muttering:

— I love you. It is the will of heaven.

And those were not just random words. Virgilia was somewhat religious. She did not go to mass on Sundays, it is true, and I even think she only went to church on feast days and when there was a vacant pulpit somewhere. But she prayed every night, fervently, or sleepily at least. She was afraid of thunder. On those occasions, she covered her ears and mumbled all the prayers in the catechism. In her bedroom, she had a small rosewood oratory, three feet high, and with three images inside. But she never mentioned it to her friends. On the contrary, she tagged as fanatics those who were simply religious. For some time, I suspected that there was a certain annoyance with belief in her and that her religion was a kind of flannel undergarment, hidden and cozy, but I was obviously mistaken.

CHAPTER LVIII
CONFIDENCE

Lobo Neves gave me great fear at first. An illusion! He never tired of telling me how much he loved his wife. He thought that Virgilia was perfection itself, a combination of solid and refined qualities, loving, elegant, austere, a model woman. And the confidence did not stop there. From the crack that it once was, it grew to be a wide-open door. One day, he confessed to me that he had a sad worm gnawing at his existence. He needed public glory. I bolstered his spirits, told him many nice things that he listened to with that religious unction of a desire that does not want to finish dying. Then I realized that his ambition was fatigued from beating its wings and being unable to take flight. Days later, he told me about all his annoyance and weariness, the bitter pills he had swallowed, spites, intrigues, perfidy, interests, vanity. There was obviously a crisis of melancholy there. I tried to fight against it.

— I know what I am talking about — he replied, sadly. — You cannot imagine what I have been through. I went into politics because of a liking for it, the family, ambition, and a little bit because of vanity: you can see that I have in me all the reasons that lead a man into public life. All I was missing was a different way of interest. I saw the theater from the audience's side and, I swear, it was beautiful! Superb sets, life, movement and grace in the performance. I signed on. They gave me a role that... But why am I boring you with all this? Let me keep my afflictions to myself. Believe me, I spent hours, days... There is no constancy of feelings, there is no gratitude, there is nothing... nothing ... nothing...

He fell silent, deeply downcast, his eyes in the air, not seeming to hear anything unless it was the echo of his own thoughts. After a few moments, he stood up and reached out his hand to me. — You must be laughing at me, — he said — but please, forgive my letting things out. I had some business that was eating my soul. — And he laughed in a somber, sad way, then, he asked me not to mention to anyone what had passed between us. I replied that absolutely nothing had happened. Two deputies and a district leader came in. Lobo Neves greeted them effusively, at first a little artificially, but then quite naturally. After half an hour, no one would have said he was not the most fortunate of men. He chatted, joked, laughed, and everybody laughed.

CHAPTER LIX
AN ENCOUNTER

Politics must be an invigorating wine, I said to myself as I left Lobo Neves' house. And I kept walking on and on until, on the Street of *Barbonos*, I saw a carriage, and in it was one of the ministers, an old schoolmate of mine. We waved to each other affectionately, the carriage went on its way, and I kept walking on... on... on...

— Why can't I be a minister?

That idea, resplendent and great — extravagantly clad, as Father Bernardes would have said — that idea started a swirl of somersaults, and I let myself stand there watching it, finding it amusing. I was not thinking about Lobo Neves' sadness anymore, I felt the attraction of the abyss. I remembered that schoolmate, how we played around on the hills, our joys and our mischief, and I compared the boy with the man and asked myself why I could not be like him. I was turning into the promenade then, and everything seemed to be telling me the same thing.

— Why can't you be a minister, Cubas? — Cubas, why can't you be a minister of state? When I heard it, a delightful feeling refreshed my whole organism. I went in, sat down on a bench, and mulled that idea over. And how Virgilia would enjoy it! A few moments later, coming toward me, I saw a face that did not seem unknown to me. I recognized it from somewhere or another.

Imagine a man between thirty-eight and forty, tall, slim, and pale. His clothes, except for their style, looked as if they had escaped from the Babylonian captivity. The hat was a contemporary of one of Gessler's. Imagine now a frock coat broader than the needs of his frame — or, literally, that person's bones. The black color was giving way to a dull yellow. The fringe had disappeared some time ago; of the eight original buttons, three were left. The brown drill trousers had two strong knee patches, while the cuffs had been chewed by the heels of boots that bore no pity or polish. About his neck, the ends of a tie of two faded colors floated, gripping a week-old collar. I think he was also wearing a dark silk vest, torn in places and unbuttoned.

— I bet you do not know me, my good Dr. Cubas — he said.

— I am not remembering...

— I am Borba, Quincas Borba.

I drew back in astonishment... If only I had been given the solemn speech of a Bossuet or a Vieira to describe such desolation! It was Quincas Borba, the amusing boy of times gone by and my schoolmate, so intelligent and so well-off. Quincas Borba! No, impossible. It could not be. I could not believe that this filthy figure, this beard tinted white, this aging tatterdemalion, all that ruination was Quincas Borba. But it was. His eyes had something left over from other times, and his smile had not lost a certain mocking air that was peculiar to him. In the meantime, he withstood my astonishment. After a while, I turned my eyes away. If the figure repelled me, the comparison grieved me.

— I do not have to tell you a thing, you can guess it all. A life of misery, tribulation, and struggle. Remember our parties where I played the part of the king? What a fiasco! I ended up a beggar...

And, lifting his right hand and his shoulders with an air of indifference, he seemed resigned to the blows of fortune and, I do not know, was even happy maybe. Maybe... Impassive, certainly. There was no Christian resignation or philosophical acceptance in him. It seemed that misery had calloused his soul to the point of taking away the feeling of the mud. He dragged his rags along just as he had formerly done with the royal purple, with a certain indolent grace.

— Look for me; — I said — I might be able to find something for you.

— You are not the first to promise me something and I do not know if you will be the last not to do anything for me. So, what is the use? I am not asking for anything, unless it is money, money, yes, because I have to eat and eating-places do not give credit, greengrocers either. A nothing, two pennies of cornmeal porridge, the damned greengrocers will not even trust you for that... It is hell, my... I was going to say friend... A hell! Devilish! Absolutely devilish! Look, I did not have any breakfast today.

— No?

— No; I left home early. Do you know where I live? On the third landing of the Sao Francisco stairs, to the left of a person going up. You do not have to knock on the door. A cool house, extremely cool. Well, I left early, and I did not eat yet...

I took out my wallet, picked up a five banknote — the least clean one — and gave it to him. He took it with eyes that gleamed with greed. He held the note up in the air and flourished it with enthusiasm.

— *In hoc signo vinces!* — he shouted.

And then he kissed it with a great show of tenderness and such noisy carrying on that it gave me a mixed feeling of nausea and pity. He was sharp, and he understood me. He became serious and asked my forgiveness for his joy, saying that it was the joy of a poor man who had not seen a five banknote in many years.

— Well, it is in your hands to see a lot more of them — I said.
— Yes? — he hastened to say, lunging toward me.
— Working — I concluded.

He made a gesture of disdain. He fell silent for a few moments, then told me positively that he did not want to work. I was disgusted with that abjection, which was so comical and so sad, and I got ready to leave.

— Do not leave until I teach you my philosophy of misery — taking a broad stance before me.

CHAPTER LX
THE EMBRACE

I presumed that the poor devil was crazy, and I was going to leave when he grabbed me by the wrist and stared for a few seconds at the diamond I was wearing on my finger. I could feel the quivers of greed in his hand, an itch for possession.

— Magnificent! — he said.

Then he started walking all around me, examining me closely.

— You take good care of yourself — he said. — Jewelry, fine and elegant clothes, and... Just compare those shoes with mine. What a difference! There is no comparison! I tell you; you take good care of yourself. What about girls? How about them? Are you married?

— No...
— Me neither.
— I live at...
— I do not want to know where you live — Quincas Borba stressed. — If we see each other again, give me another five note. But allow me not to look at you at home. It is a kind of pride... Now, goodbye, I can see that you are impatient.

— Goodbye!
— And thank you. Let me thank you a little more warmly.

And saying that, he embraced me so swiftly that I could not avoid it. We finally separated; I took long strides, my shirt wrinkled from the embrace, annoyed and sad. The pleasant side of me no longer dominated, the other one did. I would have preferred to see him bear this misery with dignity. Yet, I could not help comparing the man of today with the one of days gone by, growing sad as I faced the abyss that separates the hopes of one time from the reality of another...

— So, goodbye! Let's have dinner — I said to myself.

I put my hand into my vest and I could not find my watch. The final disillusionment. Borba had stolen it during the embrace.

CHAPTER LXI
A PROJECT

I had dinner in sadness. It was not the loss of the watch that tormented me, it was the image of the perpetration of the theft and the remembrances of childhood, and once again, the comparison, the conclusion... Starting with the soup, the yellow, morbid flower from chapter XXV started opening up in me, and then I ate hurriedly in order to run to Virgilia's house. Virgilia was the present. I wanted to take refuge in it, so I could escape the burdens of the past, because the encounter with Quincas Borba had turned my eyes back to the past, and I had really entered it, but it was a broken, abject, beggarly, and thievish past.

I left the house, but it was early. If I went now, I would find them still at the table. I thought about Quincas Borba again, and then I got the desire to go back to the promenade and see if I could find him. The idea of regenerating him rose up in me like a strong need. I went, but I could not find him now. I inquired of the guard, who told me that, indeed, "that fellow" came around there sometimes.

— At what time?
— He does not have a set time.

It would not be impossible for me to run into him on another occasion. I promised myself I would be back. The need to regenerate him, get him back to work, and have respect for his person was filling my heart. I was starting to get a comfortable feeling, one of uplift, and admiration for myself... At that point, the night started falling. I went to meet Virgilia.

CHAPTER LXII
THE PILLOW

I went to meet Virgilia. I quickly forgot Quincas Borba. Virgilia was the pillow for my spirit. A soft, warm, aromatic pillow embroidered in cambric and lace. It was there that it was accustomed to resting away from all unpleasant feelings, those that were merely annoying or those that were even painful. And when things were put into proper balance, that was the only reason for Virgilia's existence. There could not have been any other. Five minutes were enough to forget Quincas Borba completely, five minutes of mutual contemplation, with hands clasped together. Five minutes and a kiss. And off went the memory of Quincas Borba... Scrofula of life, rag out of the past, what do I care if you exist or not, if you bother the eyes of other people, since I have ten square inches of a divine pillow on which to close my eyes and sleep?

CHAPTER LXIII
LET'S RUN AWAY!

Alas, not always to sleep. Three days later, going to Virgilia's house, — it was four in the afternoon — I found her sad and downcast. She refused to tell me what it was, but since I insisted so much:

— I think Damiao suspects something. I noticed some weird things about him lately... I do not know... He treats me well, there is no doubt about that. But his look does not seem the same. I am not sleeping well. Just last night I woke up terrified, I was dreaming he was going to kill me. Maybe it is just an illusion, but I think he suspects...

I calmed her down as best I could. I said that they might be political worries. Virgilia agreed that they might be, but she was still very distraught and nervous. We were in the living room which, as it happened, faced the yard, where we had exchanged our initial kiss. An open window let the breeze in, rustling the curtains slightly, and I sat staring at the curtains without seeing them. I was holding the binoculars of the imagination. In the distance, I could see a house of our own in which there was not any Lobo Neves or any marriage or any morality or any other bond that impeded the expansion of our will. That idea intoxicated me. With the elimination of the world, morality, and husband in that way, all we had to do was go into that angelic dwelling.

— Virgilia, — I said — I have a proposal for you.

— What is it?

— Do you love me?

— Oh! — she sighed, putting her arms around my neck.

Virgilia loved me furiously. That answer was her open wish. With her arms around my neck, silent, breathing heavily, she remained staring at me with her beautiful big eyes, which gave the singular impression of a moist light. I let myself remain watching them, looking lovingly at her mouth, as cool as dawn and as insatiable as death. Virgilia's beauty had a grandiose tone now, something it had not before she was married. She was one of those figures carved in Pentelic ivory, of noble workmanship, open and pure, tranquilly beautiful, like the statues, but neither indifferent nor cold. On the contrary, she had the warm look natures have, and it could be said that, in reality, she summed up all love. She summed it up, especially on that occasion, in which she was mutely expressing everything the human eye can say. But time was urgent. I clasped her hands, took them by the wrists, and, looking at her, asked if she had the courage.

— Courage of what?

— Courage of running away. We will go where it will be more comfortable for us, a house, big or small, according to what you want, in the country or in the city, or in Europe, wherever you think, where nobody can bother us and there will not be any dangers for you, where we can live for each other... Yes? Let's run away. Sooner or later, he is going to find out something, and you will be lost, because I will kill him, I swear.

I stopped. Virgilia had grown very pale. She dropped her arms and sat down on the settee. She remained that way for several minutes, without saying anything to me; I do not know whether she was hesitating in her choice or terrified at the idea of discovery and death. I went over to her, insisted on the proposal, told her all of the advantages of a life alone together, without jealousies, terrors, or afflictions. Virgilia listened to me in silence, then said:

— Maybe we could not run away: he would catch up with me and kill me anyway.

I pointed out to her how it would not be that way. The world was rather vast, and I had the means to live wherever the air was pure and there was a lot of sunshine. He would never get there. Only great passions are capable of great actions, and he did not love her enough to be able to find her if we were far away. Virgilia made a gesture of horror, almost indignation. She muttered that her husband loved her very much.

— Maybe, — I answered — maybe he does...

I went over to the window and started drumming my fingers on the sill. Virgilia called to me. I stayed where I was, chewing on my jealousy, wanting to strangle her husband if I had him there at hand... At that precise moment, Lobo Neves appeared in the yard. Do not tremble so, my pale lady reader. Relax, I am not going to begin this page with a drop of blood. As soon as he appeared in the yard, I gave him a friendly wave along with a gracious word. Virgilia hurriedly left the room, which he entered three minutes later.

— Have you been here long? — he asked.
— No.

He came in serious, worried, his eyes wide open in a distracted way, a habit of his, but he immediately changed it into a true expression of joviality when he saw his son arrive, the little master, the future lawyer in chapter VI. He took him in his arms, lifted him into the air, kissed him several times. I, who hated the child, drew away from both of them. Virgilia came back into the room.

— Ah! — Lobo Neves said with a deep breath as he sat down on the sofa.
— Tired? — I asked.
— Very. I made a couple of hard coups, one in the chamber and the other in the street. And we have a third one still to come — he added, looking at his wife.
— What is it? — Virgilia asked.
— A... Guess what?

Virgilia sat down beside him, took one of his hands, straightened his tie, and asked again what it was.

— Nothing less than a cabin.
— For Candiani?
— For Candiani.

Virgilia clapped her hands, stood up, gave her son a kiss with an air of childish joy, which was quite out of tune with her appearance. Then she asked if the cabin was on the side or in the middle, consulted her husband in a low voice as to what she should wear, about what opera would be sung, and I do not know what other things.

— Will you stay for dinner with us, doctor? — Lobo Neves asked.
— That is precisely why he came; — his wife confirmed — he says that you have the best wine in Rio de Janeiro.
— Even so, he does not drink very much.

At dinner, I proved he was wrong and drank more than I was accustomed to. Even so, less than necessary for me to lose my reason. I was already upset and I became a little more. It was the first great anger I felt for Virgilia. I did not look at her one single time during dinner. I talked about politics, the press, the ministry, I think I could have talked about theology (if I knew anything about it or remembered anything). Lobo Neves followed me with great calm and dignity, even with certain superior benevolence. And all of that also annoyed me, and rendered the dinner all the more bitter and long. I took my leave as soon as we got up from the table.

— See you later, right? — Lobo Neves asked.
— Maybe. And I left.

CHAPTER LXIV
THE TRANSACTION

    I wandered through the streets and retired at nine o'clock. Unable to sleep, I started reading and writing. At eleven o'clock, I was sorry I had not gone to the theater, consulted the clock, wanted to get dressed and go out. I calculated that I would get there too late, however. Besides, it would be proof of weakness. Obviously, Virgilia was beginning to be annoyed with me, I thought. And that idea made me desperate and cold successively, ready to forget her and to kill her. I could see her from there, reclining in her box with her magnificent bare arms, — the arms that were mine, only mine — fascinating everyone's eyes with the superb dress she must have had on, her milky white breast, her hair in tight curls in the style of the time, and her diamonds, less brilliant than her eyes... I saw her like that, and it pained me that others should see her. Then I started undressing her, putting the jewels and silks aside, undoing her hair with my voracious and lascivious hands, making her — I do not know whether more beautiful or more natural — making her mine, only mine, nothing but mine.

    The next day, I could not stand it. I went to Virgilia's house early and found her with eyes red from weeping.

— What happened? — I asked her.

—You do not love me — it was her answer. — You never showed me the slightest sign of love. Yesterday, you treated me as if you hated me. If I only knew what I did! But I do not know. Won't you tell me what it was?

— What? I think there was nothing.

— Nothing? You treated me like a dog...

With that word, I took her hands, kissed them, and two tears appeared in her eyes.

— It is over, it is over — I said.

I did not have the heart to argue, and, besides, argue about what? It was not her fault if her husband loved her. I told her that she had not done anything to me, that I was necessarily jealous of the other man, that I could not always bear him with a happy face. I added that maybe there was a lot of pretending on his part, and the best way to shut the door on battles and disagreements was to accept my idea of the day before.

— I thought about it. — Virgilia said — A little house all our own, by itself, in the middle of a garden on some backstreet, isn't it? I liked the idea, but why run away?

She said that with the ingenuous and casual tone of someone who can think no evil, and the smile that slackened the corners of her mouth carried the same innocent expression. Then, moving away, I answered:

— You are the one who never loved me.
— Me?

—Yes, you are selfish! You preferred to see me suffer every day... You are unspeakably selfish!

Virgilia started weeping, and so as not to attract anyone's attention, she put her handkerchief into her mouth, and suppressed her sobs. An outburst that disconcerted me. If anyone had heard her, everything would have been lost. I leaned toward her, took her by the wrists, whispered the sweetest names of our intimacy to her. I pointed out the danger. The fear calmed her down.

— I cannot; — she said after a few moments — I cannot leave my son; If I took him along, I am sure *he* would follow me to the ends of the earth. I cannot. Kill me, if you want, or let me die... Oh, Lord! Oh, Lord!

— Calm down, someone might hear you.
— Let them hear! I do not care.

She was still upset. I asked her to forget everything, to forgive me, that I was mad, but that my insanity was because of her and would end because of her. Virgilia wiped her eyes and reached out her hand. We both smiled. A few minutes later, we went back to the matter of the solitary little house on some backstreet...

CHAPTER LXV
EYES AND EARS

We were interrupted by the sound of a carriage in the yard. A slave came in to announce the arrival of Baroness X. Virgilia consulted me with her eyes.

— If you have a headache like that, madam, — I said — I think it would be better not to receive her.

— Has she gotten down already? — Virgilia asked the slave.

— Yes. She says she needs very much to talk to my lady!

— Let her in!

The Baroness entered shortly. I do not know whether she expected to see me there, but she could not have shown any greater fuss.

— How good to see you! — she exclaimed. — Where have you been hiding, sir, that you never appear anywhere? Look, just yesterday, I was surprised not to see you at the theater. Candiani was a delight. What a woman! Do you like Candiani? Naturally. Men are all alike. The baron was telling me last night in our cabin that a single Italian woman is worth five Brazilian women. Such impertinence! And the impertinence of an old man, which is worse. But why didn't you go to the theater last night?

— A migraine.

—Hah! Some love affair, don't you think, Virgilia? Well, my friend, you better hurry up because you must be forty... Or close to it... Aren't you forty years old?

— I cannot say for sure, — I answered — but if you excuse me, I will check my baptism certificate.

— Go, go... — And reaching out her hand to me: — When will we see you? We will be at home on Saturday. The baron misses you...

Out on the street, I was sorry I had left. The Baroness was one of the people who was most suspicious of us. Fifty-five years old and looking forty, sleek, smiling, vestiges of beauty, elegant bearing, and refined manners. She did not talk a lot or all the time. She possessed the great skill of listening to others, spying on them. At those times, she would sit back in her chair, unsheathe her long, sharp vision, and take her ease. The others, not knowing what was going on, talked, looked, gesticulated, while she simply looked, sometimes staring, sometimes moving her eyes, carrying the ruse to the point of looking inside herself sometimes because she let her eyelids drop. But since eyelashes were lattices, her glance continued its work, rummaging in the souls and lives of others.

The second person was a relative of Virgilia, Viegas, a worthless old man of seventy winters, sucked dry and yellowish, who suffered from a chronic case of rheumatism, no less chronic asthma, and a heart lesion. He was a walking hospital ward. His eyes, however, gleamed with plenty of life and health. Virgilia, during the first few weeks, was not afraid of him at all. She told me that, when Viegas seemed to be watching with his stare, he was simply counting money. He was, in fact, a great miser.

There was still Virgilia's cousin, Luis Dutra, whom I disarmed now by dint of talking to him about his prose and poetry and introducing him to acquaintances. When the latter, linking the name to the person, showed themselves to be pleased with the introduction, there was no doubt that Luis Dutra overflowed with happiness. And I made use of that happiness with the hope that he would never catch us. There were, finally, two or three ladies, several fops, and the servants, who naturally would avenge themselves for their servile status in that way, and all of them constituted a veritable forest of eyes and ears among which we had to slip along with the tactics and subtlety of serpents.

CHAPTER LXVI
LEGS

Now, whenever I think about those people, my legs carry me off down the street, so that without realizing it, I found myself at the door of the Hotel Pharoux. I was in the habit of having dinner there. But, not having deliberately walked there, I deserved no credit for the act, but my legs, which had done so, did. Blessed legs! And there are those who treat you with disdain or indifference. Even I, until then, held you in low esteem, getting annoyed when you tired, when you could not go beyond a certain point, leaving me with a desire to flap my wings like a hen tied by the feet.

That time, however, it was a ray of light. Yes, legs, my friends, you left the task of thinking about Virgilia to my head, and you said to one another: — He needs to eat, it is dinnertime, let's take him to the Pharoux. Let's divide up his consciousness, one part can stay with the lady, we will take over the other part so that he goes straight ahead, does not bump into people or carriages, tips his hat to acquaintances, and, finally, arrives safe and sound at the hotel. And you followed your plan to the letter, kind legs, which forces me to immortalize you with this page.

CHAPTER LXVII
THE LITTLE HOUSE

I had dinner and went home. There I found a box of cigars that Lobo Neves had sent me, wrapped in tissue paper and tied with a pink ribbon. I understood, opened it, and took out this note:

"My B...

"They suspect us. All is lost. Forget me forever. We cannot see each other again. Goodbye, forget this unhappy.

"V...a."

That letter was a blow. Nevertheless, immediately after nightfall, I ran to Virgilia's house. I was on time, she regretted it. Through an open window, she told me what had happened with the Baroness. The Baroness had told her quite frankly that there was a lot of talk at the theater the night before regarding my absence from the Lobo Neves cabin. They had commented on my relationship to the house. In short, we were the object of public suspicion. She finished by saying that she did not know what to do.

— The best thing is to run away — I hinted.

— Never — she replied, shaking her head.

I saw that it was impossible to separate two things that were completely linked to her spirit: our love and public opinion. Virgilia was capable of equal and great sacrifices to preserve both advantages, and flight left her with only one. Maybe I had felt something similar to spite, but the commotion of those two days was already great, and the spite quickly died. It is all set. Let's arrange the little house. As a matter of fact, I found it a few days later, made to order, in a corner of Gamboa. A jewel! New, freshly painted, with four windows in front and two on either side — all with brick-colored blinds — vines at the corners, a garden in front. Mystery and solitude. A jewel!

We arranged for a woman known to Virgilia, in whose house she had been a seamstress and servant, to go live there. Virgilia held a real enchantment for her. She would not tell her everything. She had easily accepted the rest.

For me, this was a new situation in our love, an appearance of exclusive possession, of absolute dominion, something that would soothe my conscience and maintain decorum. I was already tired of the other man's curtains, chairs, carpet, couch, all the other things that constantly brought our duplicity before my eyes. Now I could avoid the frequent dinners, the teas every night, and, finally, the presence of their son, my accomplice and my enemy. The house rescued me completely. The ordinary world would end at its door. From there on, there was the infinite, an eternal, superior, exceptional world, ours, only ours, without laws, without institutions, without any baroness, without eyes, without ears — one single world, one single couple, one single life, one single will, one single affection — the moral unity of all things through the exclusion of those that were contrary to me.

CHAPTER LXVIII
THE WHIPPING

Such were my reflections as I walked along *Valongo* right after seeing and arranging for the house. They were interrupted by a gathering of people. It was because of a black man whipping another one in the square. The other one did not try to run away. He only moaned these words: — Please, I am sorry, master. Master, I am sorry! But the first one paid no attention and each entreaty was answered with a new lashing.

— Take that, you devil! — he said. — Here is your apology, you drunk!
— Master! — the other one was moaning.
— Shut your mouth, you animal! — the whipper replied.

I stopped to look... Good Lord! And who did the one with the whip turn out to be? None other than my houseboy Prudencio — the one my father had freed some years ago. He came over to me, having ceased immediately, and asked for my blessing. I inquired if that black man was his slave.

— Yes, he is, little master.
— What did he do?
— He is a loafer and a big drunk. Today I left him in the grocery store while I went downtown, and he went off to a bar to drink.
— Okay, forgive him — I said.
— Of course, little master. Your word is my command. Go home, you drunk!

I left the crowd of people who were looking at me with wonder and whispering conjectures. I went on my way, unraveling an infinite number of reflections that I think I have lost completely. They would have been material for a good, and maybe happy, chapter. I like happy chapters; they are my weakness. On the outside, the *Valongo* episode was dreadful, but only on the outside. As soon as I stuck the knife of rationality deeper into it, I found it to have a happy, delicate, and even deep marrow. It was the way Prudencio had to rid himself of the beatings he had received by transmitting them to someone else. As a child, I used to ride on his back, put a bit into his mouth, and whip him mercilessly. He moaned and suffered. Now that he was free, however, he had the free use of himself, his arms, his legs, he could work, rest, sleep unfettered from his previous status. Now he could make up for everything. He bought a slave and was paying him back with high interest the amount he had received from me. Just look at the subtlety of the rogue!

CHAPTER LXIX
A GRAIN OF FOLLY

The case makes me remember a mad guy I knew. His name was Romualdo, and he said he was Tamerlane. It was his great and only mania, and he had a strange way of explaining it.

— I am the famous Tamerlane — he said. — Formerly I was Romualdo, but I got sick, and I took so much tartar, so much tartar, so much tartar, that I became a Tartar, and even king of the Tartars. Tartar has the property of producing Tartars.

Poor Romualdo! People laughed at his response, but it is likely that the reader is not laughing, and rightfully so. I do not think it is funny at all. When you first hear it, it has a touch of humor, but told like this, on paper, and with reference to a whipping received and passed on, I have to confess that it is much better to get back to the little house in Gamboa and put the Romualdos and Prudencios aside.

CHAPTER LXX
MRS. PLACIDA

Let's get back to the little house. You would not be able to enter it today, curious reader. It grew old, blackened, rotted, and the owner tore it down to replace it with another three times bigger, but, I swear to you, lesser than the first one. The world may have been too small for Alexander, but the eaves of a roof are an infinity for swallows.

Take a look now at the neutrality of this globe that carries us through space like a lifeboat heading for shore. Today, a virtuous couple sleeps on the same plot of ground that once held a sinning couple. Tomorrow, a churchman may sleep there, then a murderer, then a blacksmith, then a poet, and they will all bless that corner of earth that gave them a few illusions.

Virgilia turned the house into a jewel. She arranged for household items that were just right and placed them about with the aesthetic intuition of an elegant woman. I brought in some books, and everything was under the care of Mrs. Placida, the supposed and, in certain respects, real owner of the house.

It was very difficult for her to accept the house. She had sniffed out the intention and her position pained her, but she finally gave in. I think she wept at the beginning; she was disgusted with herself. What was certain, at least, was that she did not lift her eyes to me during the first two months. She talked to me with her look lowered, serious, frowning, sad sometimes. I wanted to win her over and did not act offended, treating her with affection and respect. I made a great effort to win her goodwill, then her trust. When I obtained her trust, I made up a pathetic story about my love for Virgilia, a situation before her marriage, her father's resistance, her husband's harshness, and I do not know how many other novelistic touches. Mrs. Placida did not reject a single page of the novel. She accepted them all. It was a necessity of her conscience. At the end of six months, anyone who saw the three of us together would have said that Mrs. Placida was my mother-in-law.

I was not ungrateful. I made her a peculium of five *contos de réis* — the five *contos de réis* found in *Botafogo* — as a nest egg for her old age. Mrs. Placida thanked me with tears in her eyes and, from then on, never ceased to pray for me every night before an image of the Virgin she had in her room. That was how her disgust ceased.

CHAPTER LXXI
THE DEFECT OF THIS BOOK

I am starting to regret this book. Not that it bothers me; I have nothing to do and, really, putting together a few meager chapters for that other world is always a task that distracts me from eternity a little. But the book is tedious, it has the smell of the grave about it; it has a certain cadaveric contraction about it, a serious fault, insignificant to boot because the main defect of this book is you, reader. You are in a hurry to grow old, and the book moves slowly. You love direct and continuous narration, a regular and fluid style, and this book and my style are like drunkards, they stagger left and right, walk and stop, mumble, yell, cackle, shake their fists at the sky, stumble, and fall...

And they do fall! Miserable leaves of my cypress of death, you shall fall like any others, beautiful and brilliant as you are. And, if I had eyes, I would shed a nostalgic tear for you. This is the great advantage of death: if it leaves no mouth to laugh, neither does it leave eyes to weep... You shall fall.

CHAPTER LXXII
THE BIBLIOMANIC

Maybe I will leave out the previous chapter. Among other reasons, because in the last lines, there is a phrase that is close to being nonsense and I do not want to provide food for future critics.

Put the case that seventy years from now, a thin, yellow, gray-haired guy who loves nothing but books leans over the previous page to see if he can discover the nonsense. He reads, rereads, reads again, disjoins the words, takes out a syllable, then another, and another still, and examines the remaining ones inside and out from all sides, up against the light, dusts them off, rubs them against his knee, washes them, and nothing. He cannot find the absurdity.

He is a bibliomaniac. He does not know the author. This name of Bras Cubas does not appear in his biographical dictionaries. He found the volume by chance in the rundown shop of a second-hand book dealer. He bought it for two hundred *réis*. He inquired, investigated, searched about, and came to discover that it was a one-and-only copy... One and only! You people who not only love books, but suffer from a mania for them know quite well the value of those words, and you can imagine, therefore, my bibliomaniac's delight. He would reject the crown of the Indies, the Papacy, all the museums of Italy and Netherlands if he had to trade that one and only copy for them and not because it is that of my *Memoirs*. He would do the same with *Laemmert's Almanac* if it was a one-and-only copy. The worst part is the absurdity. The man stays there, hunched over the page, a lens under his right eye, given over completely to the noble and wearing function of deciphering the absurdity. He already promised himself to write a brief report in which he will relate the finding of the book and the discovery of the sublimity, if there is to be one under that obscure phrase. In the end, he discovers nothing and contents himself with ownership. He closes the book, looks at it, looks at it again, goes to the window and holds it up to the sun. A one-and-only copy. At that moment, passing under the window is a Caesar or a Cromwell on the path to power. He turns his back on him, closes the window, lies down in his hammock, and slowly flips through the book, lovingly, in sips... A one-and-only copy!

CHAPTER LXXIII
THE LUNCHEON

The absurdity made me lose another chapter. How much better it would have been to have said things smoothly, without all these bumps!

I already compared my style to the walk of drunkards. If the idea seems indecorous to you, let me say that it is what my meals with Virgilia were like in the little house in Gamboa, where we had our sumptuous feast sometimes, our luncheon. Wine, fruit, jams. We ate, it is true, but it was eating punctuated by loving little words, tender looks, childish acts, an infinity of those side comments of the heart in addition to the real, uninterrupted discourse of love. Sometimes a tiff came to temper the excessive sweetness of the situation. She left me, took refuge in a corner of the settee, or went inside to listen to Mrs. Placida's pruderies. Five or ten minutes later, we picked up the thread of our conversation the way I picked up the thread of this narrative to let it unwind again. Let it be noted that far from being horrified at the method, it was our custom to invite it in the person of Mrs. Placida, to sit down at the table with us, but Mrs. Placida never accepted the invitation.

— It seems you do not like me anymore — Virgilia told her one day.

— Holy Mother of God! — the good lady exclaimed, lifting her arms up to the ceiling. — Do not I like you?! Who would I ever like in this world then?

And taking her hands, she looked into her eyes, looked and looked until her eyes watered from staring so hard. Virgilia stroked her, and I left her a small silver coin in the pocket of her dress.

CHAPTER LXXIV
THE STORY OF MRS. PLACIDA

Never regret being generous. The little silver coin brought me confidence from Mrs. Placida and, consequently, this chapter.

Days later, when I was alone in the house, we started a conversation, and she told me her story in brief terms. She was the illegitimate child of a sexton at the cathedral and a woman who sold candy on the street. She lost her father when she was ten. By then, she was shredding coconut and doing all kinds of other chores of a candies-maker fitting for her age. At fifteen or sixteen, she married a tailor who died of tuberculosis a while later, leaving her with a daughter two years old and her mother, exhausted from a life of work. She had three mouths to feed. She made sweets, which was her trade, but she also sewed, day and night, assiduously, for three or four shops, and she taught some girls in the neighborhood for ten dimes a month. The years passed that way, but not her beauty, because she never had any. Some courtships, proposals, and seductions came her way, which she resisted.

— If I could have found another husband, — she told me — I think I would have gotten married, but nobody wanted to marry me.

One of the suitors managed to get himself accepted, without being any more kind than the others, however. Mrs. Placida sent him away and, after sending him away, wept a great deal. She continued sewing for the other people and kept her pots boiling. Her mother was ill-tempered because of her age and her poverty. She railed at her daughter to take on one of the seasonal, temporary husbands who asked for her. And she shouted:

— Do you think you are better than me? I do not know where you get those stuck-up ideas of a rich person. My daughter, life does not get straightened out just by chance. You cannot eat the wind. What is this? Nice young fellows like Policarpo from the store, poor boy... Are you waiting for some nobleman to come along?

Mrs. Placida swore to me that she was not waiting for any nobleman. It was her character. She wanted to be married. She knew quite well that her mother had not been, and she knew some women who only had lovers. But it was her character, and she wanted to be married. She did not want her daughter to be anything else either. She worked hard, burning her fingers on the stove and her eyes sewing by the candleholder, in order to eat and not lose everything. She grew thin, fell ill, lost her mother, buried her with the help of charity, and kept on working. Her daughter was fourteen, but she was very frail and did not do anything except flirt with the sharpers who hung around the window grating. Mrs. Placida worried a great deal, taking her daughter with her when she had to deliver sewing jobs. The people in the shops stared and winked, convinced that she had brought her along in order to catch a husband or something else. Some made bad jokes, some paid their respects. The mother came to receive offers of money...

She paused for a moment and then went on:

— My daughter ran away. She went off with a fellow, I do not even want to know about it... She left me alone, but so sad, so sad that I wanted to die. I had nobody else in the world, and I was getting old and sick. It was around that time that I got to know Lady Virgilia's family, good people who gave me something to do and even gave me a home. I was there for several months, a year, over a year, a house servant, sewing. I left when lady Virgilia got married. Then I lived as God willed. Look at my fingers, look at these hands... — And she showed her thick, wrinkled hands, the tips of her fingers pricked by needles... — You do not get this way by chance, sir. God knows how you get this way... Luckily, Lady Virgilia took care of me, and you too, doctor... I was afraid of ending up begging on the street...

As she said the last phrase, Mrs. Placida shuddered. Then, as if recovered, she seemed to be worrying about the impropriety of that confession to the lover of a married woman, and she started laughing, retracting, calling herself silly, "full of trust," as her mother used to tell her. Finally, tired of my silence, she left the room. I stayed there, staring at my shoe tops.

CHAPTER LXXV
TO MYSELF

Given the possibility that one of my readers might have skipped the previous chapter, I must observe that it is necessary to read it in order to understand what I said to myself right after Mrs. Placida left the room. What I said was this:

Well, then, the sexton of the cathedral, assisting at mass one day, saw the lady, who was to be his partner in the creation of Mrs. Placida, come in. He saw her on other days, for whole weeks, he liked her, he joshed with her, stepped on her foot as he went up to the altar on feast days. She liked him, they grew close, made love. From that conjunction of empty sensuality, Mrs. Placida came into bloom. It must be believed that Mrs. Placida still could not talk when she was born, but if she could have, she might have said to the authors of her days: — Here I am. Why did you call me? — And the sacristan and the woman would naturally have answered her: — We called you to burn your fingers on pots, your eyes on sewing, to eat poorly or not at all, to go from one place to another in drudgery, getting ill and recovering only to get ill and recover once again, sad now, then desperate, resigned tomorrow, but always with your hands on the pot and your eyes on the sewing until one day you end up in the mire or the hospital. That is why we called you in a moment of sympathy.

CHAPTER LXXXVI
MANURE

Suddenly my conscience gave me a tug, accusing me of having Mrs. Placida surrender her virtue, assigning her a shameful role after a long life of work and privation. The mediator was no better than the concubine, and I had lowered her to that position by dint of gifts and money. That was what my conscience was saying to me. I spent a few minutes not knowing how to answer it. It added that I had taken advantage of the fascination Virgilia held over the ex-seamstress, of the latter's gratitude, ultimately, of her need. It made note of Mrs. Placida's resistance, her tears during the early days, her grim expressions, her silences, her lowered eyes, and my skills at bearing up under all that until I could overcome it. And it tugged at me again in an annoyed and nervous way.

I agreed that it was how it was, but I argued that Mrs. Placida's old age was not protected from beggary. It was compensation. If it had not been for our love affair, most likely Mrs. Placida would have ended up like so many other human creatures, from which it can be deduced that vice often is manure for virtue. And that does not prevent virtue from being a fragrant and healthy flower. My conscience agreed, and I went to open the door for Virgilia.

CHAPTER LXXVII
INTERVIEW

Virgilia entered, smiling and relaxed. Time had carried away her frights and vexations. How sweet it was to see her arrive during the early days, shameful and trembling! She traveled in a carriage, her face veiled, wrapped in a kind of collared cape that disguised the curves of her figure. The first time she had dropped onto the settee, breathing heavily, scarlet, with her eyes on the floor. And — word of honor! — never, on any occasion, had I found her so beautiful, maybe because I had never felt myself more flattered.

Now, however, as I was saying, the frights and vexations were over. Our meetings were entering the chronometric stage. The intensity of love was the same, the difference was that the flame had lost the mad brightness of the early days and had become a simple beam of rays, peaceful and constant, as with marriages.

— I am very angry with you — she said, as she sat down.
— Why?
— Because you did not go there yesterday, as you told me you would. Damiao asked several times if you were not coming, at least for tea. Why you did not come?

As a matter of fact, I had broken the promise I had made, and the fault was all Virgilia's. A matter of jealousy. That splendid woman knew that she was, and she liked to hear it, whether aloud or in a whisper. Two days before at the Baroness' house, she had waltzed twice with the same dandy after listening to his courtly talk in a corner by the window. She was so merry! So open! So self-possessed! When she caught an interrogative and threatening wrinkle between my eyebrows, she showed no surprise, nor became suddenly serious, but she threw the dandy and his courtly talk overboard. Then she came over to me, took my arm, and led me into the other room, with fewer people, where she complained of being tired and said many other things with the childlike air, she was accustomed to assuming on certain occasions, and I listened to her almost without replying.

Now, once more, it was difficult for me to reply, but I finally told her the reason for my absence... No, eternal stars, I never saw such startled eyes. Her mouth half-open, her eyebrows arched, a visible, tangible stupefaction that was undeniable, such was Virgilia's immediate reply. She nodded her head with a smile of pity and tenderness that confused me completely.

— Oh, you...!

And she went to take off her hat, cheerful, jovial, like a girl just back from school. Then she came over to me where I was seated, tapped me on the head with one finger, repeating: — This, this — and I could not help laughing, too, and everything ended up in fun. It was obvious that I was wrong.

CHAPTER LXXVIII
THE PRESIDENCY

On a certain day, months later, Lobo Neves arrived home, saying that he might get the position of president of a province. I looked at Virgilia, who had grown pale. Seeing her grow pale, he asked:
— What? Didn't you like it, Virgilia? Virgilia shook her head.
— I am not too pleased — it was her answer.

Nothing more was said, but at night, Lobo Neves brought up the project again, a little more resolutely than during the afternoon. Two days later, he declared to his wife that the presidency was all set. Virgilia could not hide the dislike it caused her. Her husband replied to everything by saying he had political needs.

— I cannot refuse what they ask of me. And it even suits us, our future, our coat-of-arms, my love, because I promised that you would be a marchioness, and you are not even a baroness yet. Are you going to say I am ambitious? I really am, but you must not put any weight on the wings of my ambition.

Virgilia was disoriented. The next day, I met her at Gamboa's house, waiting for me, and I thought she was sad. She told everything to Mrs. Placida, who was trying to console her as best as she could. I was no less downcast.

— You have to come with us — Virgilia told me.

— Are you crazy? It would be foolishness.

— What then...?

— Then we have to change the plan.

— It is impossible... Has he already accepted?

— It seems so.

I stood up, tossed my hat onto a chair, and started pacing back and forth, not knowing what to do. I thought for a long time and could not come up with anything. Finally, I went over to Virgilia, who was seated, and took her hand. Mrs. Placida went over to the window.

— My whole existence is in this little hand — I said. You are responsible for it; do whatever you think is best.

Virgilia had an afflicted expression. I went over to lean against the sideboard across from her. A few moments of silence passed. We could only hear the barking of a dog and, I am not sure, the sound of the water breaking on the beach. Seeing that she was not saying anything, I looked at her. Virgilia had her eyes on the floor, motionless, dull, her hands resting on her knees with her fingers crossed in a sign of extreme despair. On another occasion, for a different reason, I would certainly have thrown myself at her feet and sheltered her with my reason and my tenderness. Now, however, it was necessary to have her make her own effort to sacrifice for the responsibility of our life together and, consequently, not shelter her, leave her to herself, and go away. That was what I did.

— I repeat, my happiness is in your hands — I said.

Virgilia tried to hold me back, but I was already out the door. I managed to hear an outburst of tears, and, I can tell you, I was on the point of going back to stanch them with a kiss, but I got control of myself and left.

CHAPTER LXXIX
COMMITMENT

I would never finish if I had to recount every detail of how I suffered during the first few hours. I vacillated between wanting and not wanting, between the compassion that was pulling me toward Virgilia's house and a different feeling — selfishness, let us suppose — that was telling me: stay here. Leave her alone with the problem, leave her alone because she will solve it in favor of love. I think those two forces were equal in intensity; they attacked and resisted at the same time, fervently, tenaciously, and neither was giving way at all. Sometimes I felt a tiny bite of remorse. It seemed to me that I was abusing the weakness of a guilty woman in love, without any sacrifice or risk on my part. And when I was about to surrender, love would come again and repeat the selfish advice to me, and I would remain irresolute and restless, desirous of seeing her and wary that the sight of her would lead me to share the responsibility of the solution.

Finally, a commitment between selfishness and compassion: I would go see her at her home, and only at her home, in the presence of her husband so as not to say anything to her, waiting for the effect of my intimation. In that way, I would be able to conciliate the two forces. Now, as I write this, I like to think that the commitment was a fraud, that compassion was still a form of selfishness, and that the decision to go console Virgilia was nothing more than a suggestion of my own suffering.

CHAPTER LXXX
AS SECRETARY

The next night I went to Lobo Neves' house. They were both at home, Virgilia was quite sad, he was quite jovial. I could swear that she was feeling a certain relief when our eyes met, full of curiosity and tenderness. Lobo Neves told me about the plans that would bring him the presidency, the local difficulties, the hopes, the solutions. He was so happy, so hopeful! Virgilia, at the other end of the table, pretended to be reading a book, but she would look at me over the page from time to time, questioning and anxious.

— The worst part — Lobo Neves told me — is that I still did not find a secretary.
— No?
— No, and I have an idea.
— Ah!
— An idea... Would you like to travel north? I did not know what to say.
— You are rich, — he went on — you do not need the paltry salary; but if you wanted to do me a favor, you would come along with me as a secretary.

My spirit gave a leap backward, as if I had seen a snake in front of me. I faced Lobo Neves, stared at him demandingly to see if some hidden thought had caught hold of him... Not a shadow of it. His look was direct and open, the calmness of his face was natural, not forced, a calmness sprinkled with joy. I took a deep breath and did not have the courage to look at Virgilia. I could feel her gaze over the page, also asking me the same. And I said yes, I would go. In all truth, a president, a president's wife, a secretary was a way of solving things in an administrative way.

CHAPTER LXXXI
RECONCILIATION

Despite everything, as I left there, I had the shadow of some doubts. I pondered whether or not it would be an insane exposure of Virgilia's reputation, if there was not some other reasonable way of combining the government and Gamboa. I could not find any. The next day, as I got out of bed, my mind was made up, and I resolved to accept the nomination. At midday, my servant came to tell me that a veiled lady was waiting for me in the living room. I hurried out. It was my sister, Sabina.

— It cannot go on like this — she said. — Once and for all, let's make peace. Our family's fallen apart; we must not go on acting like two enemies.
— But that is all I am asking you, sister! — I shouted, reaching out my arms to her. I sat her down beside me, asking her about her husband, her daughter, her business, everything. Everything was fine. Their daughter was as pretty as a picture. Her husband would come and show her to me if I allowed him.
— Come on! I will go see her for myself.
— Will you?

— Word of honor.

— So much the better! — Sabina sighed. — It is time to put an end to all of this. I thought she was fatter and maybe younger-looking. She looked twenty and she was over thirty. Charming, affable, no awkwardness, no resentments. We looked at each other, holding hands, talking about everything and nothing, like two lovers. It was my childhood coming to the surface, fresh, frisky, and golden. The years were falling away like the rows of bent playing cards I fooled with as a child, and they let me see our house, our family, our parties. I bore the memory with some effort, but a neighborhood barber c a m e to mind as he twanged on his classical fiddle and that voice — because up until then, the memory had been mute — that voice out of the past, nasal and nostalgic, moved me to such a degree that...

Her eyes were dry. Sabina had not inherited the morbid yellow flower. What difference did it make? She was my sister, my blood, a part of my mother, and I told her that with tenderness, sincerity... Suddenly, I heard someone knocking on the living room door. I went to open it. It was a five-year old little angel.

— Come in, Sara – Sabina said.

It was my niece. I picked her up, kissed her several times. The little one, frightened, pushed me off on my shoulder with her little hand, writhing to get down... At that moment, a hat appeared in the door, followed by a man, Cotrim, no less. I was so moved that I put the daughter down and threw myself into the arms of the father. That effusion may have disconcerted him a little, because he seemed awkward to me. A simple prologue. Shortly after, we were talking like two good old friends. No allusions to the past, lots of plans for the future, the promise to have dinner at each other's house. I did not fail to mention that the exchange of dinners might have to have a slight interruption because I was thinking of traveling north. Sabina looked at Cotrim, Cotrim at Sabina. Both agreed that the idea made no sense. What the hell could I expect to find up north? Because was it not in the capital, right there in the capital, that I should continue to shine, showing up the young fellows of the time? Because, really, there was not a single one of them who could compare to me. He, Cotrim, had been following me from a distance and, despite a ridiculous quarrel, he had always had an interest, pride, and vanity in my triumphs. He heard what was being said about me on the street and in salons. It was a concert of praise and admiration. And leave all that to go and spend a few months in the provinces without any need to, without any serious reason? Unless it was political...

— Political, precisely — I said.

— Not even for that reason. — And after another silence, he replied: — In any case, come and have dinner with us tonight.

— Of course, I will. But tomorrow or afterward, you have to come and have dinner with me.

— I do not know; I do not know — Sabina objected. — At a bachelor's house... You have to get married, brother. I want a niece, too, do you hear?

Cotrim stopped her with a gesture I did not understand too well. It did not matter. The reconciliation of a family is well worth an enigmatic gesture.

CHAPTER LXXXII
A MATTER OF BOTANY

Let hypochondriacs say what they want: life is sweet.

That was what I was thinking to myself as I watched Sabina, her husband, and her daughter troop down the stairs, sending lots of affectionate words up to where — on the landing — I was sending just as many others down to them. I kept thinking that I really was lucky. A woman loved me, I had the trust of her husband, I was going to be secretary to them both, and I reconciled with my family. What more could I ask for in twenty-four hours?

That same day, trying to prepare people's ideas, I started spreading that I might be going north as provincial secretary in order to fulfill certain political designs of my own. I said so on Ouvidor Street and repeated it the following day at the Pharoux and at the theater. Some people, tying my nomination to that of Lobo Neves, which was already rumored, smiled maliciously, others patted me on the back. At the theater, a lady told me that it was carrying a love of sculpture a bit far. She was referring to Virgilia's beautiful figure.

But the most open allusion I received was at Sabina's house, three days later. It was made by a certain Garcez, an old surgeon, tiny, trivial, and a babbler who was capable of reaching the age of seventy, eighty, or ninety without ever having acquired the austere bearing that marks the gentility of the aged. A ridiculous old age is maybe nature's saddest and final surprise.

— I know, this time you are going to read Cicero — he told me when he heard of the trip.

— Cicero! – Sabina exclaimed.

— What else? Your brother is a great Latinist. He can translate Virgil at sight. Note that it is Virgil and not Virgilia... Do not confuse them...

And he laughed, a gross, vulgar, frivolous laugh. Sabina looked at me, fearful of some reply. But she smiled when she saw me smile and turned her face to hide it. The other people looked at me with expressions of curiosity, indulgence, and sympathy. It was quite obvious that they had not heard anything new. The matter of my love affair was more public than I could have imagined. Nevertheless, I smiled a quick, fugitive, swallowing smile — chattering like the Sintra magpies. Virgilia was a beautiful mistake, and it is so easy to confess a beautiful mistake! At first, I was accustomed to scowling when I heard some reference to our love affair, but — word of honor — inside, I had a warm and flattered feeling. Once, however, it happened that I smiled, and I continued doing so on other occasions. I do not know if there is anyone who can explain the phenomenon. I explain it this way: in the beginning, the contentment, being inner was, in a manner of speaking, that same smile, but only a bud. With the passage of time, the flower bloomed and appeared in the eyes of others. It is a simple matter of botany.

CHAPTER LXXXIII
13

Cotrim drew me out of that pleasure, leading me to the window.

— Do you mind if I tell you something? — he asked. — Do not take that trip. It is unwise, it is dangerous.

— Why?

— You know very well why — he replied. — It is especially dangerous, quite dangerous. Here in the capital, an affair like that gets lost in the mass of people and interests. But in the provinces, it takes on a different shape. And since it is a question of political people, it is really unwise. The opposition newspapers, as soon as they sniff out the business, will proceed to print it in block letters, and out of that will come the jokes, the remarks, the nicknames...

— But I do not understand...

— You do, you do. Really, you would not be much of a friend of ours if you denied what everybody knows. I have known about it for months. I repeat, do not take a trip like that. Bear up under her absence, which is better, and avoid any great scandal and greater displeasure...

He said that and went inside. I remained there, looking at the streetlight on the corner — an old oil lamp — sad, obscure, and curved, like a question mark. What should I do? It was Hamlet's case: to suffer the slings and arrows of fortune or fight against them and subdue them. In other words, to sail or not to sail. That was the question. The streetlight was not telling me anything. Cotrim's words were echoing in the ears of my memory in quite a different way from those of Garcez. Maybe Cotrim was right. But would I be able to separate from Virgilia?

Sabina came over and asked me what I was thinking about. — Nothing — I answered that I was sleepy and was going home. Sabina was silent for a moment. — I know what you need. It is a bride. Let me arrange a bride for you. I left there oppressed, disoriented. Everything is ready for sailing — heart and soul —, and that gatekeeper of social rules appears and asks me for my card of admission. I said to hell with social rules and, along with them, the constitution, the legislative body, the ministry, everything.

The next day, I opened a political newspaper and read that, by a decree dated the 13th, Lobo Neves and I had been named president and secretary of the Province of ***. I immediately wrote to Virgilia and, two hours later, I went to Gamboa. Poor Mrs. Placida! She was getting more and more upset. She asked me if we were going to forget our old lady, if our absence would be for long, and if the province was far away. I consoled her, but I needed consolation myself. Cotrim's objections were bothering me. Virgilia arrived a short time later, lively as a swallow, but when she saw that I was downcast, she got serious.

— What is wrong?
— I am not sure — I said. — I do not know if I should accept...
Virgilia dropped onto the settee, laughing. — Why? — she asked.
— It is not proper. It is too obvious...
— But we are not going anymore.
— How so?

She told me that her husband was going to refuse the nomination, and for reasons that he only told her, charging her with the greatest secrecy. He could not admit it to anyone else. — It is childish, — he observed — it is ridiculous; but in the end, for me, it is a powerful reason. He said that the decree was dated the 13th, and that this number carried a mournful memory for him. His father had died on the 13th, thirteen days after a dinner where thirteen people had been present. The house in which his mother died was number 13. Etc. It was a fateful figure. He could not admit such a thing to the minister. He told him that he had personal reasons for not accepting. I was left — as the reader must be — a little startled at that sacrifice to a number, but since he was an ambitious man, the sacrifice must have been sincere...

CHAPTER LXXXIV
THE CONFLICT

Fateful number, can you remember how many times I blessed you? That, too, must have been the way the red-haired virgins of Thebes blessed the mare with a red mane that took their place in Pelopidas' sacrifice — a charming mare who died there covered with flowers without anyone's ever having given her a word of fond remembrance. Well, I give you one, pitiful mare, not only because of the death you suffered, but because, among the spared maidens, it is not impossible that a grandmother of the Cubas figured... Fateful number, you were our salvation. Her husband did not confess the reason for his refusal to me. He also told me that it was because of personal business, and the serious, convinced face, with which I listened to him, did honor human hypocrisy. He was the only one who had trouble covering up the sadness eating him. He spoke little, was self-absorbed, stayed home reading. On other occasions, he received and then he talked and laughed a lot, with noise and affection. Two things were oppressing him — ambition, which had its wings clipped by a scruple and immediately followed doubt and maybe regret, but regret that would return if the hypothesis were repeated, because the superstitious basis still existed. He had his doubts about the superstition without arriving at its rejection. The persistence of a feeling that was repugnant to the individual himself was a phenomenon worthy of some attention. But I preferred that she could not bear seeing a toad turn on its back.

— What is there about that? — I asked him.
— It is evil — that was his answer.

Only that, the single answer that was worth as much as the book with seven seals for her. It is evil. They had told her that when she was a child, with no other explanation, and she was content with the certainty of harm. The same thing happened when there was talk of pointing at a star. That she knew perfectly well could cause a wart.

A wart or anything else, what was that to someone who had lost the presidency of a province? A gratuitous or cheap superstition can be tolerated. What cannot be is one that carries away part of your life. That was the case with Lobo Neves along with doubt and the terror of having been ridiculous. And the added fact that the minister had not believed in any personal reasons. He attributed Lobo Neves' refusal to political maneuvers, a complicated illusion because of certain aspects. He treated him shabbily, conveyed his lack of trust to colleagues. Incidents arose. Finally, with time, the resigned president went over to the opposition.

CHAPTER LXXXV
THE SUMMIT

A person who escapes danger loves life with new intensity. I started loving Virgilia even more ardently after being on the brink of losing her, and the same things happened to her. In that way, the presidency had only given new life to our original affection. It was the drug with which we made our love more delightful and also more esteemed. During the first days, following that episode, we entertained ourselves by imagining the pain of separation had there been a separation, how sad we both would have been, how far the sea would have stretched out between us like an elastic cloth. And just as children snuggle up to their mother's breast to escape a simple scowl, we fled the imagined danger by squeezing each other with hugs.

— My wonderful Virgilia!
— My love!
— You are mine, aren't you?
— Yours, yours...

And thus, we picked up the thread of our adventure, the same as the Sultaness Scheherazade had done with the thread of her stories. That was, to my mind, the high point of our love, the summit of the mountain from where, for a time, we could make out the valleys to the east and west and the quiet blue sky above us. Having rested for that time, we started descending the slope, holding hands or apart, but descending, descending...

CHAPTER LXXXVI
THE MYSTERY

As I perceived her to be somewhat different on the way down, I did not know whether she was downcast or something else, I asked her what was wrong. She was silent, with an expression of annoyance, upset, fatigue. I persisted, and she told me that... A thin fluid ran through my whole body, a strong, quick, singular sensation that I will never be able to put down on paper. I grasped her hands, pulling her softly to me, and kissed her on the brow with the solemnity of Abraham. She shuddered, took my head between her hands, stared into my eyes, then stroked me with a maternal gesture... There is a mystery there. Let's give the reader time to decipher that mystery.

CHAPTER LXXXVII
GEOLOGY

A disaster occurred around that time: the death of Viegas. Viegas had passed through by chance, his seventy years oppressed by asthma, disjointed by rheumatism, and a damaged heart. He was one of the delicate observers of our adventure. Virgilia nourished great hopes that this old relative, avaricious as a tomb, would protect her son's future by means of some legacy. And if her husband had similar thoughts, he would cover them or choke them off. Everything must be said: there was a certain fundamental dignity in Lobo Neves, a layer of rock that resisted dealing with people. The others, the outer layers, loose earth and sand, had been brought to him by life in its perpetual overflow. If the reader remembers chapter XXIII, they will observe that this is the second time I compared life to an overflow, but they must also notice that this time I added an adjective: perpetual. And God knows the strength of an adjective, above all in new, hot countries.

What is new to this book is Lobo Neves' moral, geology, and probably that of the gentleman reading me. Yes, these layers of character that life alters, preserves, or dissolves according to their resistance, these layers deserve a chapter that I am not going to write so as not to make the narration too long. I am only going to say that the most honest man I ever met in my life was a certain Jacob Medeiros or Jacob Valadares, I cannot remember his name too well. Maybe it was Jacob Rodrigues, in any case, Jacob. He was probity personified. He could have been rich by going counter to the tiniest scruple, and he refused. He let no less than four hundred *contos de réis* slip through his fingers. His probity was so exemplary that it got to be punctilious and wearisome. One day, as we were alone together at his place in the midst of a pleasant chat, they came to tell him that Doctor B., a boring fellow, was looking for him. Jacob told them to say he was not at home.

— It will not work, — a voice roared in the hallway — I am already inside.

And, indeed, it was Doctor B. who appeared at the living room door. Jacob got up to receive him, stating that he thought it was someone else, not him, adding that he was very pleased with his visit, which subjected us to an hour and a half of deadly boredom and no more because Jacob took out his watch. Doctor B. then asked him if he was going out.

— With my wife — Jacob answered.

Doctor B. left, and we gave a sign of relief. Once we got through with our sighing, I told Jacob that he had just lied four times in less than two hours. The first time by contradicting himself, the second by showing happiness at the presence of the intruder, the third by saying that he was going out, the fourth by adding that it was with his wife. Jacob reflected for a moment, then confessed the accuracy of my observation, but he defended himself by saying that absolute veracity was incompatible with an advanced social state and that the peace of cities could only be obtained at the cost of reciprocal deceit... Ah! Now I remember. His name was Jacob Tavares.

CHAPTER LXXXVIII
THE SICK MAN

Needless to say, I refuted such a pernicious doctrine with the most elementary arguments, but he was so annoyed with my observation that he resisted to the end, displaying a certain fictitious heat, perhaps in order to confuse his conscience.

Virgilia's case was a bit more serious. She was less scrupulous than her husband. She openly showed the hope she had for the legacy, showering her relative with all manner of courtesies, attentions, and allurements that could bring on a codicil at the very least. Properly speaking, she flattered him, but I observed that women's flattery is not the same as that of men. The latter tends toward servitude, while the former is mingled with affection. The gracefully curved figure, the honeyed word, their very physical weakness gives women's flattery a local hue, a legitimate look. The age of the person being flattered does not matter. A woman will always have a certain air of mother or sister for his — or even that of a nurse, another feminine position in which the most skilled of men will always lack a *quid*, a fluid, something.

That was what I was thinking when Virgilia broke out into a warm greeting for her old relative. She went to meet him at the door, talking and laughing, took his hat and cane, gave him her arm and led him to a chair, or to the chair, because in the house it was "Viegas' chair," a special piece of work, cozy, made for ill or elderly people. She went to close the nearest window if there was a breeze or open it if it was hot, but carefully saw to it that he would not get a draft.

— So? You are a little stronger today...

— Hah! I had a rotten night. I cannot shake off this hellish asthma.

And the man was puffing, gradually recovering from the fatigue of arriving and climbing the steps, not from the walk because he always came in a carriage. Beside him, a little to the front, Virgilia sat on a stool, her hands on the sick man's knees. In the meantime, the young master came into the room without his usual leaping about, more discreet, meek, serious. Viegas liked him a lot.

— Come here, young fellow — he said to him, and with great effort, he put his hand into his wide pocket, took out a pillbox, put one in his mouth, and gave another to the boy. Asthma pills. The boy said they tasted very good.

This was repeated with variations. Since Viegas liked to play checkers, Virgilia followed his desire, enduring it for a long spell as he moved the pieces with his weak, slow hand. At other times, they went to stroll in the yard, with her offering him her arm, which he would not always accept, saying that he was solid and capable of walking a league. They walked, sat down, walked again, talked about different things, sometimes about some family matter, sometimes about drawing-room gossip, sometimes, finally, about a house he was thinking of building for his own residence, a house of modern design because his was an ancient one, going back to the time of King John VI, like some that can still be seen today (I think) in the *Sao Cristovao* district with their thick columns in front. He thought that the big house where he was living could be replaced, and he had already ordered a sketch from a well-known mason. Ah! Then indeed, Virgilia would see what an old man of good taste was like.

He spoke, as can be imagined, slowly and with difficulty, with pauses for gasping, which were uncomfortable for him and for others. From time to time, he had a coughing attack. Bent over, groaning, he lifted his handkerchief to his mouth and inspected it. When the attack had passed, he went back to the plans for the house, which would have this and that room, a terrace, a carriage house, a thing of beauty.

CHAPTER LXXXIX
IN EXTREMIS

— Tomorrow I am going to spend the day at Viegas' house — she told me once. — Poor thing! He has no one...

Viegas had been put to bed once and for all. His married daughter had fallen ill precisely at that time and could not keep him company. Virgilia went there from time to time. I took advantage of the occasion to spend the whole day next to her. It was two in the afternoon when I got there. Viegas was coughing so hard that it made my chest burn. Between attacks, he was haggling over the price of a house with a skinny fellow. The fellow was offering him thirty *contos de réis*, Viegas demanded forty. The buyer kept insisting, like someone afraid of missing a train, but Viegas would not give in. First, he refused the thirty *contos de réis*, then two more, then three more, and finally fell into a severe attack that shut off his speech for fifteen minutes. The buyer was most solicitous to him, rearranging his pillows, offering him thirty-six *contos de réis*.

— Never! — the sick man groaned.

He asked for a bundle of papers on his desk. Not having the strength to take off the rubber band that held the papers, he asked me to do it. I did. They were the accounts for the construction of the house: bills from the mason, the carpenter, the painter. Bills for the wallpaper in the living room, the dining room, the bedrooms, the studies. Bills for the hardware, the cost of the lot. He was opening them one by one with a trembling hand, and he asked me to read them, and I did.

— See? One thousand two hundred, paper at one thousand two hundred a piece. French hinges... Look, it is a giveaway — he concluded after the last bill was read.

— Well, alright... bit...

— Forty *contos de réis*; I will not give it to you for anything less. The interest alone… Add up the interest...

He coughed out those words in gushes, syllable by syllable, as if they were the crumbs of a crumbling pair of lungs. In their deep sockets, his eyes rolled and flashed, reminding me of a nightlight. Under the sheet, the bony outline of his body was sketched out, coming to points in two places, his knees and his feet. His yellowed, slack, wrinkled skin barely covered the skull of an expressionless face. A white cotton cap covered the cranium that had been shaved by time.

— So? — the skinny fellow said.

I signaled him not to go on, and he was silent for a few moments. The sick man stared at the ceiling, silent, gasping hard. Virgilia turned pale, got up, went to the window. She sensed death and was afraid. I made an attempt to talk about other things. The skinny fellow told an anecdote, but got onto the house again, raising his bid.

— Thirty-eight *contos de réis* — he said.

— Huh?... — the sick man grunted.

The skinny fellow went over to the bed, took his hand, and it felt cold. I went to the sick man, asked him if he felt like something, if he wanted a glass of wine.

— No... no... for... fort... for... for...

He had a coughing attack, and it was his last. Shortly thereafter, he expired, to the great consternation of the skinny fellow, who confessed to me afterward that he was ready to offer forty *contos de réis*. But it was too late.

CHAPTER XC
THE ANCIENT DIALOGUE BETWEEN ADAM AND CAIN

Nothing. No remembrance in the will, not even an asthma pill, so that when it was all over, he would not seem ungrateful or forgetful. Nothing. Virgilia swallowed that bit of failure in anger, and she told me with a certain caution, not because of the matter itself, but because she had mentioned it to her son, whom she knew I did not like very much or very little. I suggested that she should not give any more thought to such a thing. It was best to forget the deceased, an imbecile, a damned skinflint, and think about happy things. Our child, for example...

There, I revealed the deciphering of the mystery, that sweet mystery of a few weeks before, when Virgilia seemed a bit different from what she normally was. A child. A being made from my own being! That was my only thought from that moment on. The eyes of the world, the suspicions of her husband, the death of Viegas, nothing interested me at that time, neither political conflicts, nor revolutions, nor earthquakes, nor anything. I only thought about that anonymous embryo of obscure paternity, and a secret voice told me: it is your child. My child! And I repeated those two words with a certain indefinable voluptuous feeling, and I do not know how many feelings of pride there were. I felt myself a man.

The best thing was that we both talked, the embryo and I, talking about present and future things. The rascal loved me, he was a funny little rogue, giving me little pats on the face with his chubby little hands or then sketching out the shape of a lawyer's robe, because he was going to be a lawyer, and he would make a speech in the chamber of deputies. And his father would listen to him from a tribune, his eyes gleaming with tears. From lawyer he would go back to school again, tiny, slate and books under his arm, or then he would drop into his cradle and stand up again as a man. I sought in vain to fix the spirit in one age, one appearance. That embryo had my eyes, all of my forms, and all of my gestures. He suckled, he wrote, he waltzed, he was interminable in the limits of a quarter-hour — baby and deputy, schoolboy and dandy. Sometimes, beside Virgilia, I forget about her and everything. Virgilia shook me, scolded me for my silence. She said that I did not love her anymore at all. The truth is that I was having a dialogue with the embryo. It was the ancient dialogue between Adam and Cain, a conversation without words, between life and life, mystery and mystery.

CHAPTER XCI
AN EXTRAORDINARY LETTER

Around that time, I received an extraordinary letter accompanied by an object that was no less extraordinary. Here is what the letter said:

"My dear Bras Cubas, "Some time ago, on the Promenade, I borrowed a watch from you.

It gives me great satisfaction to return it to you with this letter. The difference is that it is not the same watch, but another one, I will not say better, but equal to the first. Que *voulez-vous, monseigneur,* — as Figaro said, — *c'est la misère.* Many things happened since our encounter. I will tell them in detail if you do not slam the door on me. Know, then, that I am not wearing those caduceus boots nor put on a famous frock coat whose flaps have been lost in the night of the ages. I gave up my step on the Sao Francisco stairs. Finally, I had lunch.

With that said, I ask your permission to come by one of these days to place a piece of work before you, the fruit of long study, a new philosophical system that not only explains and describes the origin and consummation of things, but takes a great step beyond Zeno and Seneca, whose stoicism was really a child's play alongside my moral recipe. This system of mine is singularly astonishing. It rectifies the human spirit, suppresses pain, assures happiness, and will fill our country with great glory. I call it Humanitism, from *Humanitas*, the guiding principle of things. My first inclination showed great presumption. It was to call it *Borbism*, from Borba, a vain title as well as being crude and bothersome. And it was certainly less expressive. You will see, my dear Bras Cubas, you will see that it is truly a monument. And if there is anything that can make me forget the bitterness of life, it is the pleasure of finally having grasped truth and happiness. There they are in my hand, those two slippery things. After so many centuries of struggle, research, discovery, systems, and failures, they are now in the hands of man. Goodbye for now, my dear Bras Cubas. Remembrances from

Your old friend,

JOAQUIM BORBA DOS SANTOS".

I read this letter without understanding it. It was accompanied by a pouch containing a handsome watch with my initials engraved on it, along with these words: *A Remembrance of Old Quincas*. I went back to the letter, read it slowly, attentively. The return of the watch excluded any idea of a scam. The lucidity, the serenity, the conviction — a touch boastful, of course — seemed to eliminate any suspicion of lunacy. Naturally, Quincas Borba came into an inheritance from some relative of his in Minas Gerais and the abundance had given him back his early dignity. I will not say entirely so. There are things that cannot be recouped completely, but, still, regeneration was not impossible. I put the letter and the watch away and waited for the philosophy.

CHAPTER XCII
AN EXTRAORDINARY MAN

Let me put an end to extraordinary things now. I had just put away the letter and watched when a thin, middling man came to see me with a note from Cotrim inviting me to dinner. The bearer was married to a sister of Cotrim's and had just arrived from the north a few days before. His name was Damascene, and he had been involved in the revolution of 1831. He himself told me that within the space of five minutes. He had left Rio de Janeiro because of a disagreement with the Regent, who was an ass, a little less of an ass than the minister who served under him. Furthermore, revolution was knocking at the door again. At that point, even though his political ideas were somewhat muddled, I managed to get an organized and formulated idea of the government of his preference: it was moderate despotism — not with sweet talk, as they say elsewhere, but with the plumed helmets of the National Guard, except that I could not tell whether he wanted a despotism of one, three, thirty, or three hundred people. He had opinions on many different things, among them the development of the African slave trade and the expulsion of the English. He liked the theater very much. As soon as he arrived, he went to the Sao Pedro Theater where he saw a superb drama, *Maria Joana*, and a very interesting comedy, *Kettly, or the Return to Switzerland*. He had also enjoyed *Deperini* very much in *Sappho* or *Anna Boleyn*, he could not remember which. But Candiani! Yes, sir, she was a top-drawer. Now he wanted to hear *Ernani*, which his daughter sang at home to the piano: *Ernani, Ernani, involami...* — And he said that standing up and half-singing; those things only reached the north as an echo. His daughter was dying to hear all the operas. His daughter had a lovely voice. And taste, very good taste. Oh, he had been so anxious to return to Rio de Janeiro. He had already gone up and down the city, filled with nostalgia... He swore that in some places, he felt like crying. But he would never sail again. He got very sick on board, like all the other passengers, except for an Englishman ... The English could go to hell! Things would never be right until they all went to hell. What can England do to us? If he could find some stout-hearted men, he could expel those Limeys in one night... Thank God he was a patriot — and he pounded his chest — which was not surprising, because it was in the family. He was descended from a very patriotic old captain-major. Yes, he was not a nobody. If the occasion arose, and he had to show what kind of wood his boat was made of... But it was getting late, and I told him that I would not miss dinner and for him to expect me there for a longer chat. I took him to the living room door. He stopped, saying that he felt very close to me. When he got married, I was in Europe. He knew my father, an upright man, he had joined in a dance at a famous ball at *Praia Grande*... Things! Things! He would talk about it later, it was getting late, and he had to carry the answer to Cotrim. He left. I closed the door behind him...

CHAPTER XCIII
THE DINNER

What torture the dinner was! Fortunately, Sabina seated me next to Damascene's daughter, Ms. Eulalia, or, more familiarly, Ms. Lolo, a charming girl, a little bashful at first, but only at the beginning. She lacked elegance, but she made up for it with her eyes, which were superb and had the only defect of being fixed on me, except when they went down to her plate. But Ms. Lolo ate so little that she scarcely looked at her meal. Later in the night, she sang. Her voice was, as her father had said, "quite lovely." Nevertheless, I slipped away. Sabina came to the door with me and asked me what I thought of Damascene's daughter.

— Nice enough.

— Very nice, don't you think? — she put in. — She needs a little refining, but what a good heart! She is a pearl! She could be a good bride for you.

— I do not like pearls.

— Grumpy! When are you going to settle down? When you fall off the tree, when you are ripe, I know. Well, my fine fellow, whether you want it or not, you are going to marry Ms. Lolo.

And as she said that, she tapped my face with her fingers, light as a dove, and at the same time, firm and resolute. Good Lord! Could that have been the reason for the reconciliation? I was a bit disconsolate with the idea, but a mysterious voice was calling me to the Lobo Neves' house. I said goodbye to Sabina and her threats.

CHAPTER XCIV
THE SECRET CAUSE

— How is my dear mother?

At that word, Virgilia pouted as always. She was by a window, all alone, looking at the moon, and she greeted me merrily, but when I mentioned our child, she pouted. She did not like that mention; she was bothered by my anticipated paternal caresses. I, for whom she was now a sacred person, a divine ampulla, left her alone. I imagined at first that the embryo, that unknown figure entering into our adventure, had brought back her sense of sin. I was wrong. Virgilia had never seemed more expansive, less reserved, or less concerned about other people and her husband. There was no remorse. I also imagined that the conception might have been nothing but an invention, a way of tying me to her, a resource that would not last long and maybe was beginning to bother her. The hypothesis was not absurd. My sweet Virgilia sometimes lied, and so gracefully!

That night I discovered the real reason. It was fear of childbirth and the annoyance of pregnancy. She had suffered a great deal with the birth of her first child. During that hour, made up of minutes of life and minutes of death, she had experienced the chills of the gallows in her imagination. As for the annoyance, it was complicated all the more by the forced deprivation of certain habits of her elegant life. That must have been it, most certainly. I told her to understand, scolding her a little for my rights as a father. Virgilia stared at me. She immediately turned her eyes away and smiled in an incredulous way.

CHAPTER XCV
FLOWERS OF YESTERYEAR

Where are they, the flowers of yesteryear? One afternoon, after a few weeks of gestation, the whole structure of my paternal dreams crumbled. The embryo went away at the point when you could not tell Laplace from a turtle. I got the news from the mouth of Lobo Neves, who left me in the living room and accompanied the doctor to the bedroom of the frustrated mother. I leaned against the window, looking out into the yard where the orange trees were green, with no flowers. Where had they gone, the flowers of yesteryear?

CHAPTER XCVI
THE ANONYMOUS LETTER

I felt a touch on my shoulder. It was Lobo Neves. We faced each other for a few minutes, mute, inconsolable. I asked about Virgilia, then we stayed chatting for half an hour. At the end of that time, a letter was brought to him. He read it, turned very pale, and folded it with a trembling hand. I think I noticed a movement in him as if he wanted to pounce on me, but I cannot remember well. What I remember clearly is that over the following days, he greeted me coldly and taciturnly. A few days later, in Gamboa, Virgilia finally told me everything.

Her husband had shown her the letter as soon as she recovered. It was anonymous, and it informed about us. It did not say everything. It said, for example, of our outside meetings. It limited itself to cautioning him about our intimacy and added that the suspicions were a matter of public knowledge. Virgilia read the letter and said with indignation that it was vile slander.

— Slander? — Lobo Neves asked.
— Vile.

Her husband took a deep breath, but as he went back to the letter, it seemed that every word in it was making a negative sign with its finger, every letter was crying out against his wife's indignation. That man, otherwise intrepid, was now the most fragile of creatures. Maybe his imagination was showing him that famous eye of public opinion staring sarcastically at him from a distance with its rascal look. Maybe an invisible voice was repeating into his ear the hints that he had previously heard or mentioned. He demanded that his wife confess everything to him, because he would forgive her everything. Virgilia saw that she was safe. She pretended to be irritated over his insistence, swore that she had only heard words of jest and courtesy from me. The letter must have been from some luckless suitor. And she named a few— one who had flirted with her openly for three weeks, another who had written her a letter, and still others, and others. She gave him their names, the circumstances, studying her husband's eyes, and ended up saying that in order not to give the slander any room, she would treat me in such a way that I would not go back there.

I listened to all this a little perturbed, not by the addition of the dissimulation it would be necessary to employ from then on until I kept completely away from the Lobo Neves house, but by Virgilia's moral calm, her lack of upset, fear, memories, and even remorse, Virgilia noticed my concern, lifted my head, because I was staring at the floor then, and told me with a certain bitterness:

— You do not deserve the sacrifices I am making for you.

I did not say anything to her. It was useless to have her ponder how a little despair and terror would give our situation the caustic taste of the early days. But if I told her that it could have been possible that, slowly and artificially, she would reach that touch of despair and terror. I did not say anything to her. She was tapping the floor nervously with the tip of her shoe. I went over and kissed her on the forehead. Virgilia drew back as if it had been the kiss of a dead man.

CHAPTER XCVII
BETWEEN THE MOUTH AND THE FOREHEAD

I can sense that the reader shuddered — or should have shuddered. Naturally, the last words suggested three or four reflections for him. Take a good look at the picture. In a little house in Gamboa, two people who love each other for a long time, one leaning over the other, one giving her a kiss on the forehead, and the other drawing back as if she felt the contact of the mouth of a corpse. There you have in the short space between mouth and forehead, before the kiss and after it, there you have enough room for a lot of things — the contraction of resentment — the wrinkle of mistrust — or, finally, the pale and drowsy nose of satiety...

CHAPTER XCVIII
SUPPRESSED

We separated in a happy mood. I had dinner and reconciled with the situation. The anonymous letter brought back the salt of mystery and the pepper of danger to our adventure, and in the end, it was good that Virgilia had not lost her self-control in that crisis. That night, I went to the Sao Pedro Theater. They were putting on a great play in which Estela was bringing out tears. I went in, ran my eyes over the cabins. In one of them, I saw Damascene and his family. The daughter was dressed in a new elegance and a certain stylishness, something difficult to explain because the father only earned enough to go into debt. Maybe that was the reason.

I went to visit them during intermission. Damascene greeted me with lots of words, his wife with lots of smiles. As for Ms. Lolo, she did not take her eyes off me. She seemed prettier to me than at the time of the dinner. I found in her a certain ethereal softness wedded to the polish of earthly forms — a vague expression worthy of a chapter in which everything must be vague. Really, I do not know how to tell you, but I did not feel too bad besides the girl who was dressed smartly in a fine dress, a dress that gave me the itching of a Tartuffe. As I contemplated how it chastely and completely covered her knee, I made a subtle discovery, namely, that nature foresaw human clothing, a condition necessary for the development of our species. Habitual nudity, given the multiplicity of the works and cares of the individual, would tend to dull the senses and retard sex, while clothing, deceiving nature, sharpens and attracts desires, activates them, reproduces them, and, consequently, drives civilization. A blessed custom that gave us Othello and transatlantic packets!

I had an urge to suppress this chapter. This is a slippery slope. But, after all, I am writing my memoirs and not yours, my peaceable reader. Alongside the charming maiden, I seemed to be taken with a double and indefinable feeling. She was the complete expression of Pascal's duality, *l'ange et la bête*, with the difference that the Jansenist would not admit the simultaneity of the two natures, while there they were quite together, — *l'ange*, who was saying certain heavenly things — and *la bête*, who... No, I am most certainly going to suppress this chapter.

CHAPTER XCIX
IN THE AUDIENCE

In the audience, I found Lobo Neves chatting with some friends. We talked superficially, coldly, both constrained. But during the next intermission, with the curtain about to go up, we ran into each other in one of the corridors where there was nobody about. He came over to me with great affability and laughter, pulled me into one of the theater's bay windows, and we talked for a long time, mostly he, who seemed the quietest of men. I got to ask him about his wife. He answered that she was fine, but then he turned the conversation to general matters, expansive, almost jolly. Whoever wants, make a guess as to the cause of the difference. I fled from Damascene, who was spying on me from the door of his cabin.

I did not hear any of the second act, neither the words of the actors nor the applause of the audience. Leaning back in my chair, I was picking the shreds of my conversation with Lobo Neves out of my memory, re-creating his manners, and I concluded that the new situation was much better. All we needed was Gamboa. Visiting the other house would only sharpen suspicions. We could rigorously go without speaking every day. It was even better; it put the longing during our breaks back into our love. Besides, I was going on forty, and I was not anything, not even a district elector. It was urgent that I do something, if only for the love of Virgilia, who would be proud to see my name shine... I think that there was loud applause at that moment, but I cannot swear to it. I was thinking about something else.

Multitude, whose love I coveted until death, was how I got my revenge on you sometimes. I let mankind bustle around my body without hearing them, just as the Prometheus of Aeschylus did with his torturers. Oh, did you try to chain me to the rock of your frivolity, your indifference, or your agitation? Fragile chains, my friends. I would break them with the action of a Gulliver. It is quite ordinary to go off to ponder in the wilderness. The voluptuous, extraordinary thing is for a man to insulate himself in a sea of gestures and words, of nerves and passions, and declare himself withdrawn, inaccessible, absent. The most they can say when he becomes himself again — that is, when he becomes one of the others — is that he comes down from the world of the moon. But the world of the moon, that luminous and prudent garret of the brain, what else is it if not the disdainful affirmation of our spiritual freedom? For God, that is a good way to end a chapter.

CHAPTER C
THE PROBABLE CASE

If this world was not a region of inattentive spirits, it would not be necessary to remind the reader that I am only attesting to certain laws when, in truth, I possess them. With others, I restrict myself to the admission of their probability. An example of the second case is the basis of the present chapter, whose reading I recommend to all people who love the study of social phenomena. It would seem, and it is not improbable, that there exists between the events of public life and those of private life a certain reciprocal, regular, and maybe periodic action — or, to use an image, something similar to the tides on the beach in Flamengo and others equally surging. Indeed, when the wave attacks the beach, it floods it for several feet inland. But those same waters return to the sea with variable force and go on to form part of the wave about to come, which must return the same as the first. That is the image. Let's have a look at its application.

I said elsewhere that Lobo Neves, nominated for president of a province, had turned down the nomination because of the date of the decree, which was the 13th. A serious act whose consequence was the break between the minister and Virgilia's husband. In that way, the private event of the evil omen of a number produced the phenomenon of political discord. It remains to be seen how, sometimes afterward; a political event determines a cessation of motion in private life. Since it is not suitable to the method of this book to describe that other phenomenon immediately, I shall limit myself, for now, to say that Lobo Neves, four months after our meeting in the theater, made peace with the minister, a fact that the reader must not lose sight of if he wishes to penetrate the subtlety of my thought.

CHAPTER CI
THE DALMATIAN REVOLUTION

It was Virgilia who gave me the news of her husband's political turnaround one certain October morning between eleven o'clock and noon. She talked to me about meetings, conversations, a speech...

— So, this time you are going to become a baroness — I interrupted.

She turned down the corners of her mouth and shook her head from side to side. But that gesture of indifference was contradicted by something less definable, less clear, an expression of pleasure and expectation. I do not know why, but I imagined that the imperial letter of nomination was capable of drawing her into virtue, I will not say because of virtue in herself, but out of gratitude for her husband. Because she was sincerely in love with nobility. One of the greatest displeasures to come up in our lives was the appearance of a dandy from a legation — let us call it the legation of Dalmatia — Count B.V., who chased after her for three months. That man, a genuine nobleman by blood, had turned Virgilia's head a little, for she, among other things, had a diplomatic vocation. I cannot get to what might have become of me if a revolution had not broken out in Dalmatia that overthrew the government and cleaned out its embassies. The revolution was bloody, painful, formidable. With every ship arriving from Europe, the newspapers described the horrors, calculated the bloodshed, counted the heads. Everybody was seething with indignation and mercy... Not I; inside, I blessed the tragedy that had removed a pebble from my shoe. And, then, Dalmatia was so far away!

CHAPTER CII
AT REST

But this same man, who was overjoyed by the departure of the Other, a while later practiced... No, I will not talk about it on this page. Let that chapter wait for when my annoyance is at rest. A crass, low act, with no possible explanation... I repeat it, I am not going to explain the matter on this page.

CHAPTER CIII
DISTRACTION

— No, sir, it is wrong. Excuse me, but it is wrong.

Mrs. Placida was right. No gentleman arrives an hour late to the place where his lady is waiting for him. I came in panting, Virgilia had left. Mrs. Placida told me that she had waited a long time, that she had gotten annoyed, that she had wept, that she had sworn contempt for me, and other things that our housekeeper said with sobs in her voice, asking me not to abandon her lady, that it was being very unfair to a girl who had sacrificed everything for me. I explained to her then that it was a mistake... And it was not. I think that it was only a distraction. A word, a conversation, an anecdote, anything. Only a distraction.

Poor Mrs. Placida! She was really upset. She was walking back and forth, shaking her head, breathing heavily, peeping through the blind. Poor Mrs. Placida! With what skill she tucked in, caressed, and pampered the wiles of our love! What a fertile imagination for making the hours more pleasurable and briefer! Flowers, candies — the delicate candies of other times — and lots of laughter, lots of caressing, laughter and caressing that grew with time, as though she wanted to preserve our adventure or give it back its first bloom. Our confident and housekeeper forgot nothing, not even lies, because she mentioned signs and longings she had not witnessed. Nothing, not even calumny, because once she even accused me of a new love. — You know I could not love any other woman – that was my answer, when Virgilia talked to me about something similar. And those simple words, with no protest or reproof, dissipated Mrs. Placida's calumny and left her sad.

— All right — I said, after a quarter of an hour. — Virgilia must recognize that I was not at all to blame... Do you want to write a letter to her right now?

— She must be very sad, the poor thing! Look, I do not want anyone to die, but if you, sir, but if you ever get to where you could marry my lady, then, yes, you will see what an angel she is.

I remember that I turned my face away and looked at the floor. I recommend that gesture to people who do not have an answer ready, or even those who are reluctant to face the pupils of other eyes. In such cases, some prefer to recite a stanza from the *Lusiads*, while others adopt the resource of whistling *Norma*. I kept the gesture mentioned. It is simpler, and it calls for less effort.

Three days later, everything had been explained. I imagine that Virgilia was a little startled when I asked forgiveness for the tears she had shed on that occasion. I cannot remember if inside I attributed them to Mrs. Placida. Indeed, it could have been that Mrs. Placida had wept when she saw her disappointment, and through a phenomenon of vision, the tears she had in her own eyes seemed to be falling from Virgilia's. Whatever it was, everything had been explained, but not forgiven, much less forgotten. Virgilia had some harsh things to say to me, threatened me with separation, and ended up praising her husband. He was a worthy man, quite superior to me, charming, a model of courtesy and affection. That is what she said while I, sitting with my hands on my knees, looked at the floor, where a fly was dragging an ant that was biting its leg. Poor fly! Poor ant!

— But, will not you say anything? — Virgilia asked, standing in front of me.

— What is there for me to say? I explained everything. You insist on getting angry. What is there for me to say? Do you know what I think? I think you are tired, that you are bored, that you want to stop...

— Exactly!

She put on her hat, her hand trembling, enraged... — Goodbye, Mrs. Placida – she shouted. Then she went to the door. She was going to leave. I grabbed her by the waist. — It is all right, it is all right – I said to her. Virgilia still struggled to leave. I held her back, asked her to stay, and told her to forget about it. She came away from the door and sat down on the settee. I sat down beside her, told her a lot of loving things, some humble, some funny. I am not sure whether our lips got as close as a cambric thread or even closer. That is a matter of dispute. I remember that, during the agitation, one of Virgilia's earrings had fallen off and I leaned over to pick it up and that the fly of a little while back had climbed onto the earring, still carrying the ant on its leg. Then I, with the inborn delicacy of a man of our century, took that pair of mortified creatures into the palm of my hand. I calculated the distance between my hand and the planet Saturn and asked myself what interest there could be in such a wretched episode. If you conclude from it that I was a barbarian, you are wrong, because I asked Virgilia for a hairpin in order to separate the two insects. But the fly guessed my intention, opened its wings, and flew off. Poor fly! Poor ant. And God saw that it was good, as Scripture says.

CHAPTER CIV
IT WAS HIM!

I gave the hairpin back to Virgilia, and she returned it to her hair, and was ready to leave. It was late, it was already three o'clock.

Everything was forgotten and forgiven. Mrs. Placida, who had been watching for the right moment to leave, suddenly shut the window and exclaimed:

— Holy Mother of God! Here comes my lady's husband!

The moment of terror was short, but complete. Virgilia turned the color of the lace on her dress. She ran to the door of the bedroom. Mrs. Placida, who had closed the blind, was also trying to close the inside door. I got ready to wait for Lobo Neves. That short instant passed. Virgilia returned to her senses, pushed me into the bedroom, and told Mrs. Placida to go back to the window. The confident lady obeyed.

It was him. Mrs. Placida opened the door with all sorts of exclamations of surprise: — You're here, sir! Honoring the house of your old woman? Please come in. Guess who is here... You do not have to guess; that is the only reason you came... Come out, my lady.

Virgilia, who was in a corner, ran to her husband. I was spying on them through the keyhole. Lobo Neves came in slowly, pale, quiet, with no furor, and cast a glance about the room.

— What is this? — Virgilia exclaimed. — What are you doing here?

— I was passing by and I saw Mrs. Placida in the window, so I came to say hello to her.
— Thank you so much — Mrs. Placida hastened to say. — And they say old women are worthless... Just look! My lady looks jealous. — And, stroking her: — This angel is the one who never forgot old Placida. Poor thing! She has her mother's exact face. Sit down, sir...
— I cannot stay.
— Are you going home? — Virgilia asked — We can go together.
— I am.
— Give me my hat, Mrs. Placida.
— Here it is.

Mrs. Placida went to get a mirror, opened it in front of her, Virgilia put on her hat, tied the ribbons, fixed her hair, while talking to her husband, who was not saying anything in reply. Our good old lady was prattling too much. It was a way of covering up the shaking in her body. Virgilia, having overcome the first moment, had regained control of herself.

— I am ready! — she said. — Goodbye, Mrs. Placida. Do not forget to come by, did you hear? — The other one promised she would, and she opened the door for them.

CHAPTER CV
THE EQUIVALENCY OF WINDOWS

Mrs. Placida closed the door and dropped onto a chair. I immediately left the bedroom and took two steps on my way out to the street to tear Virgilia away from her husband. That was what I said, and it was good that I said it, because Mrs. Placida held me back by the arms. After a while, I got to imagine that I had only said it so she held me back. But simple reflection is enough to show that after ten minutes in the bedroom, it could only have been a most genuine and sincere gesture. And that was because of the famous law of the equivalency of windows that I had the satisfaction of discovering and formulating in chapter LI. It was necessary to air out one's conscience. The bedroom had a closed window. I opened another one with the gesture of leaving, and I breathed.

CHAPTER CVI
A DANGEROUS GAME

I breathed and sat down. Mrs. Placida was clamoring with exclamations and wailing.

I listened without saying anything. I was pondering to myself whether it might have been better to have shut Virgilia up in the bedroom and to have stayed in the living room. But I immediately realized that it would have been worse. It would have confirmed suspicions, reached the point of an explosion and a bloody scene... It had been so much better that way. But what about afterward? What was going to happen to Virgilia? Would her husband kill her, beat her, lock her up, or throw her out? Those questions ran slowly through my brain, the way little specks and dark commas run across the field of vision of sick or tired eyes. They came and went, with their dry and tragic looks, and I could not grasp one of them and say: it is you, you, and no other.

Suddenly, I saw a black shape. It was Mrs. Placida, who had gone inside, put on her cloak, and was offering to go to the Lobo Neves' house for me. I cautioned her that it was risky, because he would be suspicious of such a quick visit.

— Do not worry — she interrupted me. — I will know how to do it. If he is at home, I will not go in.

She left. I remained there, pondering what had happened and the possible consequences. In the end, it seemed to me that I was playing a dangerous game, and I asked myself if it was not time to stand up and take a little walk. I felt taken by a longing for marriage, by a desire to straighten my life out. Why not? My heart still had things to explore. I did not feel incapable of chaste, austere, pure love. In reality, adventures are the torrential and giddy part of life, the exception, that is. I was weary of them. I may even have felt the prick of some remorse. As soon as I thought about that, I let myself go to follow my imagination. I immediately saw myself married, alongside an adorable woman, looking at a baby sleeping in the arms of a nursemaid, all of us in the back of a shady green yard, and peeping at us through the trees was a strip of blue sky, an extremely blue sky...

CHAPTER CVII
A NOTE

"Nothing happened, but he suspects something. He is very serious and not talking. He just went out. He smiled only once, at our son, after staring at him for a long time, frowning. He did not treat me either badly or well. I do not know what is going to happen. God willing, this will pass. Be very cautious for now, very cautious."

CHAPTER CVIII
THAT IS NOT UNDERSTOOD

There is the drama, there is the tip of Shakespeare's tragic dog ear. That little scrap of paper, scribbled on in part, crumpled by hands, was a document for analysis, which I am not going to do in this chapter, or in the next, or maybe in all the rest of the book. Could I rob the reader of the pleasure of noting for himself the coldness, the perspicacity, and the spirit of those few lines jotted down in haste and, behind them, the storm of a different brain, the concealed rage, the despair that brings on constraint and meditation, because it must be solved in the mud, in blood, or in tears?

As for me, if I tell you that I read the note three or four times that day, believe it, because it is the truth. If I tell you, further, that I reread it the next day, before and after breakfast, you can believe it; it is the naked truth. But if I tell you about how upset I was, you might doubt that assertion a bit and not accept it without proof. Neither then nor even now have I been able to make out what I felt. It was fear, and it was not fear. It was pity, and it was not pity. It was vanity, and it was not vanity. In the end, it was love without love, that is, without delirium, and all that made for a rather complex and vague combination, something that you probably do not understand, as I did not understand it. Let's just suppose that I did not say anything.

CHAPTER CIX
THE PHILOSOPHER

Since it is known that I reread the letter before and after breakfast, it is known, therefore, that I had breakfast, and all that remains to be said is that the breakfast was one of the most frugal of my life: an egg, a slice of bread, a cup of tea. I did not forget that small circumstance. In the midst of so many important things that were obliterated, that breakfast escaped. The main reason might have been my disaster, but it was not. The main reason was a reflection given to me by Quincas Borba, who visited me that day. He told me that frugality was not necessary in order to understand Humanitism, much less to practice it. That philosophy enjoyed easy accommodation with the pleasures of life, including table, theater, and love, and that, quite the contrary, frugality could be an indication of a certain tendency toward asceticism, which was the perfect expression of human foolishness.

— Look at Saint John, — he went on, — he lived off grasshoppers, in the desert, instead of growing fat peacefully in the city and make the Pharisaism in the synagogue lose weight.

God spare me the narration of Quincas Borba's story, which I listened to in its entirety on that sad occasion, a long, complicated yet interesting story. And since I will not be telling the story, I will also dispense with describing his person, which is quite different from the one that appeared to me on the Promenade. I shall be silent. I will only say that if a man's main characteristic is not in his features but in his clothing, he was not Quincas Borba: he was a judge without a robe, a general without a uniform, a businessman without a budget. I noted the perfection of his frock coat, the whiteness of his shirt, the shine of his shoes. His very voice, hoarse before, seemed to have been restored to its original sonority. As for his mannerisms, without having lost the previous vivacity, they no longer had the disorder and were subject to a certain method. But I do not wish to describe him. If I were to speak, for example, about his gold stickpin and the quality of the leather in his shoes, it would initiate a description that I am omitting in the name of brevity. Be satisfied to know that his shoes were made of patent leather. Know, furthermore, that he had inherited a few braces of *contos de réis* from an old uncle in the city of *Barbacena*.

My spirits (allow me a child's comparison here!), my spirits on that occasion were a kind of shuttlecock. Quincas Borba's narration hit it, it went up, and when it was about to drop, Virgilia's note hit it again, and it was hurled into the air once more. It descended, and the episode on the Promenade received it with another stroke, equally firm and effective. I do not think I was born for complex situations. That pushing and pulling of opposite things was getting me off balance. I had an urge to wrap up Quincas Borba, Lobo Neves, and Virgilia's note in the same philosophy and send them to Aristotle as a gift. Nevertheless, our philosopher's narrative was instructive. I especially admired the talent for observation with which he described the gestation and growth of vice, the inner struggles, the slow capitulations, the use of mud.

— Look, — he observed, — the first night I spent on the Sao Francisco stairs, I slept all night long as if it was the softest feather. Why? Because I went gradually from a bed with a mattress to a wooden cot, from my own bedroom to the police station, from the police station to the street...

Finally, he wanted to explain the philosophy to me. I asked him not to. — I am terribly worried today, and I would not pay attention. Come back another time. I am always home. — Quincas Borba smiled in a sly way. Maybe he knew about my affair, but he did not say anything more. He only said these last words to me at the door:

— Come to Humanitism. It is the great bosom for the spirit, the eternal sea into which I dove to bring out the truth. The Greeks made it come out of a well! What a base conception! A well! But that is precisely why they never hit upon it. Greeks, Sub-Greeks, Anti-Greeks, the whole long series of mankind leaned over that well to watch the truth come out, but it was not there. They wore out ropes and buckets. Some of the more audacious ones went down to the bottom and brought up a toad. I went directly to the sea. Come to Humanitism.

CHAPTER CX
31

A week later, Lobo Neves was named president of a province. I clung to the hope of a refusal if the decree was again dated 13th. The date was the 31st, however, and that simple transposition of ciphers eliminated any diabolical substance in them. How deep are the springs of life!

CHAPTER CXI
THE WALL

As it is not my habit to cover up or hide anything, on this page I will talk about the wall. They were ready to embark. In the meantime, at Mrs. Placida's house, I caught sight of a small piece of paper on the table. It was a note from Virgilia. She said she would expect me at night in the yard, without fail. And she ended: "The wall is low on the alley side." I made a gesture of displeasure. The letter seemed uncommonly audacious to me, poorly thought out, even ridiculous. It was not just inviting scandal; it was inviting ridicule along with it. I pictured myself climbing over the wall, even though it was low on the alley side. And just as I was about to get over it, I saw myself in the clutches of a policeman, who took me to the station house. The wall is low! And what if it was low? Virgilia did not know what she was doing, naturally. It was possible that she was already sorry. I looked at the piece of paper, wrinkled, but inflexible. I had the itch to tear it up into thirty thousand pieces and throw them to the wind as the last remnants of my adventure. But I retreated in time. Self-respect, the vexation of running away, the idea of fear... There was nothing to do but go.

— Tell her I will go.
— Where? — Mrs. Placida asked.
— Where she said she expects me.
— She did not say anything to me.
— On this piece of paper.

Mrs. Placida widened her eyes: — But this piece of paper, I found it in your drawer this morning, and I thought that...

I had a strange feeling. I reread the piece of paper, looked at it, and looked at it again. It was, indeed, an old note of Virgilia received during the beginning of our love affair, a certain meeting in the yard, which had, indeed, led to my leaping over the wall, a low and discreet wall. I put the paper away... I had a strange feeling.

CHAPTER CXII
THE PUBLIC OPINION

But it was written that the day was to be one of dubious moves. A few hours later, I ran into Lobo Neves on Ouvidor Street. We talked about the presidency and politics. He took advantage of the first acquaintance who passed and left me after all manner of pleasant words. I remember that he was withdrawn, but it was a withdrawal he was struggling to hide. It seemed to me then (and may the critics forgive me if this judgment of mine is too bold), it seemed to me that he was afraid — not afraid of me, or of himself, or of the law, or of his conscience. He was afraid of public opinion. I imagined that the anonymous and invisible tribunal in which every member accuses and judges was the limit set for Lobo Neves' will. Maybe he did not love his wife anymore, and therefore it was possible that his heart was indifferent to its indulgence in her latest acts. I think (and again, I beg the critics' goodwill), I think he was probably prepared to break up with his wife, as the reader has probably broken with many personal relationships, but public opinion, that opinion that would drag his life along all the streets, would open a minute investigation into the matter, would put together, one by one, all circumstances, antecedents, inductions, proofs, would talk about them in idle backyard conversations, that terrible public opinion, so curious about bedrooms, stood in the way of a family breakup. At the same time, it made vengeance, which would be an admission, impossible. He could not appear resentful toward me without also seeking a conjugal breakup. Therefore, he had to pretend the same ignorance as before and, by deduction, similar feelings.

I think it was quite hard for him. In those days, especially, I saw how hard it must have been for him. But time (and this is another point in which I hope for the indulgence of men who think!), time hardens sensibility and obliterates the memory of things. It was to be supposed that the years would dull the thorns, that removal from events would smooth the sore spots, that a shadow of retrospective doubt would cover the nakedness of reality. In short, that public opinion would occupy itself a bit with other adventures. The son, as he grew up, would try to satisfy the father's ambitions. He would be heir to all his affection. This and constant activity and public prestige and old age, then illness, decline, death, a dirge, an obituary, and the book of life was closed without a single bloody page.

CHAPTER CXIII
WELD

The conclusion, if the previous chapter has one, is that public opinion is a good weld for domestic institutions. It is not entirely impossible that I will develop that thought before finishing the book, but it is also not impossible that I will leave it the way it is. One way or another, public opinion is a good weld, both in domestic order and in politics. Some bilious metaphysicians have arrived at the extreme of presenting it as the simple product of foolish or mediocre people. But it is obvious that even when a concept as extreme as that does not bring out an answer by itself, it is enough to consider the salutary effects of public opinion and conclude that it is the superfine work, of the flower of mankind, namely, the greatest number.

CHAPTER CXIV
END OF A DIALOGUE

— Yes, it is tomorrow. Are you going to come on board?
— Are you crazy? It is impossible.
— So, goodbye!
— Goodbye!
— Do not forget Mrs. Placida. Go see her from time to time. Poor thing! She came to say goodbye to us yesterday. She cried a lot; said I would never see her again... She is a good person, isn't she?
— Certainly.
— If we have to write, she will receive the letters. Goodbye for now, then, until...
— Two years, maybe?
— Oh, no! He says it is only until the elections.
— Is that so? So long, then. Watch out; they are looking at us.
— Who?
— Over there on the sofa. We better move away.
— It is awfully hard for me.
— But we have to. Goodbye, Virgilia!
— See you soon. Goodbye!

CHAPTER CXV
THE LUNCH

I did not see her leave, but at the designated hour, I felt something that was not pain or pleasure, a mixed thing, relief and longing all mixed in together in equal doses. The reader should not be annoyed by this confession. I know quite well that in order to titillate the nerves of fantasy, I should have suffered great despair, shed a few tears, and not eaten lunch. It would have been like a novel, but it would not have been a biography. The naked truth is that I ate lunch, as on every other day, succoring my heart with the memories of my adventure and my stomach with the delicacies of M. Prudhon...

... Old people from my time, maybe you remember that master chef at the Hotel Pharoux, a fellow who, according to what the owner of the place said, had served in the famous Very and Vefour in Paris and later on in the palaces of the Count Mole and the Duke de la Rochefoucauld. He was famous. He arrived in Rio de Janeiro along with the polka... The polka, M. Prudhon, the Tivoli, the foreigners' ball, the Casino, there you have some of the best memories of those times, but above all, the master's delicacies were delicious.

They were, and on that morning, it was as if the devil of a fellow had sensed our catastrophe. Never had ingenuity and art been so favorable to him. What a delight in spices! What a delicacy of meat! What refinement in the shapes! You ate with your mouth, with your eyes, and with your nose. I cannot remember the bill from that day. I know that it was expensive. Oh, the sorrow of it! I had to give a magnificent burial to my love affair. It was going off there, out to sea, off into space and time, and I was staying behind at a corner table with my forty-odd years old, so lazy and so hazy. It was left for me never to see them again, because she might come back, and she came back, but who asked for an outpouring of morning from the evening sunset?

CHAPTER CXVI
THE PHILOSOPHY OF OLD AGES

The end of the last chapter left me so sad that I was capable of not writing this one, of taking a little rest, purging my spirit of the melancholy that encumbers it, and then continuing on. But no, I do not want to waste any time.

Virgilia's departure left me with a sample of what it is like to be widowed. During the first few days, I stayed home, catching flies like Domitian, if Suetonius is telling the truth, but catching them in a particular way, with my eyes. I took them one by one, lying in the hammock in the rear of a large room with an open book in my hands. It was everything: nostalgia, ambitions, a bit of tedium, and a lot of aimless daydreaming. My uncle, the canon, died during that interval, along with two cousins. I did not feel shocked. I took them to the cemetery as one takes money to the bank. What am I saying? As one takes letters to the post office. I sealed the letters, put them in the box, and left it to the postman to see that they were delivered to the right hands. It was also around that time that my niece Venancia, Cotrim's daughter, was born. Some were dying, others were being born. I continued with the flies.

At other times, I was agitated. I opened drawers, shuffled through old letters from friends, relatives, sweethearts (even those from Marcela), and opened all of them, read them one by one, and revived the past... Uninstructed reader, if you do not keep the letters from your youth, you will not get to know the philosophy of old pages someday, and you will not enjoy the pleasure of seeing yourself from a distance, in the shadows, with a three-cornered hat, seven-league boots, and a long Assyrian beard, dancing to the sound of anacreontic pipes. Keep the letters of your youth!

Or, if the three-cornered hat does not suit you, I will use the expression of an old sailor, a friend of Cotrim. I will say that if you keep the letters of your youth, you will find a chance to "sing a bit of nostalgia." It seems that our sailors give that name to songs of the land sung on the high seas. As a poetic expression, it is something that can make you even sadder.

CHAPTER CXVII
THE HUMANITISM

Two forces, however, along with a third, compelled me to return to my usual agitated life. Sabina and Quincas Borba.

My sister was pushing the conjugal candidacy of Ms. Lolo in a truly impetuous way. When I became aware, I practically had the girl in my arms. As for Quincas Borba, he finally laid out Humanitism for me. It was a philosophical system destined to be the ruination of all others.

— Humanitas, — he said — the principle of things, is nothing but man himself divided up into all men. Humanitas has three phases: *the static*, previous to all creation; *the expansive*, the beginning of things; *the dispersive*, the appearance of man; and it will have one more, *the contractive*, the absorption of man and things. The expansion, starting the universe, suggested to Humanitas the desire to enjoy it, and from there the *dispersion*, which is nothing but the personified multiplication of the original substance.

Since that explanation did not seem sufficiently clear to me, Quincas Borba developed it in a deep way, pointing out the main lines of the system. He explained to me that on the one side, Humanitism was related to Brahmanism, namely, in the distribution of men throughout the different parts of the body of Humanitas, but what had only a narrow theological and political meaning in the Indian religion, in Humanitism was the great law of personal worth. Thus, descending from the chest or the kidneys of Humanitas, that is, being strong, was not the same as descending from the hair or the tip of the nose. Therefore, it is necessary to cultivate and temper muscles. Hercules was only an anticipatory symbol of Humanitism. At that point, Quincas Borba pondered whether or not paganism might have reached the truth if it had not been debased by the gallant part of its myths. Nothing like that will occur with Humanitism. In this new church there will be no easy adventures, or falls, or sadness, or puerile joys. Love, for example, is a priestly function, the reproduction of a ritual. Since life is the greatest reward in the universe and there is no beggar who does not prefer misery to death (which is a delightful infusion of Humanitas), it follows that the transmission of life, far from being an occasion of lovemaking, is the supreme moment of the spiritual mass. From all of this, there is truly only one misfortune: that of not being born.

— Imagine, for example, that I had not been born. — Quincas Borba went on — It is positive that I would not be having the pleasure of chatting with you now, of eating this potato, of going to the theater, or, to put it all into one word, living. Note that I am not making a man a simple vehicle of Humanitas. He is a vehicle, a passenger, and a coachman, all at the same time. He is Humanitas itself in a reduced form. Hence, the need for him to worship himself. Do you want proof of the superiority of my system? Think about envy. There is no moralist, Greek or Turkish, Christian or Muslim, who does not thunder against the feeling of envy. Agreement is universal, from the fields of Idumea to the heights of Tijuca. So, then, let go of old prejudices, forget about shabby rhetoric, and study envy, that ever-so-subtle and noble feeling. With every man being a reduction of Humanitas, it is clear that no man is fundamentally opposed to another man, whatever his contrary appearances may be. Thus, for example, the headsman who executes the condemned man can excite the vain clamor of poets. But substantially, it is Humanitas correcting in Humanitas an infraction of the law of Humanitas. I will say the same of an individual who disembowels another. It is a manifestation of the force of Humanitas. There is nothing to prevent (and there are examples) his being disemboweled just the same. If you understood well, you easily understood that envy is nothing but admiration that fights, and since fighting is the main function of mankind, all bellicose feelings are the ones that best serve its happiness. Hence, envy is a virtue.

Why deny it? I was stupefied. The clarity of the exposition, the logic of the principles, the rigor of the deductions, all of that seemed great to the highest degree, and it became necessary for me to break off the conversation for a few minutes while I digested the new philosophy. Quincas Borba could not conceal the satisfaction of his triumph. He had a chicken wing on his plate, and he was gnawing on it with philosophical serenity. I voiced a few objections still, but they were so feeble that he did not waste much time knocking them down.

— In order to understand my system well. — he concluded — it is necessary never to forget the universal principle, distributed and summed up in every man. Look. War, which looks like a calamity, is a convenient operation, which we could call the snapping of Humanitas' fingers; hunger (and he sucked philosophically on his chicken wing), hunger is proof that Humanitas is subject to its own entrails. But I do not need any other documentation of the sublimity of my system than this chicken right here. It nourished itself on corn, which was planted by an African, let us suppose, imported from Angola. That African was born, grew up, and was sold. A ship brought him here, a ship built of wood cut in the forest by ten or twelve men, propelled by sails that eight or ten men sewed together, not to mention the rigging and other parts of the nautical apparatus. In that way, this chicken, which I have lunched on just now, is the result of a multitude of efforts and struggles carried out with the sole aim of satisfying my appetite.

Between cheese and coffee, Quincas Borba demonstrated to me how his system meant the destruction of pain. Pain, according to Humanitism, is a pure illusion. When a child is threatened with a stick, even before being struck, he closes his eyes and trembles. That *predisposition* is what constitutes the basis of the human illusion, inherited and transmitted. It is not enough, of course, to adopt the system in order to do away with pain immediately, but it is indispensable. The rest is the natural evolution of things. Once man gets it completely into his head that he is Humanitas itself, there is nothing else to do but raise his thought up to the original substance in order to prevent any painful sensation. The evolution is so deep, however, that it can only take place over a few thousand years.

A few days later, Quincas Borba read me his great work. It consisted of four handwritten volumes, a hundred pages each, in a cramped hand and with Latin quotations. The last volume was a political treaty based on Humanitas. It was, maybe, the most tedious part of the system, since it was conceived with a formidable rigor of logic. With society reorganized by his method, not even then would war, insurrection, a simple beating, an anonymous stabbing, hunger, or illness be eliminated. But since those supposed plagues were actually errors of understanding, because they were nothing but external movements of the internal substance destined not to have any influence over man except as a simple break in universal monotony, it was clear that their existence would not be a barrier against human happiness. But even when such plagues (a basically false concept) corresponded in the future to the narrow conception of former times, not even then would the system be destroyed, and for two reasons: first, because Humanitas is the creative and absolute substance, every individual would find the greatest delight in the world in sacrificing himself to the principle from which he descends; second, because even then it would not diminish man's spiritual power over the earth, invented solely for his recreation, like the stars, breezes, dates, and rhubarb. Pangloss, he said to me as he closed the book, was not as dotty as Voltaire painted him.

CHAPTER CXVIII
THE THIRD FORCE

The third force that called me into the bustle was the pleasure of making a show and, above all, the incapacity to live by myself. The multitude attracted me; applause was my love. If the idea of the poultice had come to me at that time, who knows? I might not have died so soon and would have been famous. But the poultice did not come. What came was a desire to be active in something, with something, and for something.

CHAPTER CXIX
PARENTHESIS

I want to leave in parentheses, here, half a dozen maxims from the many I wrote down around that time. They are yawns of annoyance. They can serve as epigraphs to speeches that have no subject:

Bear your neighbor's cramp with patience.

———

We kill time; time buries us.

A philosophical coachman used to say that the pleasure of a carriage would be less if we all traveled in carriages.

Believe in yourself, but do not always doubt others.

It is beyond understanding why a Botocudo Indian pierces his lip to adorn it with a piece of wood. This is the reflection of a jeweler.

Do not be annoyed if you are poorly paid for a service. It is better to fall down from the clouds than from a third-story window.

CHAPTER CXX
COMPELLE INTRARE

— No, sir, right now, like it or not, you have to get married — Sabina told me. — What a pretty future! An old bachelor with no children.

No children! The idea of having children gave me a start. The mysterious fluid was running through me again. Yes, it was fitting for me to be a father. The life of a celibate may have certain advantages of its own, but they would be tenuous and purchased at the price of loneliness. No children! No, impossible! I was ready to accept everything, even the alliance with Damascene. No children! Since I had already placed great trust in Quincas Borba by then, I went to see him and laid out my inner movement toward paternity to him. The philosopher listened to me with great excitement. He declared to me that Humanitism was at work in my chest. He encouraged me to get married. He pondered the fact that there were some more guests knocking at the door, etc. *Compelle intrare*, as Jesus said. And he would not leave me without proving that the allegory in the Gospels was nothing but a foretoken of Humanitism, mistakenly interpreted by priests.

CHAPTER CXXI
DOWNHILL

At the end of three months, everything was going along marvelously. The fluid, Sabina, the girl's eyes, the father's desires were among the many impulses driving me toward marriage. The memory of Virgilia appeared at the door from time to time, and with it came a black demon who held a mirror up to my face, in which I saw Virgilia, far away, drowning in tears. But a different demon came, pink, with another mirror in which the figure of Ms. Lolo was reflected, tender, luminous, angelic.

I will not talk about the years. I did not feel them. I will even add that I put them aside one certain Sunday when I went to mass at the chapel on *Livramento* Hill. Since Damascene lived in *Cajueiros*, I accompanied him to mass many times. The hill was still bare of houses except for the old mansion on top, where the chapel was. So, one Sunday as I was descending with Ms. Lolo by the arm, some kind of phenomenon, I do not know what, took place, taking off two years here, four there, then five further on, so that when I got down, I was only twenty years old, just as lively as I had been at that age.

Now, if you want to know under what circumstances the phenomenon took place, all you have to do is read this chapter to the end. We were coming from mass, she, her father, and I. Halfway down the hill, we came upon a group of men. Damascene, who was walking beside us, noticed what it was and went ahead, all excited. We followed along. And this is what we saw: men of all ages, sizes, and colors, some in shirtsleeves, others wearing jackets, others in tattered frock coats, in different positions, some squatting, others with their hands on their knees, these sitting on stones, those leaning against the wall, and all watching the center, with their souls leaning out of the pupils.

— What is it? — Ms. Lolo asked me.

I signaled her to be quiet, carefully opened a path, and they all made room for me with none of them really seeing me. The center held their eyes. It was a cockfight. I saw the two contenders, two roosters with sharp spurs, fiery eyes, and filed beaks. Both were shaking their bloody combs, The breasts of both were without feathers and ruddy- colored; weariness was coming over them. But they kept on fighting, eyes staring at eyes, beak down, beak up, a peck from this one, a peck from that, quivering and enraged. Damascene did not know anything else.

The spectacle had eliminated the whole universe for him. I told him, in vain, that it was time to go down. He did not answer, he did not hear; he was concentrating on the duel. Cockfights were one of his passions.

It was on that occasion that Ms. Lolo tugged me softly on the arm, saying we should be on our way. I accepted her advice and went on with her. I already said that the hill was uninhabited at the time. I also said that we were coming from mass, and since I did not say it was raining, it was clear that the weather was good, a delightful sun. And strong. So strong that I immediately opened the umbrella, held it by the center of the handle, and tilted in a way that was an aid to a page out of Quincas Borba's philosophy: Humanitas kissed Humanitas... That was how the years fell away from me on the way downhill.

We stopped at the base for a few minutes, waiting for Damascene. He arrived after a while, surrounded by bettors and commenting about the fight. One of them, the holder of the bets, was distributing a bundle of old ten banknotes, which the winners took with redoubled joy. As for the roosters, they came along under the arms of their respective owners. One of them had his comb so badly pecked away and bloody that I recognized him immediately as the loser, but I was mistaken — the loser was the other one, who had no comb at all. They both had their beaks open and had trouble breathing, exhausted. The bettors, on the other hand, were merry despite the strong commotion of the fight. They recounted the lives of the contenders, and recalled the deeds of both. I went along in vexation. Ms. Lolo was especially vexed.

CHAPTER CXXII
A VERY DELICATE INTENTION

What had upset Ms. Lolo was her father. The ease with which he had joined the bettors brought out old habits and social affinities, and Ms. Lolo had become afraid that a father-in-law like him would seem unworthy to me. The difference she was making in herself was notable. She studied herself and studied me. An elegant and polished life attracted her, mainly because she thought it was the surest way to blend our personalities. Ms. Lolo observed, imitated, and guessed. At the same time, she undertook an effort to conceal her family's inferiority. On that day, however, her father's manifestation was so great that it made her quite sad. I then sought to get her mind off the matter, telling her a string of jokes and jests, all in good taste. A vain effort that did not make her any happier. Her depression was so deep, she was so obviously downcast, that I came to see in Ms. Lolo the positive intention of separating her cause from her father's cause in my mind. I thought that was a mostly elevated feeling. It was one more affinity we had in common.

— There is no other way — I said to myself. — I am going to pluck that flower out of that swamp.

CHAPTER CXXIII
THE REAL COTRIM

Despite my forty-odd years old, since I loved harmony in the family, I understood that I should not bring up the matter of marriage without first speaking to Cotrim. He listened to me and answered seriously that he had no opinions when it came to his relatives. They might imagine some special interest if he happened to praise the rare qualities of Ms. Lolo. That is why he kept quiet. Furthermore, he was sure that his niece had a real passion for me, but if she consulted him, his advice would be negative. It was not brought about by any hate, he appreciated my good qualities — they could not be more praiseworthy, it was true, and as for Ms. Lolo, he could never deny that she was an excellent bride, but from there to advise marriage there was a wide gap.

— I wash my hands of it completely — he concluded.
— But the other day, you thought I should get married as soon as possible...
— That was something else. I think it is indispensable that you get married, especially with your political ambitions. You must know that celibacy is a drawback in politics. As to the bride, though, I cannot approve, I do not want to, I should not, it is against my honor. I think Sabina went too far, giving you certain hints, according to what she said. But, in any case, she is not a blood relative of Ms. Lolo like me. Look... but no... I will not say...
— Say it.
— No; I will not say anything.

Maybe Cotrim's scruples will seem excessive to someone who does not know that he possesses an extremely honorable character. I myself was unfair to him during the years following my father's will. I recognize now that he was a model. They accused him of avarice, and I think they were right, but avarice is only the exaggeration of a virtue, and virtues should serve as evaluations. Oversupply is better than a deficit. Since he was very cold in his manners, he had enemies who even accused him of being a barbarian. The only fact alleged in that particular case was his frequent sending of slaves to the dungeon, from where they emerged dripping blood. But, alongside the fact that he only sent recalcitrants and runaways, it so happens that, having been long involved in the smuggling of slaves, he had become accustomed to a certain way of dealing that was a bit harsher than the business required, and one cannot honestly attribute to the original nature of a man what is simply the effect of his social relations. The proof that Cotrim had pious feelings could be found in his love for his children and the grief he suffered when Sara died a few months after that. Irrefutable proof, I think, and not the only one. He was the treasurer of a confraternity and brother in several brotherhoods, and even a redeemed brother in one of them, which is not consistent with his reputation for avarice. The truth is that the beneficence did not fall on the ground: the brotherhood (of which he was a judge) ordered a portrait of him in oils to be painted. He was not perfect, needless to say. He had, for example, the bad habit of letting the press know about his several charities — a reprehensible and not praiseworthy custom, I must agree. But he defended himself by saying that good works were contagious when done in public. An argument that is not without some weight. I do believe (and here I give him the highest praise) that he only practiced those occasional charities with the aim of arousing the philanthropy of others, and if such was his intent, I must confess that publicity is a *sine qua non*. In short, he may have been owing a few courtesies, but he did not owe anyone a penny.

CHAPTER CXXIV
AS AN INTERLUDE

What is there between life and death? A short bridge. Nevertheless, if I had not put this chapter together, the reader would have suffered a strong shock, quite harmful to the effect of the book. Jumping from a portrait to an epitaph can be a real and common act. The reader, however, is only taking refuge in the book to escape life. I am not saying the thought is mine. I am saying that there is a grain of truth in it and the form, at least, is picturesque. And, I repeat, it is not mine.

CHAPTER CXXV
EPITAPH

HERE LIES

MS. EULALIA DAMASCENA DE BRITO

DEAD

AT THE AGE OF NINETEEN

PRAY FOR HER!

CHAPTER CXXVI
DISCONSOLATION

The epitaph says everything. It is worth more than my telling you about Ms. Lolo's illness, her death, the despair of the family, the burial.

Just know that she died. I will add that it was on the occasion of the first outbreak of yellow fever. I will not say anything more except that I accompanied her to her final resting place and said goodbye sadly, but without tears. I concluded that maybe I did not really love her.

See now how excess can lead to unawareness. I was pained a little by the blindness of the epidemic that was killing right and left, and also carrying off a young lady who was to be my wife. I could not get to understand the necessity of the epidemic, much less that death. I think that I felt it to be even more absurd than all the other deaths. Quincas Borba, however, explained to me that epidemics were useful for the species, even though disastrous for a certain portion of individuals. He made me take notice that, as horrible as the spectacle might be, there was a very weighty advantage: the survival of the greater number. He got to ask me in the midst of the general mourning if I did not feel some secret joy in having escaped the clutches of the plague. But that question was so absurd that it remained unanswered.

Since I did not talk about the death, I will not tell you about the seventh-day mass. Damascene's sadness was deep. The poor man looked like a ruin. I was with him two weeks later. He was still inconsolable, and he said that the great pain God had inflicted upon him was increased all the more by that inflicted on him by men. He did not tell me anything else. Three weeks later, he got back onto the subject, and then he confessed to me that, in the midst of the irreparable disaster, he would have liked to have had the consolation of the presence of his friends. Only twelve people, and three-quarters of them Cotrim's friends, had accompanied the corpse of his beloved daughter to her grave. And he had sent out eighty notices. I argued that with the losses being so widespread, he could easily forgive that apparent lack of concern. Damascene shook his head in an incredulous and sad way.

— Ah! – he moaned – they abandoned me. Cotrim, who was present, said:

— The ones who came were the ones who had a true interest in you and in us. The eighty would have come as a formality; they would have talked about the government's inertia, druggists' panaceas, the price of houses, or something like that...

Damascene listened in silence, shook his head again, and sighed:

— But they should have come!

CHAPTER CXXVII
FORMALITY

It is a great thing to have received a particle of wisdom from heaven, the gift of finding the relationship between things, the faculty of comparing them, and the talent for drawing a conclusion! I had a psychic distinction. I am thankful for it, even now, at the bottom of my grave. In fact, the ordinary man, if he had heard Damascene's last words, would not remember them when sometime later he had to look at a print showing six Turkish ladies. But I remembered. They were six ladies from Constantinople — modern — in street clothes, faces covered not by a thick cloth that really covered them, but by a thin veil that pretended to reveal only the eyes and, in reality, exposed the whole face. And I was amused by that cunningness of Muslim coquetry, which in that way hides the face and follows usage but does not cover it, displaying its beauty. There is apparently nothing to connect the Turkish ladies and Damascene, but if you are a deep and penetrating spirit (and I doubt very much that you will deny me that), you will understand that in both cases there arises the tip of a rigid yet gentle companion of social man...

Yes, pleasant Formality, you are the staff of life, the balm of hearts, the mediator among men, the link between heaven and earth. You wipe away the tears of a father; you capture the indulgence of a Prophet. If grief falls asleep and conscience is accommodated, to whom, except you, is that huge benefit owed? The esteem that extends to the hat on one's head does not say anything to the soul, but the indifference that courts it leaves it with a delightful impression. The reason is that, contrary to an old absurd formula, it is not the letter that kills; the letter gives life, the spirit is the object of controversy, of doubt, of interpretation, and consequently of life and death. You live, pleasant Formality, for the peace of Damascene and the glory of Mohammed.

CHAPTER CXXVIII
IN THE CHAMBER

And take good notice that I saw the Turkish print two years after Damascene's words, and I saw it in the Chamber of Deputies, in the midst of a great hubbub while a deputy was discussing an opinion of the budget commission, for I was also a deputy. For those who have read this book, there is no need to discuss my satisfaction further, and for the others, it is equally useless. I was a deputy, and I saw the Turkish print as I leaned back in my seat between a colleague who was telling a story and another who was sketching the profile of the speaker in pencil on the back of an envelope. The speaker was Lobo Neves. The wave of life had brought us to the same beach as two bottles from shipwrecked sailors; he was holding his resentment, I was holding my remorse, maybe. And I use that suspensive, doubtful, or conditional form meaning to say that there was nothing to be held there unless it was my ambition to be a minister.

CHAPTER CXXIX
NO REMORSE

I had no remorse. If I had the proper chemical apparatus, I would include a page on chemistry in this book because I would break down remorse into its most simple elements, with the aim of knowing in a positive and conclusive way the reason

for Achilles' dragging the corpse of his adversary around the walls of Troy, and Lady Macbeth's walking around the room with her spot of blood. But I do not have any chemical apparatus, just as I did not have remorse. What I had was the desire to be a minister of state. Therefore, if I am to finish this chapter, I must say that I did not want to be either Achilles or Lady Macbeth, and that if I had to be either one, better Achilles, better dragging the corpse in triumph than carrying the spot. Priam's supplications are finally heard, and a nice military and literary reputation is gained. I was not listening to Priam's supplications, but to Lobo Neves' speech, and I had no remorse.

CHAPTER CXXX
TO BE INTERSPERSED IN CHAPTER CXXIX

The first time I was able to talk to Virgilia after the presidency was at a ball in 1855. She was wearing a superb gown of blue grosgrain and was displaying the same pair of shoulders as in previous times. It was not the freshness of her early years, quite the contrary, but she was still beautiful, with an autumnal beauty enhanced by the night. I remember that we talked a lot without referring to anything from the past. Everything was understood. A remote, vague comment or a look, maybe, and nothing else. A short while later, she left. I went to watch her go down the steps, and I do not know by what means of cerebral ventriloquism (I beg the forgiveness of philologists for this barbarous expression) I murmured to myself the profoundly retrospective word:

— Magnificent!

This chapter should be interspersed between the first and second sentences of chapter CXXIX.

CHAPTER CXXXI
CONCERNING A SLANDER

Just after I had said that to myself through the ventriloquy-cerebral process — or what was simple opinion and not remorse — I felt someone put his hand on my shoulder. I turned. It was an old friend, a naval officer, jovial, impudent in his manners. He smiled maliciously and said to me:

— You old devil! Memories of the past, eh?

— Hurray for the past!
— You got your old job back, naturally.
— Easy, you rogue! — I said, threatening him with the finger.

I must confess that the dialogue was an indiscretion — especially my last response. And I confess it with so much greater pleasure because women are the ones who have the fame of being indiscreet, and I do not wish to end the book without setting that notion of the human spirit straight. In matters of love adventures, I have found men who smiled or had trouble denying it, in a cold way, with monosyllables, and so forth, while their female equivalents would not admit it and would swear by the Holy Gospels that it was all slander. The reason for this difference is that women (excepting the hypothesis in CHAPTER CI and other hypotheses) surrender out of love, whether it be either Stendhal's love-passion, or the purely physical love of certain Roman ladies, for example, or Polynesian, Laplander, Kaffir, and possibly those of other civilized races. But men — I am talking about men belonging to an elegant and cultured society — men couple their vanity with another feeling. In addition to that (and I am still referring to forbidden cases), women, when they love another man, think they are betraying a duty and therefore must conceal it with the greatest skill, and they must refine the perfidy, while men, enjoying being the cause of the infraction and the victory over the other man as well, are legitimately proud and immediately pass on to that other less harsh and less secret feeling —that fine fatuousness that is the luminous sweat of merit.

But whether my explanation is true or not, it is enough for me to leave on this page, for the use of the ages, that the indiscretion of women is a trick invented by men. In love, at least, they are as silent as the tomb. They have been ruined many times by being clumsy, restless, unable to stand up in the face of looks and gestures, and that is why a great lady and delicate spirit, the Queen of Navarre, somewhere employed a metaphor to say that all love adventures will of necessity be discovered sooner or later: "There is no puppy so well-trained that we do not hear its bark in the end."

CHAPTER CXXXII
WHICH IS NOT SERIOUS

By quoting the Queen of Navarre, it occurs to me that among our people, when a person sees another annoyed, it is customary to ask: "Say, who killed your puppies?" as if to say, "Who exposed your love affair, your secret adventure, etc.?" But this chapter is not serious.

CHAPTER CXXXIII
HELVETIUS' PRINCIPLE

We were at the point where the naval officer got the confession of my affair with Virgilia out of me, and here I will improve on the Helvetius' principle — or if not, I will explain it. It was in my interest to keep quiet. To confirm the suspicions of an old thing was to arouse some forgotten hate, give rise to a scandal, at most to acquire the reputation of an indiscreet person. It was in my interest, and if I superficially understood the Helvetius' principle, that is what I should have done. But I have already given the reasons for masculine indiscretion: before that interest in security, there was another, that of pride, which is more intimate, more immediate. The first was reflexive, with the supposition of a previous syllogism. The second was spontaneous, instinctive, it came from the subject's insides. Finally, the first had a remote effect, the second a close one. Conclusion: Helvetius' principle is true in my case. The difference is that it was not a case of apparent interests, but of hidden ones.

CHAPTER CXXXIV
FIFTY YEARS OLD

I still have not told you — but I will say it now — that when Virgilia was going down the steps and the naval officer touched me on the shoulder, I was fifty years old. It was, therefore, my life that was going downstairs — or the best part of it at least, a part full of pleasures, agitations, and frights — disguised with dissimulation and duplicity — but, all in all, the best if we must speak in the usual terms. If, however, we employ other, more sublime ones, the best part was what remained, as I shall have the honor of telling you in the few pages left in this book.

Fifty! It was not necessary to confess it. You are already getting the feeling that my style is not as nimble as it was during the early days. On that occasion, when the conversation with the naval officer came to an end, and he put on his cape and left, I must confess that I was left a bit sad. I went back to the main room. I felt like dancing a polka, being intoxicated by the lights, the flowers, the chandeliers, the pretty eyes, and the quiet and sprightly bubble of individual conversations. And I am not sorry. I was rejuvenated. But a half hour later, when I left the ball at four in the morning, what did I find inside the carriage? My fifty years. There they were, insistent, not numb from the cold, not rheumatic — but dozing off from fatigue, a little longing for bed and rest. Then — and just look to what point the imagination of a sleepy man can reach — then I seemed to hear from a bat who was climbing up the roof of the vehicle: "Mr. Bras Cubas, the rejuvenation was in the room, the chandeliers, the lights, the silk — in short, in other people."

CHAPTER CXXXV
OBLIVION

And now I have the feeling that if some lady has followed along these pages, she closes the book and does not read the rest. For her, the interest in my love, which was love, has died out. Fifty years old! It is not invalidism yet, but it is no longer sprightliness. With ten more years, I will understand what an Englishman once said, I will understand that "it is a matter of not finding anyone who remembers my parents and the way in which I must face my own OBLIVION." Put that name in small caps. OBLIVION! It is only proper that all honor be paid to a character so despised and so worthy, a last-minute guest at the party, but a sure one. The lady who dazzled at the dawn of the present reign knows it, as does, even more painfully, the one who displayed her charms in bloom during the Parana ministry, because the latter is closer to triumph, and she is already beginning to feel that others have taken her carriage. So, if she is true to herself, she will not persist in a dead or expiring memory. She will not seek in the looks of today the same greeting as in yesterday's looks, when it was others who took part in the march of life with a merry heart and a swift foot. *Tempora mutantur.* She understands that this whirlwind is like that, it carries off the leaves of the forest and the rags of the road without exception or mercy. And if she has a touch of philosophy, she will not envy, but will feel sorry for the ones who have taken her carriage because they too will be helped down by the footman called OBLIVION. A spectacle whose purpose is to amuse the planet Saturn, which is quite bored with it.

CHAPTER CXXXVI
USELESSNESS

But either I am very wrong or I have just written a useless chapter.

CHAPTER CXXXVII
THE SHAKO

Not really. It sums up the reflections I made to Quincas Borba the following day, adding that I felt downhearted and a thousand other sad things. But that philosopher, with the elevated good sense he had at his disposal, shouted at me that I was sliding down the fatal slope of melancholy.

— My dear Bras Cubas, do not let yourself be overcome by those vapors. Good Lord! Be a man! Be strong! Fight! Conquer! Dominate! Fifty is the age of science and government. Courage, Bras Cubas. Do not turn a fool on me. What have you got to do with that succession from ruin to ruin, from flower to flower? Try to savor life. And be aware that the worst philosophy is that of the weeper who lies down on the riverbank to mourn the incessant flow of the waters. Their duty is never to stop. Make an adjustment to the law and try to take advantage of it.

The value of the authority of a great philosopher is found in the smallest things. Quincas Borba's words had the special virtue of shaking me out of the moral and mental torpor I was caught up in. Let's get to it. Let's get into the government, it is time. Up until then, I had not participated in the great debates. I was courting a minister's portfolio by means of flattery, teas, commissions, and votes. And the portfolio never came. It was urgent that I make a speech.

I started slowly. Three days later, during the discussion of the budget for the Ministry of Justice, I took advantage of an opening to ask the minister modestly if it would not be useful to reduce the size of the National Guard's shakos. The object of the question was not far-reaching, but even so, I demonstrated how it was not unworthy of the cogitations of a statesman, and I mentioned Philopaemen, who ordered the replacement of his troops' shields, which were small, by other larger ones, and also their spears, which were too light, a fact that history did not find out of line with the gravity of its pages. The size of our shakos called for a deep cut, not only to make them more stylish but also to make them more hygienic. In the sun, the excessive heat they produce could be fatal. Since it was a well-known fact that it was a precept of Hippocrates that a person should keep his head cool, it seemed cruel to force a citizen, from the simple consideration of being in uniform, to risk his health and his life, and, consequently, the future of his family. The chamber and the government should keep in mind that the National Guard is the rampart of freedom and independence, and that a citizen called up for service freely given, frequent, and arduous, had the right to have the onus of it lessened by a decree calling for a light and easy-fitting uniform. I added that the shako, because of its weight, lowered a citizen's head, and the nation needed citizens whose brow could be raised, proud and serene, in the face of power. And I concluded with this idea: the weeping willow, which bends its branches toward the earth, is a graveyard tree. The palm tree, erect and firm, is a tree of the wilderness, public squares, and gardens.

The impressions made by the speech varied. As regards the form, the quick eloquence, the literary and philosophical parts, the opinion was unanimous. Everyone told me it was perfect and that no one had ever been able to extract so many ideas from a shako. But the political part was considered deplorable by many. Some thought my speech was a parliamentary disaster. Lastly, they told me that others now considered me in the opposition, among them oppositionists in the chamber who went so far as to hint that it was a convenient moment for a vote of no confidence. I energetically rejected such an interpretation, which was not only erroneous but libelous in view of my prominent support of the cabinet. I added that the need to reduce the size of the shako was not so great that it could not wait a few years, and, in any case, I was ready to compromise in the extent of the cut, being content with three-quarters of an inch or less. In the end, even though my idea was not adopted, it was enough for me to have it introduced in parliament.

Quincas Borba, however, made no restrictions. I am not a political man, he told me at dinner, I do not know whether you did the right thing or not. I do know that you made an excellent speech. And then he noted the most outstanding parts, the strong arguments, with that modesty of praise that is so fitting in a great philosopher. Then he took the subject into account and attacked the shako with such strength, such great lucidity, that he ended up by effectively convincing me of its danger.

CHAPTER CXXXVIII
TO A CRITIC

My dear critic,

A few pages back when I said I was fifty, I added: "You are already getting the feeling that my style is not as nimble as it was during the early days." Maybe you find that phrase incomprehensible, knowing my present state, but I call your attention to the subtlety of that thought. I do not mean I am older now than when I started the book. Death does not age. I mean that in each phase of the narration of my life, I experience the corresponding sensation. Good Lord! Do I have to explain everything?

CHAPTER CXXXIX
HOW I WAS NOT A MINISTER OF STATE

. . . .
. . . .
. . . .
. . . .

CHAPTER CXL
WHICH EXPLAINS THE PREVIOUS ONE

There are things that are better said in silence. Such is the material in the previous chapter. Unsuccessful ambitious people will understand it. If the passion for power is the strongest of all, as some say, imagine the despair, the pain, the depression on the day I lost my seat in the Chamber of Deputies. All my hopes were left: me, my political career was over. And take note that Quincas Borba, through the philosophical inductions he made, found that my ambition was not a true passion for power but a whim, a desire to have some fun. In his opinion, that feeling, no less deep than the other one, is much more vexing because it matches the love women have for lace and coiffures. A Cromwell or a Bonaparte, he added, for the very reason that they were burning with passion for power, got there by sheer strength, either by the stairs on the right or the ones on the left. My feelings were not like that. Not having that same strength in themselves, they did not have certainty in the results, and that was why there was greater affliction, greater disappointment, greater sadness. My feelings, according to Humanitism...

— Go to hell with your Humanitism! — I interrupted him — I am sick and tired of philosophies that do not get me anything.

The harshness of the interruption in the case of a philosopher of his standing was the equivalent of an insult. But he forgave the irritation with which I spoke to him. They brought us coffee. It was one o'clock in the afternoon, and we were in my study, a lovely room that looked out on the backyard, with good books, art objects, a Voltaire among them, a bronze Voltaire who, on that occasion, seemed to be accentuating the sarcastic little smile with which he was looking at me, the scoundrel, excellent chairs. Outside the sun, a big sun, which Quincas Borba, I do not remember whether as a jest or as poetry, called one of nature's ministers. A cool breeze was blowing, the sky was blue. In each window — there were three — hung a cage with birds, who were trilling their rustic operas. Everything had the appearance of a conspiracy of things against man: and even though I was in *my* room, looking at *my* yard, sitting in *my* chair, listening to *my* birds, next to *my* books, lighted by *my* sun, it was not enough to cure me of the longing for that other chair that was not mine.

CHAPTER CXLI
DOGS

— So, what do you plan to do now? — Quincas Borba asked me, going over to put his empty coffee cup on one of the windowsills.

— I do not know; I am going to hide out in Tijuca, get away from people. I am disgraced, disgusted. So many dreams, my dear Borba, so many dreams, and I am nothing.

— Nothing? — Quincas Borba interrupted me with a gesture of indignation. In order to take my mind off it, he suggested we go out. We went in the direction of *Engenho Velho*, on foot, philosophizing about things. I will never forget how beneficial that walk was. The words of that great man were the stimulating brandy of wisdom. He told me that I could not run away from the fight. If the oratorical rostrum was closed to me, I should start a newspaper. He came to use less elevated speech, showing that philosophical language can, now and then, fortify itself with the slang of the people. Start a newspaper, he told me, and "bring down that whole stinking mess."—A great idea! I am going to start a newspaper. I am going to shatter them into a thousand pieces. I am going to...

— Fight. You can shatter them or not; the essential thing is for you to fight. Life is a fight. A life without fight is a dead sea in the center of the universal organism.

A short while later, we came upon a dogfight. Sometimes that would be of no consequence in the eyes of an ordinary man. Quincas Borba made me stop and watch the dogs. There were two of them. I noticed that there was a bone under their feet, the motive for their war, and I could not help having my attention called to the fact that there was no meat on the bone. Just a naked bone. The dogs were biting each other, growling, with fury in their eyes... Quincas Borba put his cane under his arm and seemed ecstatic.

— How beautiful this is! — he said from time to time.

I wanted to get away from there, but I could not. He was rooted to the ground and he only started walking again when the fight was completely over and one of the dogs, bitten and defeated, took his hunger off somewhere else. I noticed that Quincas had been truly happy, even though he held his happiness in as befits a great philosopher. He made me observe the beauty of the spectacle, recall the object of contention, and concluded that the dogs were hungry. But deprivation of food was nothing to do with the general effects of philosophy. Nor he forgot to remember that, in some parts of the world, the spectacle is on a grander scale: human beings are the ones who fight with dogs over bones and other less appetizing tidbits. A fight that becomes quite complicated because entering into action is man's intelligence along with the whole accumulation of sagacity that the centuries have given him, etc.

CHAPTER CXLII
THE SECRET REQUEST

So many things in a minuet! — as the saying goes. So many things in a dogfight! But I was no servile or weak-hearted disciple who was not about to make one or another adequate objection. As we walked along, I told him that I had some doubts.

I was not too sure of the advantage of fighting with dogs over a meal. He answered with exceptional softness:

— It is more logical to fight over it with other men, because the status of the contenders is the same and the stronger one gets the bone. But why shouldn't it be a grand spectacle to fight over it with dogs? Locusts are eaten voluntarily, as in the case of the One Who Goes Before or, even worse, that of Ezequiel, therefore, what is awful is edible. It remains to be seen whether it is more worthy for a man to fight over it by virtue of a natural necessity or to prefer it in obedience to religious, that is, mutable, exaltation, while hunger is eternal, like life and like death.

We were at the door of my house. I was given a letter, which they said was from a lady. We went in, and Quincas Borba, with the discretion proper to a philosopher, went over to read the spines of the books on a shelf while I read the letter, which was from Virgilia:

"My good friend,

"Mrs. Placida is very sick. I am asking you the favor of doing something for her. She is living on the *Beco das Escadinhas (Stairs Alley)*. Could you see if you can get her admitted to Mercy Hospital?

Your sincere friend,

V."

It was not Virgilia's delicate and correct hand, but heavy and uneven. The V of the signature was nothing but a scribble with no alphabetical intent, so, from the looks of the letter, it was very hard to attribute its authorship to her. I turned the piece of paper over and over. Poor Mrs. Placida! But I had left her with the five *contos de réis* from the beach at Gamboa, and I could not understand why...

— You will understand — Quincas Borba said, taking a book off the shelf.

— What? — I asked, startled.

— You will understand that I was telling nothing but the truth. Pascal is one of my spiritual grandfathers, and even though my philosophy is worth more than his, I cannot deny that he was a great man. Now, what does he say on this page? — And, with his hat still on his head and his cane under his arm, he pointed out the place with his finger. — What does he say? He says that "man has a great advantage over the rest of the universe; he knows that he is going to die, while the universe is completely ignorant of the fact." Do you see? The man who fights over a bone with a dog has the great advantage over him of knowing that he is hungry. And that is what makes it a grand fight, as I was saying. "He knows that he is going to die" is a deep statement, but I think my statement is deeper: he knows that he is hungry. Because the fact of death limits, in a manner of speaking, human understanding. The consciousness of extinction lasts only for a brief instant and ends forever, while hunger has the advantage of coming back and prolonging the conscious state. It seems to me (at the risk of some immodesty) that Pascal's formula is inferior to mine, without ceasing to be a great thought, however, or Pascal a great man.

CHAPTER CXLIII
I AM NOT GOING

While he was putting the book back on the shelf, I reread the note. At dinner, seeing that I was not talking very much, chewing without really swallowing, staring into a corner of the room, or at the edge of the table, or at a plate, or at an invisible fly, he said: — Something is not right with you; I bet it was that letter! — It was. — I felt really bothered, annoyed with Virgilia's request. I had given Mrs. Placida five *contos de réis*. I doubt very much that anyone has been more generous than I, or even equally generous. Five *contos de réis*! And what had she done with them? She had thrown them away, naturally, squandered them at big parties, and now she is ready for Mercy Hospital and I am the one to get her in! You can die anywhere. Furthermore, I did not know or did not recall any *Beco das Escadinhas*. But judging from its name as an alley, I imagined it to be some dark and narrow corner of the city. I would have to go there, attract neighbors' attention, knock on the door, and all that. What a nuisance! I am not going.

CHAPTER CXLIV
RELATIVE USEFULNESS

But the night, which is a good counselor, reflected that courtesy demanded I obey the wishes of my former lady.

— Bills that fall due have to be paid — I said as I stood up.

After breakfast, I went to Mrs. Placida's place. I found a bundle of bones wrapped in rags lying on an old and revolting cot. I gave her some money. The next day, I took her to Mercy Hospital, where she died a week later. I correct myself: she was found dead in the morning. She had sneaked out of life just the way she had come into it. I asked myself again, as in chapter LXXV, if that was why the sexton of the cathedral and the candymaker had brought Mrs. Placida into the world at a specific moment of affection. But I realized immediately that if it had not been for Mrs. Placida, my affair with Virgilia might have been interrupted or broken off suddenly in its full effervescence. Such, therefore, was the usefulness of Mrs. Placida's life. Relative usefulness, I admit, but what is absolute in this world?

CHAPTER CXLV
A SIMPLE REPETITION

As for the five *contos de réis*, it is not worth mentioning that a neighborhood stonemason pretended to be in love with Mrs. Placida, succeeded in arousing her feelings or her vanity, and married her. At the end of a few months, he invented some business deal, cashed in their savings, and fled with the money. It is not worth it. It is a case like Quincas Borba's dogs: a simple repetition of a chapter.

CHAPTER CXLVI
THE PROSPECTUS

It was urgent that I found the newspaper. I drew up the prospectus, which was a political application of Humanitism. Except that since Quincas Borba had not published his book yet (which he went on perfecting year by year), we agreed not to make any reference to it. Quincas Borba only asked for a signed and confidential declaration that certain principles applied to politics had been drawn from his still unpublished book.

It was the fine flower of prospectus, it promised a cure for society, an end to abuses, and a defense of the sound principles of liberty and conservation. It appealed to commerce and to labor. It quoted Guizot and Ledru-Rollin and ended with this threat, which Quincas Borba found petty and local: "The new doctrine that we profess will inevitably bring down the present ministry." I must confess that, given the political climate of the moment; the prospectus looked like a masterpiece to me. The threat at the end, which Quincas Borba found petty, was shown to him to be saturated with the purest Humanitism, and later on he himself allowed that it was. Since Humanitism excluded nothing, the Napoleonic Wars and a fight between goats, according to our doctrine, possessed the same sublimity, with the difference being that Napoleon's soldiers knew that they were going to die, something that apparently was not true with the goats. So, I was only applying our philosophical formula to the circumstances: Humanitas wanted to replace Humanitas for the consolation of Humanitas.

— You are my beloved disciple, my caliph — Quincas Borba roared with a touch of tenderness I had not heard in him till then. — I can say, like the great Mohammed: even if the sun and the moon come against me, I will not turn back from my ideas. Believe me, my dear Bras Cubas, this is the eternal truth, before the world and after the ages.

CHAPTER CXLVII
MADNESS

I immediately sent a discreet notice to the press saying that within a few weeks, an opposition paper edited by Dr. Bras Cubas would begin its publication. Quincas Borba, to whom I read the notice, picked up a pen and, with true humanistic brotherhood, added this phrase after my name: "one of the most glorious members of the previous Chamber of Deputies."

The next day, Cotrim entered my house. He was a little upset, but he hid it, demonstrating calm and even happiness. He had seen the news about the paper and felt that, as a friend and relative, he should dissuade me from an idea like that. It was a mistake, a serious mistake. He pointed out how I would be putting myself in a difficult situation and, in a certain way, locking the doors of parliament for me. The government not only seemed excellent to him, which could not be my opinion, of course, but it would also certainly endure for a long time. So, what could I gain by making it unfavorable to me? He knew that some of the ministers liked me. It was not impossible to fill a vacancy, and... I interrupted him at that point to tell him that I had meditated a great deal about the step I was going to take and that I would not retreat an inch. I got to the point of suggesting that he read the prospectus, but he refused vehemently, saying that he did not want to share the tiniest part of my madness.

— It is real madness, — he repeated — think about it for a few days, and you will see it is madness.

Sabina said the same thing at the theater that night. She left her daughter in the cabin with Cotrim and took me out into the corridor.

— Brother Bras, what are you doing? — she asked me with affliction. — What kind of idea is that, provoking the government for no reason when you could...

I explained to her that it was not for me to go about begging for a seat in parliament, that my idea was to bring down the government because I did not think it was equal to the situation — and a certain philosophical formula. I promised always to use courteous, although energetic, language. Violence was not a spice for my palate. Sabina tapped the tips of her fingers with her fan, lowered her head, and picked up the matter again, alternating between supplication and threats. I told her no, no, no. Disappointed, she threw into my face the idea that I preferred the advice of strange and envious people to hers and her husband's. — So, then, just keep on with what seems best to you — she concluded — we fulfill our obligation. She turned her back on me and returned to her cabin.

CHAPTER CXLVIII
THE UNSOLVABLE PROBLEM

I published the newspaper. Twenty-four hours later, a declaration by Cotrim appeared in other papers, saying in substance that "given the fact that he was not a member of either of the parties into which the nation was divided, he found it expedient to make it quite clear that he had no influence on or any direct or indirect part in the journal of his brother-in-law, Dr. Bras Cubas, whose ideas and political directions he disapproved of. The present government (like any other composed of equally competent members), seemed to him to be working for the public good." It was hard for me to believe my eyes. I rubbed them once or twice and reread the inopportune, unusual, and enigmatic declaration. If he had nothing to do with the parties, what was an incident as minor as the publication of a newspaper to him? Not all citizens who find a government good or bad make declarations like that to the press, nor are they forced to do so. Really, Cotrim's intrusion into that affair was a mystery, no less than his personal attack. Our relations until then had been smooth and pleasant. I could not remember any dissension, any shadow, anything, after the reconciliation. On the contrary, the memory was one of genuine goodwill. For example, when I was a deputy, I was able to obtain some supply contracts for the naval arsenal for him, contracts that he continued fulfilling with the greatest punctuality, and concerning which he talked to me about a few weeks earlier, saying that, at the end of three more years, they could bring him two hundred *contos de réis*. Well, then, should not the memory of such a large favor be enough to stop him from going public and tarnishing his brother-in-law's reputation? The reasons behind his declaration must have been very powerful in order to make him commit an act of impertinence and an act of ingratitude at the same time. I must confess, it was an unsolvable problem...

CHAPTER CXLIX
THE THEORY OF BENEFIT

... So unsolvable that Quincas Borba could not handle it despite having studied it for a long time and quite willingly.

— So, goodbye! — he concluded: — not every philosophical problem is worth five minutes' attention.

As for the censure of ingratitude, Quincas Borba entirely rejected it, not as unlikely, but as absurd, because it did not obey the conclusions of a good humanistic philosophy.

— You cannot deny one fact, — he said — that the pleasure of the benefactor is always greater than that of the beneficiary. What is a benefit? It is an act that brings to an end a certain deprivation of the one who got the benefit. Once the essential effect has been produced, once the deprivation has ceased, that is, the organism returns to its previous state, a state of indifference. Just suppose that the waist of your trousers is too tight. In order to relieve the uncomfortable situation, you unbutton the waist, you breathe, you enjoy an instant of pleasure, the organism returns to indifference, and you forget about the fingers that performed the operation. If there is nothing that lasts, it is natural that memory disappears, because it is not an aerial plant, it needs earth. The hope for other favors, of course, always holds the beneficiary in a remembrance of the first one, but that fact, also one of the most sublime that philosophy can find in its path, is explained by the memory of deprivation or, using a different formula, by deprivation's continuing on in memory, which echoes the past pain and advises alertness for an opportune remedy. I am not saying that, even without this circumstance, it does not sometimes happen that the memory of the favor will persist, accompanied by a certain more or less intense affection. But they are true aberrations with no value whatsoever in the eyes of a philosopher.

— But, — I replied — if there is no reason for the memory of the favor to last in the favored, there must be even less in relation to the one who did the favor. I would like you to explain that point for me.

— What is obvious by its nature cannot be explained — Quincas Borba replied. But I will say one more thing. The persistence of the benefit in the memory of the one performing it is explained by the very nature of the benefit and its effects. In the first place, there is the feeling of a good deed and, deductively, the awareness that we are capable of good acts. In the second place, a conviction of superiority over another being is received, a superiority in status and means, and this is one of the most legitimately pleasant things for the human organism, according to the best opinions. Erasmus, who wrote some good things in his *In Praise of Folly*, called attention to the complacency with which two donkeys rub against each other. I am far from rejecting that observation by Erasmus, but I shall say what he did not say, namely, that if one of the donkeys rubbed better than the other, he would have some special indication of satisfaction in his eyes. Why is it that a pretty woman looks into a mirror so much if not because she finds herself pretty and, therefore, it gives her a certain superiority over a multitude of women who are less pretty or absolutely ugly? Conscience is just the same. It looks at itself quite often when it finds itself pretty. Nor is remorse anything else but the twitch of a conscience that sees itself as repugnant. Do not forget that since everything is a simple irradiation of Humanitas, a benefit and its effects are perfectly admirable phenomena.

CHAPTER CL
ROTATION AND TRANSLATION

Every enterprise, attachment, or age contains a complete cycle of human life. The first number of my paper filled my soul with a vast awakening, crowned me with garlands, restored the quickness of youth to me. Six months later, the hour of old age struck, and two weeks later, that of death, which was in secret, like Mrs. Placida's. On the day the paper was found dead in the morning, I sighed deeply, like a man who had come back from a long journey. So, if I were to say that human life feeds other more or less ephemeral lives, the way a body feeds its parasites, I do not think I would be saying something completely absurd. But in order not to risk a less neat and adequate image like that, I prefer an astronomical one: man executes, at the turn of the wheel of the great mystery, a double movement of rotation and translation. Its days are unequal, like those of Jupiter, and they comprise its more or less long year. At the moment I was finishing my movement of rotation, Lobo Neves was concluding his movement of translation. He died with his foot on the ministerial step. It had been rumored for several weeks that he was going to be a minister. And since the rumor filled me with a great deal of annoyance and envy, it is not impossible that the news of his death left me with a touch of tranquility, relief, and one or two minutes of pleasure. Pleasure may be an exaggeration, but it was true. I swear to the ages that it was absolutely true.

I went to the funeral. In the mortuary room, I found Virgilia by the casket, sobbing. When she lifted her head, I saw that she was really weeping. Before leaving the funeral, she embraced the coffin with affliction. They came to pull her off and take her away. I tell you; the tears were genuine. I went to the cemetery, and, to say it outright, I did not feel much like speaking. A stone was stuck in my throat or in my conscience. At the cemetery, most of all, when I dropped the shovel of lime onto the coffin at the bottom of the grave, the dull thud of the lime gave me a shudder, a fleeting one, it is true, but unpleasant. And afterwards, the afternoon had the weight and color of lead. The cemetery, the black clothing...

CHAPTER CLI
THE PHILOSOPHY OF EPITAPHS

I left, keeping away from the groups of people and pretending to read the epitaphs. Besides, I like epitaphs. Among civilized people, they are an expression of that pious and secret selfishness that induces us to pull out of death a shred at least of the shade that has passed on. That may be the origin of the inconsolable sadness of those who know their dead are in potter's field. They feel the anonymous rotting reaching themselves.

CHAPTER CLII
VESPASIAN'S COIN

They all went away. Only my carriage was waiting for its owner. I lighted a cigar. I left the cemetery behind. I could not shake the burial ceremony from my eyes or Virgilia's sobs from my ears. The sobs, most of all, had the vague and mysterious sound of a problem. Virgilia had betrayed her husband, sincerely, and now she was weeping for him, sincerely. There you have a difficult combination whose trajectory I was unable to follow completely. At home, however, getting out of the carriage, I suspected that the combination was possible and even easy. Gentle Nature! The tax of grief is like Vespasian's coin: it does not smell of its origins and can be collected just as well from evil as from good. Morality might condemn my accomplice. That is of no account, implacable friend, once you have punctually received the tears. Gentle, thrice gentle Nature!

CHAPTER CLIII
THE ALIENIST

I started getting pathetic, and I preferred sleeping. I slept, I dreamed that I was a Nawab, and I woke up with the idea of being a Nawab. I sometimes liked to imagine those contrasts of region, status, and belief. A few days earlier, I had thought about the hypothesis of a social, religious, and political revolution that transformed the Archbishop of Cantuaria into a simple tax collector in Petropolis, and I made long calculations to find out if the tax collector eliminated the archbishop or if the archbishop rejected the tax collector, or what portion of an archbishop could remain in a tax collector, or what amount of a tax collector could combine with an archbishop, and so forth. Insoluble questions, apparently, but in reality, perfectly soluble if one considers that there can be two archbishops in one archbishop —the one from the bull and the other one. It is all set; I am going to be a Nawab.

It was nothing but drollery. I mentioned it to Quincas Borba, who looked at me with a certain caution and sorrow, being so good as to inform me that I was crazy. I laughed at first, but the noble conviction of the philosopher instilled a certain fear in me. The only objection to Quincas Borba's words was that I did not feel crazy, but since crazy people generally have no other concept of themselves, such an objection was worthless. And see now if there is not some basis for the popular belief that philosophers are men who are far removed from petty things. The next day, Quincas Borba sent an alienist to see me. I knew him, I was terrified.

He, however, behaved with the greatest delicacy and poise, taking his leave so merrily that it encouraged me to ask him if he really thought I was crazy.

— No, — he said, smiling — there are few men so much in command of their faculties as you.

— So, Quincas Borba was wrong?

— Completely. — And then: — On the contrary, if you are his friend... I ask you to distract him... Because...

— For God's sake! Do you think?... A man of such spirit, a philosopher!

— That makes no difference. Madness can enter any house.

You can imagine my affliction. The alienist, seeing the effect of his words, realized that I was a friend of Quincas Borba and tried to lessen the gravity of the warning. He observed that it might not be anything and added even that a grain of folly, far from doing harm, gives a certain spice to life. Since I rejected that opinion with horror, the alienist smiled and told me something extraordinary, so extraordinary that it deserves no less than a chapter of its own.

CHAPTER CLIV
THE SHIPS OF THE PIRAEUS

— You must remember — the alienist told me — that famous Athenian maniac who imagined that all ships entering Piraeus were his property. He was nothing but a poor wretch who probably did not even have a Diogenes' tub to sleep in, but the imaginary ownership of the ships was worth all the drachmas in Hellas. Well, we all have an Athenian madman in us. And anyone who swears that he did not possess at least two or three schooners mentally, has to know that he swears falsely.

— Including you? — I asked.
— Including me.
— Including me?

— Including you; and your servant as well, if that man shaking rugs out the window is your servant.

As a matter of fact, it was one of my servants who was beating rugs while we were talking in the garden alongside. The alienist then noted that he had opened all the windows wide and kept them that way, had raised the curtains, and had revealed the richly furnished room as much as possible so it could be seen from outside, and he concluded: — That servant of yours has the Athenian's mania. He thinks that the ships are his. One hour of illusion that gives him the greatest happiness on Earth.

CHAPTER CLV
A CORDIAL REFLECTION

— If the alienist is right, — I said to myself — there is not much to pity in Quincas Borba. It is a question of degree. Still, it is only proper to keep an eye on him and prevent manias of other origins from entering his brain.

CHAPTER CLVI
THE PRIDE OF SERVANTHOOD

Quincas Borba differed with the alienist regarding my servant. — It is possible as an image, — he said — to attribute the Athenian's mania to your servant, but images are not ideas or observations taken from nature. What your servant has is a feeling that is noble and perfectly in line with the laws of Humanitism: it is the pride of servanthood. His intention is to show that he is not just *anybody's* servant. — Then he called my attention to the coachmen in great houses, haughtier than their masters, to hotel servants, whose solicitude depends upon the social variations of the guest, etc. And he concluded that all of it was an expression of that delicate and noble feeling — full proof that so many times man, even when shining shoes, is sublime.

CHAPTER CLVII
A BRILLIANT PHASE

— You are the sublime one — I shouted, throwing my arms around his neck.

Indeed, it was impossible to believe that such a deep man could have reached dementia. That was what I told him after my embrace, revealing the alienist's suspicions to him. I cannot describe the impression that the revelation made on him. I remember that he trembled and turned pale.

It was around that time that I became reconciled once again with Cotrim, without getting to know the cause of our falling out. An opportune reconciliation, because solitude was weighing on me, and life for me was the worst kind of weariness, which is weariness without working. A short time later, I was invited by him to join a Third Order, which I did not do without first consulting Quincas Borba:

— Go ahead if you want, — he told me — but temporarily. I am trying to attach a dogmatic and liturgical part to my philosophy. Humanitism must also be a religion, the one of the future, the only true one. Christianity is good for women and beggars, and the other religions are not worth much more. They are all equal, with the same vulgarity or weakness. The Christian paradise is a worthy emulation of the Muslim one. And as for Buddha's Nirvana, it is nothing more than a concept for paralytics. You will see what humanistic religion is. The final absorption, the contractive phase, is the reconstitution of substance, it is not annihilation, etc. Go where you are called, but do not forget that you are my caliph.

And now have a peek at my modesty. I joined the Third Order of ***, and filled a few positions in it. That was the most brilliant phase of my life. Nevertheless, I shall be silent, I shall not say anything, I will not talk about my service, what I did for the poor and the sick, or the reward I received, nothing; I shall say absolutely nothing.

Maybe the social economy could profit somewhat if I were to show how each and every outside reward is worth little alongside the subjective and immediate reward. But that would be breaking the silence I have sworn to maintain at this point. Besides, the phenomena of conscience are difficult to analyze. On the other hand, if I told one thing, I would have to tell everyone who is connected to it, and I would end up writing a chapter on psychology. I shall only state that it was the most brilliant phase of my life. The pictures in it were sad. They had the monotony of misfortune, which is as boring as that of pleasure, maybe worse. But the joy given to the souls of the sick and the poor is a recompense of some value. And do not tell me that it is negative because the only one receiving it is the one taken care of. No. I received it in a reflexive way, and even then, it was great, so great that it gave me an excellent idea of myself.

CHAPTER CLVIII
TWO ENCOUNTERS

After a few years, three or four, I'd had enough of the service, and I left it, not without a substantial donation, which gave me the right to have my portrait hung in the sacristy. I will not finish this chapter, however, without mentioning that, in the hospital of the Order, I witnessed the death of — guess who ...? — the beautiful Marcela. And I watched her die on the same day that, while visiting a slum to distribute alms, I found... You are incapable of guessing now... I found the flower of the shrubbery, Eugenia, the daughter of Ms. Eusebia and Vilaca, as lame as I had left her and even sadder.

When she recognized me, she turned pale and lowered her eyes. But it was only a matter of an instant. She immediately raised her head and looked straight at me with dignity. I understood that she would not accept alms from my pocket, and I held out my hand to her as I would to the wife of a capitalist. She greeted me and shut herself up in her tiny room. I never saw her again. I learned nothing about her life or whether her mother was dead or what disaster had brought her to such poverty. I know that she was lame and sad. It was with that deep impression that I reached the hospital where Marcela had been admitted the day before and where I saw her expire a half hour later, ugly, thin, decrepit...

CHAPTER CLIX
SEMIDEMENTIA

I understood that I was old and needed some strength. But Quincas Borba had left for Minas Gerais six months earlier, and he had taken the best of philosophies with him. He returned four months later and came into my house one certain morning, almost in the state in which I had seen him in the Promenade. The difference was that his gaze was different. He was demented. He told me that in order to perfect Humanitism, he had burned the whole manuscript and was going to start all over again. The dogmatic part was finished, although it was not written down. It was the true religion of the future.

— Do you swear by Humanitas? — he asked me.
— You know I do.

My voice could barely come out of my chest, and, besides, I had not discovered the whole cruel truth. Quincas Borba was not only mad, but he knew that he was mad, and that remnant of awareness, like a dim lamp in the midst of the shadows, greatly complicated the horror of the situation. He knew it and was not bothered by the illness. On the contrary, he told me, it was one more proof of Humanitas, which in that way was playing with itself. He recited long chapters of the book to me, and antiphonies, and spiritual litanies. He even got to go through a sacred dance he had invented for the rites of Humanitism. The lugubrious grace with which he lifted and shook his legs was singularly fantastic. At other times, he sulked in a corner with his eyes staring into space, eyes in which, at long intervals, a persistent ray of reason glowed, as sad as a tear...

He died a short time later, in my house, swearing and repeating always that pain was an illusion and that Pangloss, the slandered Pangloss, was not as dotty as Voltaire supposed.

CHAPTER CLX
ON NEGATIVES

Between Quincas Borba's death and mine, the events narrated in the first part of the book took place. The main one was the invention of the *Bras Cubas Poultice*, which died with me because of the illness I had contracted. Divine poultice, you would have given me first place among men above science and wealth because you were the genuine and direct inspiration of heaven. Fate determined the contrary. And so, all of you must remain eternally hypochondriac.

This last chapter is all about negatives. I did not reach the fame of the poultice, I was not a minister, I was not a caliph, I did not get to know marriage. The truth is that, alongside these lacks, I had the good fortune of not having to earn my bread by the sweat of my face. Furthermore, I did not suffer the death of Mrs. Placida or the semidementia of Quincas Borba. Putting one and another thing together, any person will probably imagine that there was neither a lack nor a surfeit and, consequently, that I went off squared with life. And they imagine it wrongly. Because on arriving at this other side of the mystery, I found myself with a small balance, which is the final negative in this chapter of negatives: — I had no children; I did not transmit the legacy of our misery to any creature.